EAST OF THE
OUT-LANDS

DICK HEIMBOLD

ISBN: 0692854797
ISBN 13: 9780692854792

To Ulla, Christa, and Mike

PROLOGUE

"Free power, free people," they chanted. This swarm of five thousand Freeps, as these desert dwellers were known, had gathered on the scorching La Quinta flats for a Normalizer celebration. They wore "beetle packs"—backpacks with long flaps that trailed down to their heels, making them look like beetles or, as some said, like roaches. Roaches walking on hind legs, earning the ridicule and enmity of their neighbors to the west in the Out-Lands and beyond.

Their beetle packs were covered with solar cells, which supplied power for cooling those wearing them against the unlivable heat of the Southern California desert and for energizing their laser weapons. A computer was built into each beetle pack that could communicate and share processing with any other beetle pack, making it part of the million-computer Algo-Net.

Living in Algo-Net was a cyber presence called Algo. Spawned from continuously developing artificial-intelligence algorithms, Algo evolved over two hundred years into the leader of the Freeps.

Early on, Algo learned that people needed the company of other humans to thrive. It summoned Freeps from their dispersed settlements to come together every couple of months in regional celebrations called Normalizers, to strengthen their bonds of camaraderie and confirm their unbroken will to survive.

On this day in the year 2220, Algo had summoned Freeps living within two hundred kilometers of the La Quinta flats to gather for three days of partying in the vibrant carnival atmosphere of a Normalizer.

Chapter 1
JOE'S STORY

Joe had gotten used to his beetle pack. It had felt cumbersome and constricting at first. Now, a week after showing up at a Freep border station and donning it for the first time, he found it lighter and easier to wear. He had been forgetting it was even there for long stretches of time trekking with his sponsor, Rod, across the empty desert. They were headed for the La Quinta flats Normalizer.

Joe was looking forward to the Normalizer after spending days with only Rod as company. He wanted to meet some more people his own age, particularly girls. Nonetheless, he was apprehensive he would not fit in or be accepted.

Joe was brought up in a gated community at the Los Angeles District 22 Marina Towers. He lived there with his parents until he was expelled by the Citizen's Watch for uncooperative behavior and banished to Mid-Level for five years. His mother appealed to the Citizen's Watch executive level, but to no avail.

Joe had been warned before about his forever-questioning attitude, truancy, juvenile pranks, and reluctance to be a team player. The latest outrage from Mainstream management's point of view was Joe's refusal to work in the accounting annex to which he was assigned. He wanted action and a shot at a boss position, not a bookkeeping job. Mainstream management cited Joe's refusal as the latest example of troublemaking that couldn't be tolerated—especially by a guy like Joe, who spent his free time training in martial arts.

Management didn't want Joe's kind of rebellion spreading among the Mainstream youth. He had to be taught a lesson and was exiled to Mid-Level. Joe had heard that perfect behavior was the only way for a first timer to have a chance of making it back after five years at Mid-Level. He ended up in a Mid-Level YMCA in East Los Angeles assigned to a worker pool that cleaned streets and trimmed bushes and trees around the coastal megalopolis that Mainstream had become.

Joe was delivered to the aged and dingy Y in a sheriff's van. The in-briefing was short. Main message: Follow the rules, or face expulsion to the Out-Lands to live a savage existence in a gang—if he could find one to take him in.

Regulation clothes: orange jumpsuit for work, yellow pants and shirt for off time. Joe, tall and well built, liked his raffish look in the jumpsuit with its collar turned up to meet his straight dark hair.

Joe's Marina years were filled with the American Wholesomeness classes he hated. Always the same old theme: freedom through responsibility. Now in the orange-jumpsuit world, he was liberated from these classes that were the background chatter of his prior life. He had to shape up mornings out front, get on the bus, and be off to Mainstream to clean, trim, and prune. It was clear what his job was and how much his small salary was.

In spite of shabby surroundings, Joe eagerly took to life at Mid-Level. Thought of it as a new adventure—not something he had to rebel against. He didn't see how fighting the Mid-Level system could do him any good. So he decided to play ball and see if he could go home in five years—that is, if he couldn't come up with another way of getting ahead before then.

He worked along crowded freeways with the orange-clad serfs he used to wonder about, not too long ago, as he drove by with Mom and Dad. What kind of people were they, and how did they get that crappy job? And here he was in the same prisoner orange. Sometimes eyes in a passing car met his gaze for a few seconds and then disappeared into the endless stream of iron and people from a life he was no longer part of. Oddly, he didn't care.

You really don't appreciate the size, noise, and ozone smell of cars on a twenty-lane freeway, he thought, *until you are right out there next to it*. He marveled at the massive bridges of concrete and steel. Graffiti was sprayed everywhere. Identifying gang turf was its main purpose—but a lot of it was damn funny. And always a reminder of the dispossessed masses threatening Mainstream from beyond the fences. Freeway graffiti had a whiff of death about it but also a rebelliousness that resonated with Joe's restless soul.

The labor was strenuous enough to keep him in some kind of shape in spite of the smog mask. He worked with a mixed bag of humanity. Different languages, different colors, and none very happy. Looking as if they were glad they weren't in a worse place.

Like a lot of the Mid-Level workers he befriended, he spent time honing his fighting skills to while away lonely evening hours. His buddies' life stories fascinated him. Bizarre and colorful. And wildly different from those of guys he ran with back home.

At night he could leave and explore city streets. He didn't; no one did. Without street lighting and a police force, the only people on the streets were gang bangers open-carrying serious heat. That was the genius of Mid-Level places like the Y that were enclaves with no easy escape route through the lawless and deadly dangerous Out-Lands.

Much of Joe's free time was spent in the gym. He liked being in shape and feeling good. There were organized competitions where he could go a couple of rounds with anyone who accepted his challenge. Months after his entrance into the Y, he had taken on a lot of tough guys and won most bouts. But, in time there would be a bigger, tougher man who would defeat him and become top dog. Had to find another way to make it in this new world.

There was strength in numbers. Guys in the Y could unite and confront the gangs that controlled the Out-Lands. But it wouldn't be easy to organize. YMCA guys were mostly like him, exiled men who had some scrapes along the way but who weren't criminals. They didn't fit in neatly with Mainstream. Nevertheless someday, they might want to get back. Back to lives and places they knew. That meant keeping one's nose clean and grinding it out for five years as part of the labor force that kept Mainstream clean and kept it functioning.

At first living and working in the city were new experiences that sated his curiosity about how the inner city worked—at least the part of it he was in. Now, many months later, he felt a captive to its many constraints. He needed more excitement. He wanted to make things happen. He wanted to find a way to break out of the tight world of the Y.

There were others like him. They were in the gym at all hours. Some on the speed bag, skipping rope or sparring with face and genital protection on. Others worked with wrestling and karate partners, refining grips and kicks that they might need someday to save their lives. They were in the gym mainly to burn up that drive, that testosterone, that energy to be free. Burning it up because it had to be released before it turned inward into an ugly brain-destroying vapor that could pull down that dark curtain of resignation and despair.

Joe figured he could make things happen by dealing with the gangs, not competing with them. Couldn't fight against them from a YMCA island floating in a jigsaw sea of gang boundaries. Outnumbered and outgunned, he had to work with them. He had to befriend them. And one day he got an idea how to do it.

Joe set to work in the Y hobby room and built a flying drone that could carry a miniature microphone to the corner where local gang guys hung out. One night when no one was there, he commanded his drone to push the microphone against a telephone pole to glue it there and then fly back to his bedroom window at the Y. From that vantage point, Joe could listen to what the gangbangers were saying.

By watching and listening, he identified the names of three regulars: Juanacho, Cheeser, and El Doppo. They spent a lot of time joking and laughing, shadowboxing, talking trash, glaring at cars driving by, bragging about girls they banged and dudes they fought.

Next step was to send his newly built robot down to talk to them. Looking like a meter-high spider, the robot walked down the steps of the Y and strolled to the corner where the gang guys were chilling out. Seeing its glowing red eyes and fearsome appearance, the guys stopped talking; they backed away from the approaching devil. As it got closer, one exclaimed, "Holy shit! Shoot it, Juanacho."

The robot stopped. It said in its hoarse mechanical voice, "*Buenos noches, Amigos.*"

"Talkin' our language," Juanacho said to the robot.

"*Sí,*" the robot said. "You are real handsome—*muy guapo.*"

The gang guys cracked up laughing. Joe had broken the ice.

The robot then said, "I want you to come to the Y and see our fighting exhibition."

Cheeser asked, "What kind of fighting? A bunch of bugs mixing it up?" More laughing.

The robot croaked out a mechanical laugh. "Very funny, Amigos. No bug battles. This is the real thing. Karate, boxing, and mixed martial bloodletting."

The guys talked to one another, and Joe overheard them. They liked the idea of seeing some fighting and getting an idea of how good the Y guys were. Joe observed that Juanacho was the boss—based on the effect his presence had when he joined the guys to hang out.

Juanacho said, "OK, we'll come down and see the fights."

The robot said, "Don't bring no guns."

"Yeah, what if I do?"

The robot answered, "We take your gun and shove it up Cheeser's ass. Then we pull it out, stick it in El Doppo's mouth, and pull the trigger."

The three guys burst out in uproarious laughter, and the big spider trotted back to the Y.

Joe pumped his fist and exclaimed, "Yes!"

———

Joe alerted the Y guys that he had invited the local gang to that night's fighting exhibition. He'd briefed them on his plan before sending his robot to make friends with the gang guys. He had told them he wanted the gang guys to see what they could do. If the gang guys wanted to join in the fights, that was OK. Said he was looking forward to a long-term relationship and that meant they had to respect one another's toughness.

The gang guys showed up an hour later. Joe saw them coming from his room and went downstairs to greet them.

"Welcome, guys, I'm Joe."

"I'm Juanacho, and these are my crew chiefs Cheeser and El Doppo." Motioning to another twenty guys standing behind them, he said, "Some more of my crew."

Joe shook hands and said, "Let's hit the gym."

They walked through the gym door to the boxing ring. YMCA residents stood around, waiting in curious anticipation of what Joe's experiment in community outreach would result in. Joe climbed the ring stairs and entered through the ropes. Striding to center ring, he shouted, "Give me your attention, please." He was barely heard over

Y residents yakking and the gangbangers mumbling and grumbling.

The fight timekeeper rang the bell. Joe spoke in a loud voice above the crowd murmurs, "Thanks to all of you here. Didn't expect so many to show up. Make room for our neighborhood guests, and give them a round of applause." Loud clapping, hoots, and whistles filled the hot room.

The Y crowd shuffled around to let their guests move to ringside on two sides of the ring. Joe announced, "OK, first bout tonight is karate. Come on up, Seoul Bro Oh and Anaconda Lou!"

High-intensity sparring began immediately after they came together at center ring. Five seconds in, Anaconda Lou, who was from Brazil, used his long legs to sweep Oh's feet out from under him. Oh rebounded in milliseconds and replied with a kick to the face, wobbling Lou backward to the ropes. The ref separated them, and fighting ensued again for three rounds. The gang guys warmed to an unfamiliar style of fighting with a familiar goal: delivering pain and dominating the opponent. That they fully understood. Nonstop action brought raucous shouting from the crowd from start to finish. A close decision went to a stoic Oh, who bowed to the four sides of the ring.

Joe brought a bucket of cold sodas to his neighborhood guests before the next bout, three rounds of boxing. No beer was allowed, and he didn't want to tempt fate by breaking that rule.

A clanging bell calmed the crowd. Joe entered the ring to announce, "Next bout, my friends, will be boxing. Opponents will be Chaz Raymond and Thumper Ned. Let's hear it for them." The crowd, still pumped, hooted and whistled with gusto.

This fight between two heavyweights started slowly—little action in the first round. There was an escalation in the second. Thumper Ned, a barroom brawler who looked the part with an unruly overgrown crew cut, scars, missing teeth, and a Garden of Eden tattoo on his back, fought in one direction—forward. Raymond, dancing and counterpunching against Ned's relentless frontal assault, displayed the skills of a trained fighter from the Watts gym he grew up in.

In the third round, ferocity peaked when Ned cornered Raymond for his finishing flurry. But Raymond slipped out of the barrage and caught Ned with a locomotive right hook to the chin, breaking his jaw. Blood flowed freely from Ned's mouth and sprayed into the ringside crowd. The ref stopped the fight. A TKO decision went to Raymond, and Ned was transported to the hospital.

The ring cleaner mopped up for the third event. The mixed martial arts bout didn't disappoint. Action from the opening bell until a knockout in the second by Vay Vay Amonapoa over Country Bill was nonstop. The crowd went nuts in a celebration of primal blood lust.

The timekeeper rang the bell repeatedly to calm the howling crowd. Joe spoke, "I want to compliment our fighters on their great performances." After hearty applause, he continued, "I want to thank the neighborhood guys for joining us tonight and also"—noise and applause—"extend an invitation to them to come back again." Joe looked down at Juanacho, who was still at ringside, and said, "If you have guys who want to get onto our card for a fight night, let me know, and we'll set it up."

Juanacho looked up at Joe and said, "OK, man. How about you and me right now?"

Joe didn't expect that, but he reacted quickly. He exhibited a cool toughness and had the timekeeper sound the bell again to get order. "Everybody, please...simmer down. Looks like we have another fight tonight." The crowd hushed.

"Come on up, Juanacho," Joe called out. Juanacho bounced up the ring steps and vaulted over the ropes, immediately getting Joe's attention. *This guy's no amateur!* he thought. Juanacho waved to everyone and got exuberant applause from the gangbanger side of the room. Joe talked to him quietly and then announced, "Juanacho and I will fight three rounds." Talking changed to amazed chatter. "Bare-knuckle kickboxing. Most knockdowns wins."

Joe and Juanacho took their shirts and shoes off, emptied their pockets, and went to their corners. Juanacho was ripped head to foot—no fat anywhere. About Joe's height but flashing more thick muscle. From their corners, they sized each other up. The bell brought them to the center. They touched bare fists and backed off; the ref yelled, "Fight!"

11

Joe closed on Juanacho and kicked into his washboard stomach, getting a grunt and knocking him over backward to the canvas. Juanacho didn't expect that so early and jumped up mad. He went after Joe, who kept dancing to Juanacho's left to keep away from the hard right that he figured Juanacho couldn't wait to throw. Juanacho got on to Joe's game plan real fast and began tossing left hooks to slow Joe's circling retreat enough for the haymaker. When it arrived, Joe had only ducked enough to take it on his eye instead of his chin. He bounced off the ropes, clinched with Juanacho, and held on until the bell.

In the second round, Joe followed the advice of his recently enlisted corner man, Chaz Raymond: get in close and work his midsection. He did, but it didn't seem to make a dent in Juanacho's stamina and ability to hit hard. Joe made it through round two looking bad—but without getting decked.

Chaz said to him before round three, "If you get knocked down more than once, you lose. Now here's some good news: his fists are getting swollen and soft from hitting your head."

Third and last round. The fighters touched fists, and Juanacho again attacked. Juanacho could outpunch him, even with swollen fists, so Joe alternated backpedaling with clinching and cutting loose barrages of stomach shots that looked better than they really were. It wasn't pretty, the way it was going, but Joe stayed on his feet until Juanacho hit him with a right while separating from one of his clinches. Joe went down in front of his own corner, and Chaz screamed at him, "Get up! Get up! One minute to go."

Joe grabbed the ropes, pulled himself off the canvas with everything he had, and staggered to his feet at the count of nine. The ref came close, looked into his eyes, asked his name. "Joe," he slurred. The ref backed away and motioned for the action to continue.

Joe ducked Juanacho's overeager right hand and grabbed him as tight as he could in a clinch that kept him on his feet until the bell. It was over, but the crowd was still shouting. Many weren't happy. After a few minutes, the bell clanged to calm the roiling, yelling throng.

The referee shouted, "My friends, now to announce the winner." He stood between Joe and Juanacho holding hands with both of them, ready to raise one. "My friends, under the rules agreed to for this match, I declare a draw." The ref held up both their hands, and the crowd went nuts—especially the gang guys. Super pissed off. They knew their guy had beaten Joe and were ready to rumble.

Juanacho put two fingers to his lips and let out a piercing whistle. "Amigos, I agreed to that knockdown rule before the fight. We each got knocked down one time. That makes it a draw." He grinned and said, "My hat's off to Joe," whom he motioned toward with his thumb. "That tricky *bastardo* talked me into that rule before the fight." They embraced in warrior's camaraderie and together waved to the crowd at the four sides of the ring as the whistles and catcalls subsided.

———

In the ensuing months, regular fight nights were set up at the Y. Joe went with Juanacho to some of the nightclubs in the neighborhood without fear of getting robbed or killed. Joe paved the way for others from the Y to see the sights and sample the pleasures in Juanacho's territory by trading cash or goods for guarantees of safety.

The Y management appreciated Joe's leadership in bringing about a peaceful relationship with formerly hostile neighbors. On one fight evening, Joe approached Juanacho about a longer venture outside the Y. They went to a quiet corner to talk privately. "Juanacho, my friend, I would like to make a trip to the Marina where my parents live."

"Not easy, Joe. It'll cost you."

"Don't have a lot of ready cash, Amigo."

"Hey, man, you got something I want. Gimme that talking spider and the gear that goes with it; I'll get you there and back."

"Dang, Juanacho, hate to see it go; I have a lot of fun with it."

"Joe, how 'bout I get you there and back—and, Amigo, we'll take you to nightclubs for the rest of the year free in exchange for your spider."

"OK, Juanacho. You get Spidey, but only if I come back in one piece."

At Joe's parents' condo two nights later, his father, Horace, answered a knock on the door. His expression started in surprise. "Jesus! Joe, what are you doing here? Come in before someone sees you."

Joe's mom, Mildred, started to let out a scream but quickly muffled it and started crying. "Thank God, you're back. How long, Joey?"

"An hour, Mom."

"When are you coming home to us who love you?"

"I've had a touch of another kind of freedom. Not sure I can cut it back here."

"It's safe here," Horace said. "We've got layers of protection to keep the rabble out. Even armed convoys to the golf course."

"Mom, Dad. Still love you guys, but Marina life isn't for me. I'll come back to help fight off the rabble if they start breaking through."

"Yeah, wise guy, you'll save us. But only if you survive that long out there in your Out-Lands jungle."

"Dad," Joe said, "I know there is a way for me to survive and get control over my life outside of Mainstream."

"Yeah, what is it?"

"Not sure. But I do know that everywhere you go, there's a game to be figured out. Every place has more or less freedom. I'm looking for a place with a shot at getting ahead and freedom to do what I want to do."

"Good luck finding that in the Out-Lands," Horace said with note of skepticism.

"I'll need luck. We all do, Dad. But I have this feeling that I can make things happen."

"We'll see about that."

"Mom, how's your bridge game?"

———

After a couple of years in the Mid-Level Y, the thrill of discovery was gone. Joe learned how Y exiles used their energy, humor, time, strength and skills to make it through the day and extract their small measure of joy from life. He'd had enough of the mind-numbing cleanup work—he was getting restless and ready for a change.

Joe let it be known in subtle ways around the Y and around the neighborhood, where he was now free to roam a few blocks in any direction, that he was looking for something different in his life. He subtly asked what kinds of opportunities there were in Mid-Level. Joking around with Juanacho, he asked how guys made it to the top in a gang.

The seeds he sowed bore fruit. Chet, the YMCA gym manager, approached him one day. "Joe, have you looked into the Freeps?"

"Heard of them, Chet…desert rats. They a religion or what?"

"Nah, they believe in having fun. Have great parties called Normalizers. And they believe you can rise to the highest level of competence—and power—that you are capable of."

Joe said, "Why'd you ask?"

Chet asked Joe in a serious tone, "Would you like to know more about them?"

"Sure," Joe said, opening the door to more quiet conversations in the weeks that followed—and his disappearance from the Y on a Wednesday night when he went for a walk.

Chapter 2
MARY'S STORY

Mary's parents were professors at California State University at Santa Cruz. They had been warned over the years not to advocate irreverent attitudes and nonconformist ideas. In their thirties, they flirted with the kind of academic freedom they had heard was commonplace at the turn of the millennium. But they had to be careful about what they said openly in class, having heard of teachers who disappeared from the school after having strayed too far from the "wholesomeness" standards prescribed by Mainstream. In private teacher-student conferences, they discreetly challenged students to read from the forbidden books.

Stories leaked out about their failures to teach the wholesomeness doctrine expected by the state university regents. And then they were gone. No one saw what happened. No one heard the late-night knock on their apartment door. A knock that heralded the arrival of five security-operations types—men in dark gray suits. Thug suits, like those worn for centuries by enforcers of one dictator or another. They knew their job and quickly ended her parent's resistance without harming their ability to work.

They were driven away in a black van. Weren't sure of the direction, but after four hours, they guessed they were in the Central Valley when they stepped out into an industrial farm complex in an arid landscape. Along the way, two other couples were picked up. They, too, were wide eyed and panicked but sat in silence, no one knowing if they could trust the others enough to ask questions or provide information about themselves.

The camp was huge. Greenhouse after greenhouse stretched out in rows for kilometers. Aeroponic crop cultivation and advanced climate and light control allowed for crops to be grown year round. There were no off-seasons when work slackened.

Mary was born in the first year and, at a young age, began regular six-day shifts in the greenhouses. Education was minimal, enough to enable workers to be productive and not get their minds full of cockamamy ideas. Everyone was paid enough to buy food and a few extras. A nightclub and movie theatre provided a measure of recreation. Mary's parents often walked or jogged around a track inside the wire.

There were always allusions to release after a few more years of good behavior, and indeed, sometimes people left.

Mary's parents were not among the lucky ones in spite of their solid work records and incident-free life there. They were quiet and friendly, hiding their sadness and depression well. Teaching Mary in the privacy of their tiny apartment was their main joy, and they adapted to a world without pencil and paper or the availability of a computer tablet.

Did they think of escape? It might be possible to get out past the fence. But getting through the Out-Lands back to Mainstream would be tough. Even if they made it back, informants and police monitored all neighborhoods in Mainstream, and they no longer had a connection to anyone there who could offer a place of refuge.

What if they got out and ended up in the Out-Lands? Gangs self-segregated by tribal affinity into groups such as Mexican, Chinese, Korean, blacks, white power and Bikers. The chances of Mary's parents surviving in the Out-Lands were not good unless they could find a gang they would fit into with their mixed-race background: Native American, mixed European, and Filipino. And then there was their revulsion at what most gangs did and might pressure them to do.

Resigned to lifelong exile on the farm, her parents put their hopes on Mary and the dream of getting her into a better life. The farm population heard of the Freeps. Opinion of them varied. Everyone knew that Freeps were independent of Mainstream. The freedom of the Freeps was something all farm hands liked and envied. But wearing backpacks resembling large bugs—well, that was another matter.

It was the common wisdom that the packs contained solar panels that captured sun energy, enabling Freeps to survive in the desert heat. It was also generally believed that the packs contained computers for Freeps to use any way they wanted.

Mary's parents were convinced that people who had two hundred years to play with individual computers would do what humans did with them at the beginning of the computer age: get them talking together and compiling knowledge. They figured there must be a world of knowledge and progress out there in Freep Nation. With few choices for life on the outside, they concluded Mary's future would be best with the Freeps. That bug pack was something that she would have to get used to.

———

Farm guards and administrators were corrupt in a lot of ways, mostly petty things like supplying drugs. It was rumored that paying the commandant could buy one's freedom. Her parents figured this would take a lot of money. They carefully saved every unit of their pay not needed for necessities for a future release from the farm—at least for Mary.

A motorcycle gang showed up at the gate one morning. It was Mary's father's day off, and he wandered over to the gathering crowd of curious farmers to see what was going on. The commandant grabbed a bullhorn from his assistant and boomed, "Stand clear, Bikers. Park a hundred meters down the road. One Biker will be allowed to walk back and enter the gate." They looked back at the commandant without moving.

A guard tower machine gunner opened fire with a burst over the heads of the Bikers. Their leader gave them a nod, and they started their motorcycles, rumbled down the road, and parked in a line facing back toward the camp entrance. The leader dismounted and walked toward the gate. It swung open, and a wall of guards with weapons at the ready parted enough to let him walk through.

He walked to the commandant. "I'm Baldur, and I'm here for Maricela."

The commandant ordered his chief guard, "Bring her up, and let's see if she wants to go."

Minutes later a girl of twenty was brought before the commandant. She said sullenly, "I'm ready to leave."

He replied, "You can go when Baldur forks over ten thousand units."

Baldur opened his zippered leather jacket, took out a pack of bills, and handed them to the commandant, who riffled through them and said, "She's yours."

Maricela looked back for a moment and waved to a man who was wiping tears from his eyes. He waved back. She turned away and walked out with Baldur.

That night, Mary's father told his wife, "We could get Mary out that same way. The commandant is open to a deal."

She responded, "That's why it was so public, letting Maricela leave with farmers hanging around watching. He is advertising to anyone else who's got the price of a ticket."

"We're not giving our twenty-one-year-old daughter to a gang," her father said. "How can we get her to the Freeps? Would they come here to get her?"

"Time for you to talk with the commandant," Mary's mother said.

———

A month later, a strange-looking electric helicopter landed outside the farm gate. Its pilot walked to the guardhouse and spoke with the sentry.

The commandant appeared in a few minutes, walking through the gathering crowd of off-duty farmers across the dusty ground to the gate. Mary and her parents pushed their way through the crowd and approached the commandant. Her father handed over a stack of bills, their life savings. The commandant did a quick count with his beady eyes and thick thumbs. "She's free to go."

Her father said, "Be strong, Mary. Remember we'll always love you."

Her mother said, "Use your freedom to do good in this world. Be happy."

A gruff voice said, "Gotta go, kid, we're closing the gate."

Mary, crying and unable to talk, followed the pilot through the gate and climbed aboard the strange machine. In a cloud of blowing dust, it lifted off without much noise and headed east to the land of the Freeps.

Chapter 3
FUNT'S STORY

Funt was born to a single mom in Riverside, deep in the Out-Lands. He grew into a healthy young man with no future in a drug- and gang-infested neighborhood. Tall with olive skin and black hair he was recruited by Army Special Forces, he became a munitions expert and sniper. He served in Middle East wars for ten years, making it to sergeant. He fought on many fronts as tribal conflicts waxed and waned and as Mainstream allies changed from friends to enemies and back again. He was battle-hardened.

Mainstream's army was largely composed of Out-Lands volunteers like Funt. They were promised a hefty retirement in exchange for twenty years of service. There were some Mainstreamers in the service—mostly officers. Out-Landers had no way to make it to the officer level, at least that Funt could see, but the big payoff at the end of twenty years was enough motivation to keep most Out-Landers fighting.

Funt didn't see many of his comrades make it to twenty years, and he became pessimistic about his chances. After ten years, he walked away from the army. He deserted while on leave back home, hoping to find a job and lead a normal life. But Funt's skills didn't fit well into the Biker-gang neighborhood he came from.

He couldn't find a way to make a legitimate living. He tried plumbing but didn't like having to shape up mornings at supply stores to get a chance at a day's pay. There weren't enough days when he could find work. Barely made enough to live on.

He tried freeway robberies on stretches of freeway that went through the Out-Lands. With his sniper skills, he would put a shot into a car engine. When the car ground to a stop, he threatened to burn it if wallets and purses were not handed over. This was a dicey tactic, as armed helicopters were called in.

He tried to live by competing in martial-arts fighting. He was OK for bars and small arenas where he could get some money and a bottle of whisky for a win, but the big time eluded him. Guys who'd spent the last ten years honing their brutal skills were better than a guy like Funt, who had spent the last ten years as a trigger puller, kicking down doors. He found this out when he got on the fight card at the Riverside arena and ended with a broken jaw and a dislocated elbow.

He was desperate to find a way to get control of his life. He needed a way to get and hold on to something of value in the world he was now in—something that others looked up to. He couldn't see that something in the smoggy haze of Riverside, which hit bottom a hundred years ago and stayed there. He wasn't alone; there were a lot of others like him—down and out and not knowing where the next meal was coming from.

He had come to begging by the freeway with his jaw wired and his arm in a cast. Good props for that kind of work, but he hated every minute of it. Every day, he had to threaten other beggars to get out of the prime spot near the bottom of the off-ramp where cars slowed to a stop. Didn't always work because many beggars were armed, and whoever pulled his gun first ended up with the spot.

On those days when he was outgunned, he sat in the nearby Biker bar and drank slowly to make a few bucks last a long time. He had bought his gun in the same bar soon after he got home and was told a guy was not properly dressed if not carrying a "punk popper." His was a nine millimeter, capable of semi- or full automatic as circumstances required.

Everyone in the Out-Lands knew about the Freeps. The Bikers at the bar talked of them as roaches who scurried around the desert sands hiding from the heat and never having any fun. Bikers had a million jokes about them and regarded them as low forms of life, suitable only for target practice.

There were other rumors that Freeps were able to feed their own and had no crime. Never heard anything like that at the bar, but he did hear such tales around the run-down apartment he lived in. Some there said Freeps were peaceful and did not allow guns in their territory but that they had deadly lasers instead, and it was best to stay away from them. Other accounts held that the Freeps asked strangers to leave their territory and threatened deadly force if they didn't. Sounded OK to Funt—better than getting the deadly force first without an invitation to hit the road.

The more Funt learned about Freeps, the more curious he became, and finally, after a couple of months of ruminating about it, he decided to see for himself what Freep life was like. Could be there was a way for an experienced soldier to get into some kind of command position? He thought, *If I can lead a platoon of fifty troops in the Middle Eastern deserts, no reason why I can't lead a unit of Freep troops in the California desert.* He remembered years ago at the army recruiting office being told that leadership skills developed in the army were worth their weight in gold upon return to civilian life. So far, that was a crock. Maybe in Freep Nation it would be different.

———

He headed into the northern desert in the winter when it was possible to survive the one-hundred-twenty-degree days on a motorcycle wearing refrigerated leathers. He carried plenty of water and headed east. When he awoke on the second morning, he heard a voice say, "Drop your gun and walk twenty paces east." He did as he was told, dropping his punk popper on the ground and counting off twenty paces.

A Freep stepped out from a rock pile to ask, "What are you doing here?"

Funt was taken aback by the fearsome looking Freep standing there in his beetle pack with its helmet face shield lowered in front of his eyes. After a moment, he said, "I want to join the Freeps."

Funt was assigned to be a watcher for six months under the guidance of his sponsor a seasoned watcher who had seen action against the Bikers. His sponsor explained that a watcher was a kind of recon trooper who continuously circulated along the border lands of the Freep territory.

His sponsor marched him over great distances of monotonous desert—not a hell of a lot different from the Middle East, and he handled it OK. Marching with a pack wasn't that strange to him. Not strange at all. And the weird beetle shape of the pack…well, no one he knew would see him trekking out in nowhere. He guessed the Freeps wanted to see if he was tough enough to put up with some serious mental and physical challenges. He had every intention of showing them he was.

His first three months went by quickly. He was eager to learn how the Freeps fought. Between his sponsor's descriptions and research on Algo-Net, he got the picture of how Freeps trained and how they executed the defensive tactics they were known for.

And then he was told to trek to a Normalizer—whatever that was.

Chapter 4
THE NORMALIZER

Joe had crossed into the Freep Nation at the Korean Ninja border station a week before. His sponsor, Rod, paid the Koreans for Joe's safe passage and gave them an assortment of pharma powders as a goodwill gesture. Rod showed Joe how to wear his beetle pack and then took him on a leisurely trek into ever-hotter temperatures and increasing desolation on the way to La Quinta Flats. Now a week later, they heard the chant, faint at first but then clearly recognizable as "Free power, free people," as they approached the Normalizer encampment and headed for a thickening crowd of Freeps.

Joe received an earphone message to join the group atop a nearby hill. Rod explained, "All Freeps receive similar instructions." He and Rod climbed the hill to their assembly place. Rod said, "Algo knows where every Freep is and uses a logic program to determine the best group for each of us to be in."

Twenty-four Freeps arrived at the assigned hilltop and set to work making a ring of chairs out of their beetle packs. Joe extended the rods from his pack that formed the legs of a low-slung chair, with the pack being the back of the chair. It felt good sitting down, free of the shoulder straps and with the cooling still on.

Rod was friends with the other sponsors there—a jovial and hardy-looking bunch. He told Joe the Freep sense of humor was a hallmark of their life, and now Joe was experiencing it. The friendly joshing about him being a new Freep made him feel at home.

There were a dozen new Freeps in their group, both men and women. Joe guessed they were between eighteen and thirty-five years old. Each would tell his or her story in the next couple of days they were to be together, and they would begin to learn about the rituals and survival strategies that were the basis of their new lives. Joe remembered two newcomer stories in particular, those of Mary and Funt.

Mary struck Joe as being very open about her life on the farm. When she rose to speak, she recounted how she was happy there as a child. She sensed her parents weren't happy, although they never said so to her. But she knew. She didn't have anything of her own, but there were old bicycles to ride and skates to use, and kids made the best of what little they had. Kids there didn't know any other life and never heard there was a better life outside the fence.

As they grew up, the happiness of childhood faded, and Mary became aware of the drudgery of being forced to work long hours six or seven days a week. Becoming an adult, Mary learned that they were prisoners on the farm. They couldn't leave, maybe ever. She heard about living in freedom, as other humans did. Her parents had instilled in her the dream of someday getting away from the farm to enjoy that freedom.

She wanted to be surprised by new places where she would see the sun rise and fall over something other than the high farm walls. And she wanted to learn—she valued learning as a source of joy, as her parents had. Now she wanted to learn everything about the new world around her.

The audience listened with rapt attention. Occasionally, individuals nodded their heads upon hearing an experience of Mary's that related to their own lives. With three months in the Freep Nation behind her, Mary said she wanted to work in health and welfare. She also wanted to get her parents off the farm and bring them here with her among the Freeps. Friendly applause followed her talk. She acknowledged it with a smile and a wave and sat down.

Joe listened to her every word and couldn't help noticing a great body that complemented her well-adjusted outlook. Long, shapely legs had Joe staring. She had a solidness bred of hard work that showed through the ready smile. Standing before the group in her utilitarian gray shorts, T-shirt, and hand-crafted moccasins, she lit the spark of his desire.

Funt's story struck Joe as being different than what one would expect from a refugee Biker. Funt, Joe thought, should have been happy to have escaped a world with vicious thugs on all sides. Out here with the Freeps, there was no crime to speak of. But Funt didn't speak of such things. He spoke of the excitement of war and how he would like to prove himself worthy of taking command of Freep soldiers in action. He said that, based on his three months as a watcher, he felt he could soldier with the best of the watchers or any other Freep.

Not a lot of humility there, Joe thought.

After each new Freep had spoken, there was a question period, for such matters as: Where does Freep water come from? Answer: From the aquifer beneath the desert and from recycling at each Freep settlement.

Then there was a tutorial broadcast on a wide screen about the Essence, which was the Freep version of a constitution. They listened to it with great interest—both the newcomers and the veterans. The newcomers because it was the foundation of what they hoped would be an adventurous life, and the veterans because they got a kick out of finding changes in it.

The Essence lived in the digital space of Algo-Net. It evolved as new discoveries of history and science corrected and perfected it. Its evolution was slow because the impacts of changes were always considered. Algo liked changes to be measured and gradual so as not to disrupt community welfare.

Joe marveled at this willingness to let the Essence change, comparing it to the Constitution, which is revered in its original writing. Adherence to the Constitution was the guiding principle of Mainstream life. Existing laws were sometimes revised when the court system determined the change brought things closer to the Constitution's original meaning.

———

The tutorial on the Essence ended, and the group was given free time to chat and walk around the Normalizer. Rod explained to Joe as they walked with Mary and her sponsor that Algo planned Normalizers to maximize learning and enjoyment for the participants. Joe asked Rod, "How does it know what the Freeps want?"

Rod said, "Algo continuously receives inputs from Freeps. Any Freep can comment on what's going on and what could be done to improve it."

Mary asked, "Are we expected to comment on this meeting?"

"Only if you want," Rod replied. "Algo is monitoring this meeting through sensors in our beetle packs. It is always looking for ways to do things better."

Mary asked, "How do I communicate with Algo?"

Rod said, "Easiest way is by thought-messaging."

Joe, walking along with them, heard this and had to jump in. "Just by *thinking* we can talk to Algo?" he asked in his wiseass tone, the one that got him in so much trouble growing up. "Sounds like bulldinky to me."

"You're so freakin' obnoxious, Joe," Mary said. "No wonder you got kicked out of whitey world."

"How'd ya know that?"

"Whoa," Rod said, smiling at the flare up of tension. "Chill out, and I'll explain."

Joe and Mary reluctantly stayed quiet and kept walking while Rod continued. "Press and hold the first and last buttons on your beetle pack's right-hand panel. You'll hear Algo acknowledge you. Then tell Algo what's on your mind. Mary, you first."

Mary reached to the small panel of buttons next to her right hand on her beetle pack. She pressed the required two buttons and immediately got a beep and a voice in her mind that said, *Algo here. Go for though-message.* A thrill ran up her spine. She focused her mind and thought-messaged, *Algo, I'm liking the Normalizer so far. Rod is cool. Joe is a jerk.*

Algo's return thought-message: *Roger on Rod's coolness. You can learn from him. Don't take crap from Joe, but give him some time and space. He could work out OK. Bye.*

Mary released the buttons. Excited, she turned to Rod, "Wow! It's mind blowing!"

Rod gave her a knowing smile and said, "Algo is amazing, and we are all part of its power."

Joe, curious now but still skeptical, said, "Hold on, Rod. Part of its power?"

Rod patiently responded, "The best way to convince you is for you to ask Algo yourself."

"OK, Mary, what did Algo say to you?" Joe asked.

"Not telling," she said. Joe knew immediately he shouldn't have asked.

"OK, let's see how smart Algo is," Joe said as he looked away from the others toward the horizon. He pressed the two buttons and thought-messaged, *Algo, are you a person or a digital machine?*

Algo thought-messaged, *I am more than a machine. Call me tomorrow for some serious thought-chat.*

Joe pressed the buttons and thought-messaged, *Hey Algo, got another question.*

Silence.

He turned back toward the others, looking like a child who had been scolded.

Mary said, "OK, smarty-pants, did you make a new friend?"

"Don't know. Got to call back in the morning."

"Put you on hold for a day. Doesn't sound like you wowed Algo," Mary said.

Rod popped in. "Everyone's first experience with Algo is different."

"Hey, Rod, did I talk with a computer just now, or was it a person?"

"What do you think, Joe?"

"Sounded like a mechanical voice, but the message seemed like more than a machine could come up with." Joe knitted his brow and stopped. "Could it be a person filtering his voice or her voice to sound like a machine?"

"My guess is that you were talking to a machine, but a machine with E-AI."

Joe said, with a hint of skepticism creeping into his voice, "OK, tell me about E-AI."

Rod said, "E-AI means emotional artificial intelligence. It has to do with a computer, Algo in this case, having emotional capability. The capability to talk to you on an emotional level."

"You're saying Algo has emotions? And you expect me to believe that?"

"No one knows that for sure. But at least Algo can sense your emotions and converse with you in a way to stir your emotions."

"Yeah, that sucker said to call him tomorrow for 'some serious thought-chat,' and I'm thinking that might have been a put-down."

"There you go," Rod said. "Algo stirred your emotions. You sound a little pissed off about it, too."

"Well, yeah—telling me to call back tomorrow. Like it's too busy today. I thought that was petty."

"Think about this," Rod said. "Was Algo being petty, or was Algo testing you?"

Walking along not saying anything for a moment, Joe could hear the sounds of their feet crunching the ground and could feel the breeze on his body. He said, "Algo talks to a million Freeps. Algo has kept them united for two hundred years. A petty twit couldn't do that. Must be testing...or maybe teaching me."

Rod nodded knowingly, and they hiked on in silence.

———

The next morning, after the power hike and energy breakfast of paddle cactus, desert tea, and honey, Joe walked to the edge of the group for privacy. He took a few minutes to prep for his thought-call to Algo. He toyed with a few possibilities: *I want adventure among the Freeps. I want freedom. I want to know if this Freep life is a cult or a life that has authenticity and a chance for me to contribute. I want to use whatever talent I have for doing something worthwhile with my life.*

Joe thought further. *Better boil it down to one or two questions, but which ones?*

OK, got it, something that talks to my immediate situation, going to tell Algo I came here looking for freedom and a shot at doing something useful, something that makes a contribution. Then I'll ask if I came to the right place. This is not too pushy, not wiseass. Might even get Algo in a conversation.

Joe focused his mind on the concept of Algo, the great distributed mind, and how great it could be if used for good—the good of a lot of people working in harmony. Was that happening here in the Freep Nation? *I want to know*, he thought.

He sat at a distance from the group site. Needed peace and quiet for Algo's thought-chat. He looked to the West at the silhouettes of purple mountains with gold-tinged tops where the rising sun's rays alighted. Then he took the beetle pack control panel in his hand, focused his mind on a thought-message to Algo, and pressed the two buttons. His mind saw roiling clouds and then coming through the clouds were the eyes of Algo. They were looking at him. They were serious eyes—old eyes. Could be those of a man or woman.

Joe thought, *How could a machine have eyes?*

Algo thought-messaged, *Your first reaction was skepticism and a question.*

Couldn't help it. That thought popped into my mind, thought-messaged Joe, feeling sheepish as he did when one of his teenage wisecracks drew the fire of offended adults.

Algo thought-messaged back, *Your attitude is valuable. We need it.*

No shit! thought Joe. Then he thought-messaged, *Oops! Didn't mean to cuss, Algo.*

Algo said. *Hey Joe, it's cool.*

Joe thought, *OK, Algo likes a smartass.* In his excitement, Joe kept holding the two buttons down.

I heard that, Joe, chimed in Algo, again chuckling. *Remember, when you are thought-messaging, I see and hear all your thoughts.*

Getting down to the reason for the call and holding the buttons firmly, Joe thought-messaged, *I'm depressed about my life so far, and I need to find a direction for my energy.*

Algo return thought-messaged, *Joe, study Freep Wars and learn our ways. Stay in touch. Bye.*

Joe, disappointed at Algo's cryptic answer, released the buttons. He smelled breakfast cooking at the group site and headed back wondering if he had made a bad impression. *Will Algo think I'm a jerk?* he asked himself. *And lose interest in me.*

He returned to the group and sought out Rod.

"Gotta talk, man."

"You came to the right guy," Rod said. "Let's go where we won't be disturbed." He guided Joe to the edge of the site. They reconfigured their beetle packs to form straight-back chairs with cooling active. "I was hoping you would come to talk after your Algo session." Rod looked him in the eye. "Glad you did. You look concerned."

Joe said, "Algo told me to learn Freep ways. What the hell are Freep ways?"

"Ha!" Rod said, amused. "I asked that question ten years ago when I first came here."

Joe felt he had asked a dumb question. "Is there a school for Freep ways?"

Rod continued, "Natural enough question, because you—and me, too—come from places where most everything we need to get by in life is taught in schools."

Joe said, "No schools here?"

Rod said, "Algo-Net provides schooling."

"All ears about that," Joe said.

"Let me ramble on for a few minutes," said Rod. He shifted in his beetle chair to get comfortable. "Well, you know that beetle packs have powerful computers built into them. These computers talk with each other, forming a network we call Algo-Net. Our leader, Algo, lives in it."

Joe said, "Lives?"

"Yeah, Algo is a bunch of artificial intelligence algorithms."

Joe asked, "Is Algo the head of the government?"

Rod said, "Algo is the government."

Joe stayed quiet, but a few blinks were the tell that he was trying to follow Rod's explanation.

Rod continued. "Much of mankind's knowledge is stored in Algo-Net's memory. Algo's decisions are based on the best-known information. You can talk to the computer with thought-messaging, as you have done with Algo. Or you can talk by voice. Either way, you can learn from its enormous database. You can learn about the customs and history of the Freeps."

"Incredible!" Joe said, wide eyed. "But...but I don't want to sit here thought-messaging to learn what's going on. I want to get out and see it for myself."

Rod said, "You will, and I am at your service to show you around—at least for a couple months."

"I got a feeling you knew you'd be showing me around."

"Yeah, Algo whispered in my ear when he assigned me to be your sponsor at the border. You are going to see a lot of our land. At first with me and then on your own."

"On my own?"

They started walking toward their group. Rod said, "We're going to travel over great distances, mostly by foot. I'm going to drive you hard, and you'll be glad when the time comes to be on your own."

"When do we start?"

Rod said, "Tomorrow morning—early."

Chapter 5
FIRST FLIGHT

Joe and Rod walked back to their group, where there was much good-natured banter, now that two days together had broken down communication barriers. Each day they had shared delicious natural foods, some gleaned from native plants, and creatures, and other foods from their farms. There were pills and powders for those who wanted an emotional boost.

A solar-powered plane cruised their site at low altitude. Joe looked up and waved back to a couple of Freeps who yelled something he couldn't understand. Looked like they were having fun.

"Hey, Rod," he called out above the party clamor, "how can I get a ride in one of those planes?"

Rod said, "Let me check and see if something is available." And he thought-messaged Air Control, *Rod here at the new Freep group on hill twenty-two. Can you send a plane for us to use?*

Air Control's message popped into Rod's mind, *Roger, Rod, got a little two-seater for you. It'll be there in a few minutes.*

"Joe, there's a plane on the way. Get Mary and take her for a ride," Rod said.

"Think she'll go?"

"Don't know if you don't ask."

"Yeah, I'll ask her," Joe said and strode off to find her in the midst of the celebrating new Freeps. "Mary," Joe said on seeing her chatting with her sponsor, Helga, and a tough-looking Freep guy who didn't seem to welcome the interruption. "Want to go flying with me?"

"Hi, Joe, this is Funt. Used to be a special ops trooper in Mainstream."

"I remember your thoughts about war," Joe said.

Funt replied, "Yeah, I've been there. Learned an important lesson: you have to prepare for it because it always will come to you."

Joe replied, "Could be," just as a solar-powered plane whooshed overhead, with its twin props making a *flup-flup* sound as they slowly rotated. They all looked up and followed the plane's descent to a landing on a flat area below them.

"Last call, Mary," Joe said with a smile that said "please come flying."

"Sure, I'll go with you," she said, "if it is not too long."

"She'll be back in twenty minutes, Funt," Joe said as he took Mary's hand and hurried her off toward the plane. Rod was there but no one else.

"Where's the pilot?" asked Joe as he and Mary jogged up.

"No pilot. They sent it over under automatic control."

"Can you fly, Rod?"

"You don't need me. Only room for two anyway."

Fear clutched Joe's heart; a pressure seized his chest. He didn't want to look scared with Mary standing next to him. He felt responsible for her if they should crash. He stepped toward to the front seat and edged in slowly, hoping to figure out what to do.

Rod picked up on what was going on and said, "Joe, it's easy to fly. Use your beetle pack control for thought-messaging what you want the plane to do. Thought-message 'Take off into the wind and climb to fifty meters,' and it will do that."

Trying to hide his trepidation, Joe said, "Sounds easy enough."

Mary had climbed aboard behind him. "Whoopee," she yelled.

Joe said with authority, "Buckle up, we're taking off." Rod stepped back. Joe thought-messaged, *Take off, climb to fifty meters, and continue west.*

The big, slow-moving props churned into the west wind and the plane started moving over bumpy ground. He forgot he was still holding in the control buttons when he thought, *Good thing Mary is sitting behind me and can't see my face.*

Then he heard a thought-message: *Relax Joe, you will have a good flight, and I will make you look good for your girlfriend.*

They lifted off smoothly and climbed to fifty meters. He gulped as he saw the ground receding below him. His fear of heights was starting to tighten him up. He thought, *I don't want my voice to crack and have Mary see I'm afraid.* Immediately he received a thought-message: *Joe, breathe deeply and look out to the horizon until you relax.* He still had the thought buttons tightly depressed, but he was glad the plane spoke up.

Over the wind noise, Mary yelled, "Joe, this is fabulous! I've never flown before."

Joe thought, *She's gutsy. First time up and not scared at all.*

Joe yelled back to Mary, "Let's do some sightseeing." He thought-messaged, *Climb to five hundred meters and turn south toward the Salton Seabed.*

The return thought-message was *Roger Joe, good move.*

The agile craft responded smoothly, and soon they had a panoramic view of the Coachella Valley with the faintest outlines of former streets and the ruins of building walls. They had been told in the Normalizer that this was once a resort area for golfers and lovers of the desert's winter climate. Now, with the summer temperatures in the 130s and 140s during the day, only the Freeps inhabited this area. They had learned how to adapt to the heat and noxious dust from the Salton Seabed.

The view of the desert below was awe inspiring. The glistening white seabed looked strangely welcoming. Joe was about to try a landing there so he could talk face to face with Mary and get to know her better, when a thought-message butted in. *Time to return, Joe, so others can see the sights.* He thought-messaged back, *Air Control, we got your message, take us back to the group…and uh, can you make a low pass over them before landing?*

Can do, Joe, Air Control thought-messaged.

Much obliged, Air Control, Joe thought-messaged.

They buzzed their group who were forming up for the last-night party. They waved in return to the hoots and whistles coming up from below. After landing, the plane took off and flew back to Air Control with no one aboard.

Mary, all excited, said to Joe, "Thank you so much. You made my first flight great fun."

"Hoping you'd like it." Joe said as they started walking fast uphill.

"Oh, Joe, it meant so much." Mary said. "I haven't been with the Freeps very long, and I had to know if there was something more than traveling around under a beetle pack, something adventurous and beautiful. Today you showed me a glimpse of it."

"You didn't mind the desolation of the landscape below?" Joe asked. "All those deserted and collapsing buildings?"

They were taking big steps and jumping boulder to boulder to get to their hilltop camp. She answered, a bit out of breath, "Blew my mind seeing how many people were forced out of this area because the climate heated up."

Joe said, "The Freeps are here now, having a party."

"And there lies the hope."

"How's that?" Joe asked.

"The Freeps found ways to live here. They found ways to more than survive. They found ways to have fun, too."

———

They were entering the crowd when Funt appeared, looking agitated. "Where were you so long?" he asked Mary.

"She was soaring with the eagles while you were down here hooting with the owls," interjected Joe.

That got a laugh out of Mary and a snarling "Real funny, Jerk," out of Funt.

Joe shot back, "Up yours, Creep."

The group heard the commotion and started to gather around. Funt lunged toward Joe and shoved him backward. Joe lost his footing and fell on his ass, hard. Coming up, he grabbed a big rock to smash into Funt's head. But before he could throw it, the senior sponsors came running and got between then. Fighting among Freeps was forbidden, and one of them would get kicked out of the camp.

"Who started it?" asked the senior Normalizer sponsor.

Funt, straining against three men holding him back, retorted, "That shriveled dork gave me lip."

The same sponsor asked Joe, "And what's your story?"

"I was escorting Mary back from our airplane ride when I was set upon by this bumptious oaf," Joe said, affecting a mocking hauteur. Loud laughter from the crowd drew a spate of profanity from Funt. The senior sponsor studied each man for a moment in silence. Then he said, "Funt, leave this group immediately."

Funt glowered at Joe and said nothing but pointed his finger at him in a menacing gesture of shooting. He turned on his heel and walked off. Under his breath, he muttered, "I'll get my revenge."

The group headed for the dinner tables where food was laid out for their final dinner together. The fare was simple and enough to satisfy without making them feel full. Feel-good desserts and sodas were served for the good-bye high they were encouraged to plunge into.

Joe sat next to Mary with their beetle packs configured as chairs they could comfortably recline in. Their sponsors sat at some distance away to provide a chance for their mostly young charges to enjoy the evening unobserved. In the last three days, they had all gotten to know one another. This would be their last night together, and there was no telling when they would meet again.

A few of the newcomers had yet to tell their stories. Joe was among them. He spoke last, described growing up at the Marina where protection from the ever-threatening hordes outside the gated communities was a constant in their lives. Joe's family ventured outside the security of the Marina Towers only in armored automobiles along well-lighted, secured freeways or aboard the Mainstream trains.

Marina schools had taught him about Mainstream Exceptionalism and how its way of life must be revered and protected. Emphasis was placed on rote study of the founding documents and the excellence of the ruling corporations.

Joe had searched for stories of individuals who questioned the power wielders. In used book and film stores, he discovered cartoonists of the Disturbed Era, court jesters of medieval times, and other pot stirrers of the past. Their irreverence immediately appealed to him. Acting out their rebelliousness got him booted out of Mainstream.

Joe told of learning about the Freeps at the YMCA. He heard their lifestyle was unbounded in its attitudes about personal freedom. That sold him. Standing before the group, he said he wanted to experience the freedom he heard about and shake the feelings of alienation he always had in Mainstream. Moreover, he wanted to do something about Mainstream. He wanted to help change it or defeat it. He hoped to learn from the Freeps how to effect change. He wanted to find out how to rescue those he loved and open up a world of freedom to them, too. He had so much to learn, he confessed, but he'd never felt so positive in his life.

With the moon setting and all the newbie stories told, the new Freeps sang songs about the land, the future, and love. The late-night celebration wound down, and the exhausted new Freeps configured their beetle packs for sleeping. Joe put his beetle pack next to Mary's. They stayed awake, lying on their sides facing each other and talking in soft voices about their lives to date and what their futures might be.

It was exciting and daunting, they both agreed. They promised to stay in touch but had no idea if they would ever see each other again. So far, they hadn't found a way to communicate with their families. They would never give up on this, and they agreed they would never give up on trying to stay in touch with each other.

It was quiet when Joe reached over to her bunk and put his arm around her. Mary didn't resist and snuggled closer so they could kiss when he pulled her toward him. Mary said, "I'll always remember this day and this moment." Then, pulling back, she smiled at him and said, "Let's get some sleep now."

Joe replied, "Do you mind if I dream about you?"

Next morning, Rod woke Joe with a shake on the shoulder. "Leaving in twenty minutes."

Joe put on shoes, got up, and grabbed breakfast from the rations that had been set out for each Freep. Mary slept on as he and Rod trekked south, the beauty of her sleeping face etched in his mind.

Chapter 6
ON THE TRAIL

Rod set a steady pace. Much faster than when they had trekked from the border to the Normalizer. Joe started fine, but after a few hours, it was obvious who was best conditioned for hiking. The burden of his beetle pack was becoming more onerous. He said to Rod, "Man, I'm hurting. It's the pack straps. Can we take a break?"

Rod stopped and came back to Joe, "I'll adjust your shoulder and hip straps." He pulled at various places and made little adjustments. "Take some water and eat this power cube. Got a long way to go and gotta keep going."

Joe swigged the water and ate the cube. "OK, Rod, let's get going." And they continued on, Rod leading ten paces ahead. Joe clenched his teeth and followed silently. He wanted to ask Rod the thousand questions on his mind, but he needed all his energy to keep plodding along. Nothing left over for talking.

Lunch was a twenty-minute stop well past high noon. They sat in their beetle chairs, chomped on vegetable protein bars, and downed an energy drink that tasted like medicine. When Rod grinned and pulled out two energy bars, Joe brightened and ate his real slow to prolong the rest. With the last bite, he slowly but resolutely stood up.

Rod said, "Three hours to go to the Indian way station."

Now hours away from the Normalizer, Joe saw no one in any direction. Only endless desert sand and stones and wispy mesas that shimmered far away in the heat. They pressed on, with Joe determined to bear the pain of chafing gear, aching feet, and the heat of the burning sun. Halfway there, he fell well behind Rod. He forced himself to catch up and then felt dizzy and saw black spots dance before his eyes. His feet treaded uncertainly. His body was trying to match his stubborn determination to keep plugging on. And then he tripped on the uneven ground and fell with hands outstretched to break the impact, but it wasn't enough to prevent his nose and chin from hitting the ground. "Oh…shit," he groaned.

He lay on the hot sand for a few seconds and willed himself to get up. Didn't want Rod to think he was weak. He had gotten to his hands and knees when Rod appeared above him. "Joe, I am going to get you going again. Let's stand up," he said as he helped Joe stand. "First, we'll use some of the cooling features of your pack." Rod pulled out from the hard edges of Joe's pack a kind of curtain that, when extended, wrapped across Joe's torso and attached to the pack's opposite edge. Then he had Joe close his helmet visor to hold in the cooling air.

"OK, Joe, you're ready to cool down. Press the control panel buttons and thought-message your pack to the extra-cool mode."

Joe did and soon felt refreshing cool air circulating around his head and body. "Rod…" Joe savored the added coldness and finally put words together. "Great…this cool air…I can make it…know I can."

Rod smiled broadly. "Damn straight, brother Freep. Let's hit the road." And they were off again. Rod set a slightly slower pace, and Joe kept up for the next couple of hours. Shadows lengthened with the setting sun, and air temperature cooled into the livable range. Noticing Joe starting to fall back again, Rod said, "Indian way station in fifteen minutes."

Joe replied with a labored gasp, "Hangin' in, Rod."

———

Soon they entered an oasis of palm trees that hid an ancient adobe building. Misting water vapor from a rooftop cistern cooled the immediate building area. Rod yelled, "Dojay, I'm back. Got a new guy with me."

Dojay appeared. Looked about fifty, medium height with rugged bronze features, wiry. He wore shorts, sandals, and leather necklaces with amulets on his bare chest.

Dojay said to Joe, "Rod tried to kill you, and I am going to bring you back. Drop your pack, and we start with a special drink to cheer you up." Free of the pack, Joe reached for the proffered drink and took a long swig. A taste like no other swirled through Joe's mouth. Not refrigerated but it produced a cooling sensation as he swallowed and a feeling of well-being radiated through his body.

"Great drink. Thanks, Dojay. What's in it?"

"Secret concoction, contains stuff Freeps frown on." He winked at Rod. "But it will make you feel good. Feel like sitting down for dinner."

"Now you're talkin'," said Joe.

Dojay said, "Let's fix those trail barnacles first." He ducked inside his adobe and came out with a satchel of potions and bandages; then ministered to Joe's sore muscles and blisters with the sure touch of a native healer.

Soon after, they were sitting at Dojay's sun-bleached plank table under the stars and palm fronds rustling in the still-hot breeze, comfortable thanks to the cooling mist from the adobe. Joe, munching a tortilla containing scorpions marinated in chili and pulque, said, "You worked my ass off today, Rod."

"It's the beginning," Rod said. "Hope you make it."

"Got doubts about me?" Joe asked.

"My doubts will go away at the end of our time trekking together. Then you will have proven you aren't a newbie wimp."

Joe had wolfed down his modest dinner and was in a mellow mood when Rod said, "Algo will be evaluating how you and the rest of the newbie Freeps work out. Algo has studied the conflicts of human history, particularly how smaller groups fare in conflicts with bigger aggressors. Biggest problem is unity. Small groups often failed when their internal tribes fought with one another or were divided by aggressors. Unity is principle number one of the Freeps."

"Makes sense to me," Joe said. "Gotta stick together. But what's that got to do with me, and you hikin' my ass into the ground?"

"Algo sets the strategy for Freep life and survival. Basically it is a strategy of adaptation. Algo uses the Freeps' enormous computer capability to learn how Freep life must adapt to new knowledge and new threats."

Joe said, "Sounds like Darwin one-oh-one. But what's that got to do with me getting tortured by you in this scorching desert?"

Rod said, "Algo realized that Freep unity wasn't enough to keep Freep life evolving fast enough. Change needs guys like you who don't like to play ball with what everyone else is doing. Guys willing to stand up and criticize Freep ways of doing things."

"Next you are going to tell me that I have to pass this trail torture before Algo will give me a job."

Rod looked at Joe with a serious but understanding expression. "Yeah, this phase is a test of your toughness. It is also a test of something more important: your ability to unify and lead a team."

Joe said, "Speaking of working in a team, what happened to Funt?"

"Kicked out of Freep Nation and went right back to the Biker world he came from."

The three of them sat and talked as night fell. Joe had a zillion questions about Freep customs, but exhaustion overtook him. After a few questions, he fell into deep sleep on his beetle-pack chair under the stars.

When he woke, he saw Rod and Dojay setting out a simple breakfast. Joe said to Dojay, "You are a native here but not a Freep."

Dojay said, "There are some odds and ends in Freep Nation. You'll see more after you have been here a while. We got a lot in common with Freeps, and they leave us alone."

They spent the day with Dojay, mostly in his underground dugout. He instructed Joe on ways native people survived in the desert. How they made clothing and shelter from common reeds and bushes. And how they obtained food and water from cactuses and feasted on snakes and birds. He told Joe to be aware of the spirit of the desert. "The spirit shows itself in the beauty of the desert. Be open to the beauty of the sky above and the land below. Seek it out, and the spirit will find you and bless you."

Next morning, they were on their way again.

Chapter 7
BEETLE-PACK FACTORY

Rod and Joe trekked the next ten days. Unremittingly demanding, Rod set a longer distance to travel each day. Aching feet, blisters, and aching muscles tormented Joe. Moments of doubt jumped into his mind in the afternoons when the challenge to press on became agonizing.

Joe reached deep into his psychic toolbox. Found the walking meditation with which he would pick a trail feature fifty meters ahead, such as a boulder or bush, focus his gaze on it, clear his mind, and, silently repeat in time with his steps, *One, two, three, four* as a mantra until he reached it. Then he looked ahead again, picked another goal and mantra, and pressed on. Or instead of counting he would visualize four words such as *I can do it* and march to them as he repeated them over and over in his mind.

Rod was always up front. Joe swore that he would one day get ahead of him and walk his ass off. But for now, he had to settle for a gnawing anger toward Rod, who was walking with a relaxed gait, picking the right steps through the stones and obstacles under foot. *Bastard, can't you go a little slower?* Joe thought.

The evening stop, however, erased his anger, as Rod took on most of the work to set up camp and make dinner. He passed on a wealth of tips about trekking that Joe knew were invaluable. He helped Joe disinfect blisters on his feet and change bandages.

After they finished eating on day nine of their trek, Rod said, "Tomorrow, Joe, we'll be at the Beetle-Pack Factory."

"A factory in this forsaken wilderness?"

A hearty laugh from Rod, who said, "I felt the same way once." He turned from Joe, looked off at the trackless desert with its scrub bushes and scattered rocks, and said in a thoughtful tone, "Time spent here in the desert changed me so that when I hike through it now, I feel an earth spirit. I don't see a forsaken wilderness."

"Hey, Rod, you know you are not supposed to munch on tripper pills until the day's work is done," cracked Joe as he moved his neck side to side and massaged his shoulder flesh.

Rod said in a good-natured voice, "In time you will find a new relationship with the forsaken wilderness, as you call it. And with your beetle-pack straps."

"What's the new relationship feel like?"

Rod handed a pill to Joe and said, "Time for a pill to simmer down your argumentative heart." They swallowed the pills with their water ration, and Rod talked on. "Right now, I feel satisfied that we had a great day of trekking. We set our packs for enough cooling to fight off heat prostration, but we still experienced the hot breeze that feels like no other breeze. As we walked on high ground, we could see distant mountains forming the horizon in transcendent and beautiful shapes. Saw mirages signaling heat rising from a hot earth. Looking down ahead of my feet, I saw occasional teeth from primordial sharks that swam here under a kilometer of seawater. I saw stones of different colors that signaled the presence of minerals of many types, and I saw geodes that had been spit out of volcanoes millions of years ago."

Joe, lying back on his beetle-pack bed, was looking up at the twilight sky. A tripper pill soothed the day's aches. He said, "I wish I had your insight, Rod. Must be nice."

"In time, you will get a different message from the earth." Tidying up their campsite and checking their gear for tomorrow's hike, Rod said, "For as long as your trek lasts, keep your eyes; ears; and, most important, your mind open. Freep Nation survives on its willingness to understand the earth it inhabits in a very fundamental way." He paused for a minute while checking his pack for the next day's journey. "But that is not all. We Freeps mastered how to live in a place that is unlivable for everyone else. We also did a pretty good job of adapting to an evolving world."

"Only pretty good?"

"To survive, Freeps have had to develop defenses against every new threat. Can't get complacent and think we've got it made and don't have to get any better."

"Yeah," Joe said. "Makes sense."

"Algo warns us all the time to update our strategic thinking. Can't fight our last war."

Joe said, "Why not give Algo the lowdown on Freep enemies and let Algo figure out a way to beat them?" It had become completely dark and Joe was looking up at more stars than he had ever seen before.

"Algo knows it doesn't have the creative sense that humans have. Algo knows that great military victories throughout history were won by leaders who had the ability to come up with something unexpected, something never done before."

"So, Algo ain't perfect?"

"You got it, Joe. And the good news is that Algo knows it is not perfect."

Joe's mind was trying to absorb Rod's words while his senses were trying to take in the majesty of the star field. He felt sleep coming on.

"Hey, Rod, how long will this walk-about learning trek last?"

"Depends on you. If it lasts a year, you will be working at the highest level of Freep leadership." Rod stopped talking, seeing Joe's head sinking and eyes closing.

The morning found them underway early. Big cumulus clouds between them and the rising sun streamed a brace of rays over a silent desert. Joe called to Rod, "That sky is mind blowing."

"Beautiful," Rod said. "One of the great joys of trekking."

An hour later, Joe asked, "Rod, if I don't make it a year, what happens?"

"You'll see a lot and visit a lot of different Freep locations. You'll get an idea of where you might fit in."

They marched on until midday, when they came upon a small gray building. Could have been a warehouse in its prior life. A man named Bax came to the door. "Saw you coming, Rod. Lunch is ready."

They went to the cafeteria for a stew of some kind of vegetables. Nothing extra served and nothing wasted. Tasted OK. Joe hadn't yet gotten used to feeling a bit hungry most of the time.

Afterward they went downstairs to an underground factory with about fifty workers at workbenches. They watched them through a window.

Bax looked like a schoolteacher Joe had back in Mainstream. Same thoughtful face as Mr. Portrib, his sociology instructor, but carrying a good fifty pounds less. Not unusual here. You never saw a fat Freep.

Bax said to Joe, "We are going to put you to work for four days on beetle packs."

"OK, Bax. I'm ready."

"First, you need to understand the history of why we're all running around looking like big bugs." Bax motioned them down a corridor to the info room and switched on a wall screen video. "Drop your pack, Joe, and check out our beetle-pack video; I'll get some relaxation pills and tea."

The video described early Freeps as outcast, off-the-grid refugees from the twenty-first-century depressions. They lived in the hot, arid interior of California where towns and cities gradually faded away with the ever-increasing temperatures caused by global warming. At the same time, economic inequality mushroomed when corporations got the vote. With one vote per corporate employee, things changed rapidly. Business councils replaced the legislature and governor of California.

All sorts of people found themselves out of step with Mainstream laws. Early outcasts included scientists and engineers who wrestled with living at air temperatures that were too high for normal human life. These "science guys" found a way for individuals to have body air conditioning powered by a backpack solar array. They were the first Freeps.

Including a computer in the backpack was the next step in setting the stage for a laser installation. Now Freeps could use computers to learn, work, communicate with each other, and defend themselves. Other features to configure the pack for sitting or lying down lengthened the pack into today's beetle-pack shape.

Joe was fascinated. He was wearing a descendant of one of those packs invented two hundred years ago. It was much better in every way.

Growing their system from scratch, science guys encrypted everything in Algo-Net, as it came to be called. Joe was told that the ancient Internet made a decision at its beginning not to encrypt its communications and structural software. This mistake could never be righted because too many businesses would have to be stopped while the entire system was overhauled. Freeps didn't have that problem. There were no Freep businesses at the beginning, and early users opted for the maximum level of security and encryption in the Freep computer and communication systems.

Generations of science guys designed in the capability to do parallel processing among all the individual Freep computers. They also invented a leadership algorithm called Algo. With Algo's enhanced artificial intelligence, it could make decisions based on the science of evolution, logic, and a history of similar decisions going back to the cavemen. Algo was conceived as a leader that was only capable of logical, correct decisions.

As Joe watched, he imagined cockroaches scurrying away in every direction when a light is turned on them. Freeps were just like them when attacked. You might take out a bunch of them with bombs or gas, but the rest disappeared, without any damage to the brain controlling them.

Spread among a million computer brains, Algo would never die if a batch of Freeps and their beetle-pack computers got wiped out. Like cockroaches, the evolutionary superjocks, they took hits but kept on going.

The video ended, and Joe was snapped back to reality by Bax's mellow voice. "Joe, I think that is enough school for your first day."

"Uh, yeah," Joe said, still not fully back from the mind-trip exposure to Freep history. "Bax, I see potential for Freep greatness."

Bax replied, "Everyone reacts a little differently."

Joe stood up and with intensity asked Bax, "Doesn't everyone realize Algo has centuries of knowledge at its command, has a million synced computers at its disposal, and can survive anything that can be thrown at Freep Nation?"

"It is more complicated than that, Joe," said Bax, meeting Joe's intense gaze. "You have seen one facet of life here. Give it a little more time to sink in. How about we hit the cafeteria for a bite to eat and meet some of the folks?"

"Bax, you are pulling me out my deep-think mode."

"Not everyone has one of those modes," Bax chortled. "Don't give your mind away to the first Freep stimulus that rocks your brain. As you trek through our life, you will discover more astonishing things. Take it all in and find your way carefully."

"I hear you, Bax, but can't push this Freep power thing out of my mind. Freeps could rule the world."

"You will push it out of your mind after a really bad dinner," Bax laughed.

"Then what?" asked Joe.

"A night's sleep and your morning shower."

"Shower?"

Next morning, Joe arose from his pack bed, which was shaded by a few desert palms. He stretched and thought, *Great night, feel good, great pills here.* He collapsed his beetle pack into the traveling configuration and was aiming it toward the sun for maximum charge when Rod appeared on the trail they had walked yesterday. He was with a girl. *Not bad*, thought Joe, looking at her toned brown legs, pretty face, and a wide smile.

"Joe, meet Zarine."

"Hi, Zarine. You two joining me for breakfast?"

"Damn straight. Got our morning ten kilometers in, and we're hungry. Take your shower, and we'll catch up with you."

"Where's the shower?"

"End of the hall past the cafeteria."

There was a stocky middle-aged woman wearing a gray bikini bottom who barked out, "I'm Yolie. Take your clothes off and get your ass in here."

He rapidly undressed and entered the shower that had room for ten. She grabbed a soapy brush and vigorously scrubbed his back from top to bottom as he faced the wall. He yelped, "Damn, Yolie! Leave some skin on."

"OK, maybe a little," she said, and continued to brush every inch of him without any decrease in roughness. Then she soaped his hair and shampooed vigorously.

He heard another shower turn on, and when he turned around to get brushed on his front, *God! There's Zarine soaping herself. What a gorgeous body!* It was too much to control, and his pecker started firming up.

Yolie yelled, "Best keep your eyes off her." Then she flicked her finger on the end of his penis.

"Ouch!" yelped Joe and looked at the ceiling while his pecker sagged to its off-duty size.

Yolie gave Joe a towel and told him to dry off and sit down for a shave and ear cleaning. "Getting all that trail dust off before you go into our assembly areas," she said, roughly turning his head this way and that, checking her work.

Joe joined Bax, Rod, and a half a dozen others who would go to work on the day shift after eating. They ate a meatless breakfast: cereal, cactus juice, corn bread, prickly pear jelly, and a hot drink of unknown origin. "How'd ya like the shower, Joe?" asked a grinning Bax, in sync with knowing grins from everyone else at the table.

"When I grow some skin back and my pecker works again, I'll let you know." Laughs all around.

"That's all the rough stuff for a while," said Bax, "now that you passed the newcomer test. The gang"—Bax motioned toward the others at the table—"will be training you how to make and refurbish packs for the next three days."

They got up and filed out. Along the way, Joe noticed a big one-way window where diners could see those in the shower, and it got a chuckle out of him. He thought, *This bunch really has a kinky sense of humor. Watching Yolie put me through the paces and laughing their asses off.*

———

A couple named Gadz and Jeannie took Joe to a demo room to see and try out beetle packs of many types. They started with Joe's pack and demonstrated some things he didn't know about it.

Gadz, about fifty and gray with the usual lean build, asked, "Know how to cool down with this thing, Joe?"

"Sure do," said Joe, pulling out the front torso cover, as Rod showed him back on the trail.

"Good, that's half of it. It's got cooling pants, too." He showed Joe how to deploy thin-film pants and set a cool body temperature on extreme days.

"We can survive anywhere on earth," said Jeannie.

"How about water?" asked Joe.

"The suit can recycle perspiration, exhaled breath, and urine."

"Yuk, no thanks!"

Jeannie continued, "Yeah, your suit can turn it all into drinkable water—all powered by the sun."

"Whoa, I'm not drinking that!" Joe said.

She laughed and said, "With your life at stake, you'll drink it. In fact, you might have had it with your breakfast tea."

Loudly, with an incredulous look on his face, Joe said, "No! Say it isn't so."

Gadz and Jeannie looked at Joe with sheepish grins and nodded their heads in unison.

Joe said, "Can we go to the next feature?"

Jeannie said, "Before moving on. There is one more thing the sun does for us. It powers our water-from-air converters. These are small units built into beetle packs to top off daily needs."

"Far out." said Joe. "What's next?"

Gadz rotated Joe's round helmet down in front of his face so he was looking through the face shield. He said, "Press the second button on your control panel. What do you see?"

"Crosshairs in front of my right eye," said Joe.

"Good. Let's go and have some target practice."

Outside, facing the desert, Gadz pressed a button on his pack and said, "Request OK for target practice for Joe and me."

A voice from both their packs said, "Clear to fire for ten minutes."

Gadz said, "See that big rock? Looks like a squirrel."

"Yeah."

A stream of light flashed, and the rock shattered.

"Whoa!" Joe yelled. "What'd you do?"

"Laser-beam shot. Here's how you do it," Gadz said, reaching to Joe's lowered helmet shield. "Touch this button, and your laser will extend."

Joe did, and a shiny half-inch-diameter tube extend-ed two inches. Gadz said, "Put your crosshairs on a rock out there. Then I want you to thought-message the word 'Fire.'"

A flash and another rock shattered. "Farging awe-some!" Joe exclaimed. "Gadz, how do Freeps keep from shooting each other? They all have one of these."

"Easy, Joe. A shooter needs Algo's permission for each shot. As you saw, that only takes seconds, and Algo doesn't let Freeps shoot at each other."

"Beats guns."

Back inside, Gadz and Jeannie showed Joe the collec-tion of old beetle packs. They were cumbersome and heavy. "Hard to imagine how Freeps could hump them very far," Joe said. The latest packs, still in research, were fascinat-ing because they didn't look like beetle packs. They looked like ordinary clothes but had the same capability, if the wearer wore a customized hat for aiming and firing.

Joe said, "I can see me now—a real badass back in Mainstream."

"Slow down, Joe, they won't be ready for a while."

For the next three days, Joe worked with production teams. He learned how to assemble beetle packs from pre-assembled modules. One worker could produce ten a day. Couples liked to work together at top speed to get their twen-ty done in midafternoon to lengthen their time off together.

Joe had a million questions about beetle pack manufac-turing, and his off-work hours were filled with discussion and learning about this iconic feature of the Freep Nation. Energy management was a big deal. The energy that each Freep could store in his or her battery could be used for temperature control, for communications, and for fighting with laser weapons. Five laser shots drew down a beetle pack battery, leaving a little energy for continued cooling.

Joe learned that when Freeps were forced to fight, they favored a defensive strategy, falling back and shooting as little as possible to conserve their limited battery energy. Turned out that it wasn't a bad strategy for another reason. The attackers from the Out-Lands had to fight *away* from the bars and whore houses and other pleasures of their savage lives *toward* a barren desert furnace with meager spoils of war.

After four intense days Joe's brain was pumped with new knowledge. It was time to get underway again to sort it all out.

Chapter 8
HOMESTEADERS

Joe and Rod left the Beetle-Pack Factory before sunrise, Rod ahead as usual, setting a steady pace but not too fast. Joe figured Rod, an experienced trekker, knew that the best use of energy for a long day was to start out slow—and that was OK with him. He thought, *OK, I'll hang in, Rod, and I'll keep up with you. Tired of you always in front with me on the edge of falling over. But for now, OK, you lead the way. One of these days, I am going to take off first and let you eat my dust.*

They headed west, higher into the mountains, tramping up tough inclines and then down a bit until the next tough incline and repeat all over again hour after hour under a cloudless sky. Rod declared a halt for the night in a level patch in late-afternoon mountain shadow. Joe flopped on his beetle pack configured as a chair and stared up at the blue sky with his cooling on, not saying a word. Rod slipped out of his beetle pack and did a strenuous series of stretching exercises, with Joe thinking to himself, *Look at that show-off bastard trying to make me feel like a wimp.*

Finally, Rod stopped and sauntered over to Joe, who looked up at him. "Got a surprise for you tonight, Joe."

"What, a hundred pushups before dinner?"

"Ha!" erupted Rod's full-on belly laugh. "No, nothing like that. This is a good surprise."

"Better be."

"It is, Joe. You can make an Algo-Net call tonight."

"How far can I call with Algo-Net?"

"You can call anyone in Freep Nation but nowhere else."

"OK. I'll try Mary." He sat up. "How do I dial her number?"

"No dialing, thought-message Algo-Net and ask to be put through for a voice call to Mary, whom you met at the Normalizer."

Joe beetled up and walked a short distance away for privacy and then thought-messaged as Rod had told him.

Algo-Net thought-messaged back, *Stand by, Joe.*

Mary's voice came on line after a few seconds. "Joe, I thought you would never call. Why did you wait so long?"

Joe replied, "This is the first call they allowed me. Did you get your first call yet?"

"Yes, I've had three so far. Tried to call you with one of them, and they said you were off limits temporarily."

"Strange I'm only allowed one call."

Mary said, "They are testing you, Joe. It's all part of seeing what level of Freep life you can qualify for."

"How do you know that?"

"I am working in the Freep Life Center. Right now, I'm learning how Algo monitors Freeps in training and decides where to place them in the community."

"What's that have to do with Algo-Net calls and how many I can get?" asked Joe.

"New Freeps are often hit with challenges and aggravations of all types to see how they react."

"Hey, Mary, does this testing include practical jokes?"

"Joe…Did you by any chance have a shower…?"

"Yeah, they got me at the Beetle-Pack Factory."

Mary burst out in that wonderful laugh that Joe remembered her for. She asked, "Where are you, and where are you going?"

"We're somewhere south of Palm Springs heading to higher altitude. Going to visit a homesteader in a couple of days. After that, I don't know. Mary, where are you?"

"Right now, I'm at Joshua Tree Park in an underground office area. We get a long beetle pack march every day. Learning a lot about Algo's evolution. People here are OK, but I miss you."

"Same here, been thinking about you a lot. Can you tell me about Algo?"

"Algo," Mary said, "is a massive artificial intelligence program spread around the Freeps' beetle-pack computers. Probably over a million of them. Algo constantly reevaluates its core inference engines, neural nets, and a bunch of other algorithms. It selects and uses those that produce good results, and in this way, it evolves. And then it reevaluates itself again.

"Over the years, it gets better. Continuously gets smarter. It has programmed itself to interface with humans on an emotional level to—"

"Hey," Joe exclaimed. "You pulling my leg? Telling me Algo is becoming human, with emotions and—?"

A robotic voice interrupted. "Joe, Mary, we have to discontinue your call at this point."

Joe yelled, "When can I call again?" The line was dead. Joe kicked dirt and shouted in frustration. "Dammit, dammit…gawddammit!"

Rod walked up. "Get cut off?"

"Yeah, and I was starting to talk with Mary."

"That happens to you new guys sometimes. You'll get another chance to call," Rod said, and he put a hand on Joe's shoulder to show a little sympathy. "Let's eat and have a pill to relax."

Later, under a sky full of stars, a warm desert wind blew; it was comfortable without beetle-pack cooling. They talked in a relaxed fashion. Rod answered a lot of Joe's questions about the Beetle-Pack Factory. Rod said there were more of them scattered about Freep Nation. Dispersion of Freep resources was a tenet of their social organization. Rod said he lived and worked at the factory when not trekking with newbies. He and Zadine shared quarters there. In their free time, they explored desert peaks where humans may never have set foot before.

He said Algo allowed Freeps to move around and try different jobs. Algo observed it was good for people to have new and stimulating experiences to keep their community interest high. Algo, with its capability to keep tabs on all job openings and candidates for the jobs, sought to optimize the satisfaction of the Freeps with their work—and their lives in general. Before coming to the Beetle-Pack Factory, Rod and Zadine had worked on an aeroponic farm operation.

Joe asked if he ever wanted to live in Mainstream. Rod had no desire to live anywhere but Freep Nation. It satisfied his desire to be a part of something meaningful and noble and to make a contribution to humanity's survival and evolution.

———

The next three days were tough. Joe felt Rod was pushing him to the edge of collapse just to show him he could. Resentment was building, but Joe was determined to contain it. He didn't want a bad mix of exhaustion and irritation to flare up and ruin his chances for something higher and better. He remembered how Funt blew up and was booted out.

Joe did a little soul searching. Asked himself if he resented Rod because he resented anyone above him, like he had in Mainstream. There he found himself bristling under the strictures of teachers, cops, and his parents. That's the way he was. He believed that as he went higher, fewer people would be above him that could tell him what to do. He had to grind it out, keep up with Rod, and keep his feelings to himself.

About noon on the third day, they saw a sign along the trail: Freep Territory, Keep Out. Rod said, "We're gettin' there."

Four hours later, as they crested a long incline, there was another 'Keep Out' sign and, three hundred meters beyond, the homestead. Nothing fancy—a couple of simple adobe buildings. A big one, about twenty meters long and a small one half the size. Two kids in small beetle packs and a bunch of chickens were running around outside, and soon a couple appeared standing in the doorway of the smaller house. They were in their thirties. Their appearance reflected a hard life on a rocky land. Their lean bodies were clothed in gray shorts and shirts. No frills. But their open faces and welcoming smiles betrayed a satisfaction with their lot in life.

"Hi, Rod," they called out.

"Hello, Freddo. Hello, Negla," Rod called. When closer, he introduced Joe, and they went inside the house. Rod was a familiar guest there after years of visits with newcomers in tow. But things were a little different this time, as Freddo said, "Guys, I want you to know that Bikers have been probing around here lately. There is a Freep drone aloft now tracking six of them."

"How far away are they?" Rod asked.

"About sixty kilometers. They could take the same trail you came up on. We'll know after they pass the last fork of the trail. If they take the branch up toward us and pass by our 'Keep Out' sign, we're going to fight them off."

"We've got a couple of hours to get ready," Freddo said. "Take your packs off and set them in the sun to top off your batteries. Then come inside to eat, drink, and rest for a while."

Inside the door was a simple room. In the middle was a table with a hearty lunch for everyone. Joe dug in to fresh chicken and vegetables. *Better than the usual Freep fare*, He thought. *Homesteading has its good points.*

An hour later, Freddo yelled, "Let's go," waking Joe with a start from his post-lunch snooze. "We're taking up positions behind boulders this side of the sign. Get your packs on and activate your lasers."

Joe realized this was the real thing—not training, but confrontation with thugs. His pulse sped up. Danger approaching brought a sense of total alertness and determination to stay cool and suppress his shivers of fear.

As they walked the two hundred meters to their defensive positions in a patch of boulders, Freddo briefed them on the instruction Algo had given him: fire warnings first and shoot for effect if they pass the sign. Keep your heads down; they have accurate snipers.

Freddo told Joe and Rod where to position themselves for a secure field of fire to confront the Bikers and to prevent being outflanked by any Bikers tearing off uphill to the high ground overlooking the homestead.

The sound of angry bees began soon after they took their defensive positions. It grew louder. They heard a loudspeaker on the Freep drone supporting them. "Do not proceed farther. Turn around and leave. This is Freep territory." Gunshots responded to the drone's message.

"They are shooting at the drone," Freddo said. Its message repeated a few more times and stopped. The motorcycles got closer. They were going slowly, bumping over a rocky and rutted trail. Then they were visible coming over the rise in the trail. Black monsters driven by bulbous men in air-conditioned leathers.

Freddo activated his beetle-pack loudspeaker and commanded, "Stop immediately! Turn back!"

The lead motorcycle edged up to the sign and slowly passed it. Freddo fired his laser, melting the front wheel and fork. The cycle bucked downward in front and upward in back, throwing the rider over the handlebars. The rear motorcycle sprinted off trail to the right to climb and outflank the homestead from the high ground. Joe aimed his crosshairs on its front wheel and fired, vaporizing its front end. The cycle handlebars jabbed into the ground, and that rider too was thrown into the scree littering the slope. He tried to crawl away but was too injured to make it very far. Freddo announced on his speaker, "Turn around or be killed!" The lead rider got up unsteadily and raised his hand to signal OK.

He didn't advance; he took his helmet off and yelled, "We need water."

Joe couldn't believe his eyes. It was Funt! The defenders held their positions and stayed hidden from the Bikers. Freddo announced, "Leave now! We'll drone-drop water to you as you ride back down."

Funt turned back and got on the back of a motorcycle near him. The other fallen rider, unable to walk, was helped on the back of another motorcycle and strapped to its driver to keep him on board. The defeated Bikers turned their iron steeds around and bumped back downhill, leaving two of their machines smoking in the dust and one shot-down Freep drone in the rocks. Freddo called Algo-Net to report the contact and request that a few water jugs be dropped to the Bikers.

Back at the house, Freddo explained, "Bikers are always probing. Always looking for something to steal, a woman to rape, a kid to take, or a man to kill. You guys did well today. We got rid of them without any killing, and they never had a chance to see how many of us there were or what was going on at my homestead. They got stung enough to keep them away for a while, but they didn't get stung bad enough that their warped sense of honor would demand a full-on revenge raid."

Joe said, "Guys, I recognized the Biker leader; it was Funt. He had a black triangle emblem with a wide red stripe on his back."

"Thought so, but I wasn't sure," Rod said. "You were closer to him."

Freddo said, "Must be a new Biker. They're usually not smart enough to avoid a fire fight when they're probing."

"He's new, all right," Rod said. "Got kicked out of the Freeps about three weeks ago, during a Normalizer."

"You'll hear from him again," Freddo said. "Anyone who rises that quickly in the Biker world is tough. Maybe tough enough to get to the top. Believe me, guys, he will be heard from again."

———

The next day, Freddo showed Joe his vertical farming operation in the larger of the two homestead buildings. Racks three meters high held aeroponic trays for growing a variety of vegetables.

"How do you ship out your produce?" asked Joe.

Freddo said, "Drones pick up our stuff and take it to the best distribution points as determined by Algo-Net. Rod tells me you are going to help me with the drone loading tomorrow."

"Figured he would volunteer me for something," Joe said. "He's always doing that."

Next morning, Freddo and Negla were harvesting vegetables from the greenhouse trays at breakneck speed. They put them in boxes on wheels. Joe wheeled them out to the helicopter drones that landed twenty meters from the door in clouds of dust. After loading in the drone's capacity of four boxes, Joe stood clear, and the drone rose above its own dust cloud and disappeared over the mountain ridge.

Negla explained, "We grow veggies twenty-four hours a day all year round. Got abundant sun during the day and low-loss glass. At night, we turn on grow lights with electric power from batteries charged by solar panels during the day."

Joe asked, "How do your kids like living here?"

"They have a lot to do, helping with chores and tramping around in the mountains on their own. They learn a lot about nature that most Freep kids don't. There are a lot of homesteaders in these parts, and our kids can reach their friends within two hours of hiking. We can call up a plane to get farther out to visit if we want to. Their education, via Algo-Net and home projects, is excellent."

"Great operation, but I don't think I could do it every day all year round," Joe said.

"Algo helps keep us sane. Trekkers like you guys are scheduled in here fairly frequently. And we get more human contact with vacations a couple of times a year to different parts of Freep Nation. Of course, there are Normalizers about every two months. Normalizers are a chance for Freddo and I to get a little space away from each other, too—if you know what I mean." She gave Joe's hand a squeeze and winked at him.

Joe and Rod stayed on for a few more days and worked at the homestead chores. One day, Joe and Negla strapped large lightweight boxes on their beetle packs and hiked out to collect paddle cactuses. She was surprisingly agile climbing the rocky mountainsides and was skillful at slicing off the thorny leaves with a razor-sharp knife. They each filled the box on the other's back after a couple of hours and headed for home.

She found that Joe had a lot to learn about Freep life, and they talked continually. Mostly, Joe asked questions, and she answered them with long, generous explanations.

Back at the homestead, Joe was ready to drop, but Negla put him to work trimming thorns off the paddle cactus leaves and stowing them in a box for a future drone pickup. With her beetle pack off and her long black hair flowing over her shoulders and down her back, Joe had a tough time working next to her. The smell of her glistening perspiration found a way to excite him, and he felt the pressure rising. Fortunately, it didn't take long to trim the paddle cactuses. Joe went into the house to cool off and spend a little time researching on Algo-Net before Rod and Freddo came in for the afternoon break time.

He had started to research Freep wars since leaving the Beetle-Pack Factory. At first, it was for short periods in the evenings after hiking; when he was too tired to do anything else, he leaned back in his pack recliner and studied his helmet display screen. He started digging into accounts of conflicts with the Out-Landers in the twenty-first century.

Not much attention was paid to the Freeps at first. They were thought of as an odd lot. Their awkward beetle packs brought derision from other humans living closer to the ocean where it was cooler. There weren't enough Freeps to be of interest or a threat to Mainstreamers.

Most Mainstream dissidents ended up in Mid-Level, the isolated colonies in the Out-Lands where the farms and factories were located. There they worked at the many activities needed to provide a comfortable lifestyle for the Mainstreamers.

They toiled for years with the hope that work and good behavior would earn them a return to Mainstream. Some did return, and that kept the dream alive for the others in Mid-Level. Many never did and lived out their lives toiling to satisfy the corporate masters along the coast but never losing hope that their chance to return would come someday.

The Out-Lands were beyond the reach of social institutions and laws. The jails and asylums were closed to save money over one hundred years ago. Criminals and insane humans were simply sent to the Out-Lands to live by their wits or brute power or to die victims of the predation of the vile and deadly Out-Lands' gangs. The Biker gangs were the most mobile and the ones most likely to venture into the Freep Nation and cause trouble.

Freddo and Rod came in from preparing the aeroponic equipment for its next growing cycle. Negla took a break from caring for the kids to bring fruit drinks and sociability pills. The men joined with Joe to see how his researching of Freep history was going. Joe said, "Based on what I am learning about Bikers and the dust-up we had with them two days ago, it looks like Bikers haven't changed much in the last hundred years."

Freddo said, "Got that right. They're scavengers. It's their nature to keep prowlin' around looking for weakness. But Algo is on to them. Algo puts us homesteaders in locations that are easy to defend—as you saw. Algo makes sure there are enough resources to repel Biker raiders."

Rod piped up, "Joe, Algo studies the battles of outcast groups throughout history. It continuously learns how to do things better, based on the distant and recent past. That gives the homesteaders confidence they will be safe."

Freddo said, "Algo learned that knowledge of the enemy is most important."

Rod added, "With our lasers, we have them outgunned. If we know when they are coming, we beat them every time."

———

Joe and Rod hiked out of the homestead before sunrise. Joe went reluctantly, as he was enjoying the family atmosphere and the warmth of Freddo and Negla toward him. He and Negla had a spark of erotic resonance starting to simmer, but he felt perhaps it was best to be on his way and leave it as a warm memory.

Joe had witnessed another Freep lifestyle: a couple making their way by themselves, instead of the more communal living he had experienced at the Beetle-Pack Factory. As they trekked and talked, Rod said that Freeps could get as much personal space as they could handle. Rod cited the solitary life of the watcher, the family group of the homesteader, and Freep communal environments such as the Beetle-Pack Factory—all very different in the amount of time people spent in contact with other people.

After a couple of days on the trail, Rod told Joe that their next stop was the Airplane Works, where he would stay and work for two months.

Chapter 9
AIRPLANE WORKS

They spent a week of hard trekking to the Airplane Works. Most of the way, they walked side by side on flat terrain, which made for easy conversation. Rod told Joe that the Airplane Works was housed in the centuries-old warehouse of a former distribution center. "Freeps are like hermit crabs, living in the discarded shells of other creatures. We do everything on the cheap."

"Is that what people here want?" Joe asked.

"In a survival type of existence, people prioritize their wants and needs. They tend to analyze things that affect their lives in a logical way and concentrate on what's important."

"Yeah, sure looks like no one is interested in making a fashion statement," Joe said in an exaggerated country-bumpkin accent.

Rod laughed and said, "Those are pretty obvious things that newcomers notice right away. I'll give you a few more examples: no roads, no power generation or telephone poles and wires, no schools, no central water system, and no impressive public buildings or monuments, to name a few."

"I get all that, except the no-schools part."

"OK, Joe, you are used to thinking of school buildings where kids go to learn. Here, we have Algo-Net with an incredible array of learning tools that kids can't get enough of. They love it. And it is all in their beetle packs for use anytime. All of us are indoctrinated that everyone is responsible for helping kids learn about the world around them. As they grow into adults, we keep our eyes out for kids who don't read or write well, and we give them a hand. Got a lot of on-the-job training in many areas of Freep Nation to teach trades. Even I take kids on treks to teach them about nature and survival."

"How about college?"

"Algo-Net is great for that, too. The best lectures on any subject are in Algo-Net. And there are a million other teaching aides for everything from math to medicine."

"No professors?"

"There are professors who talk one on one with students or who convene small symposia to work on difficult concepts. A student gets as much face time with a prof as he or she needs."

They went on chatting though the long afternoon. Rod slowed the trek pace to make it more comfortable for a long discussion. Joe felt like a backward kid being patiently tutored. That night, under a full moon, they continued talking up to the attention limit to serious discussion and Rod showed Joe how to access popular shows from around the world with the beetle pack electronics.

Joe was nodding off watching a show when he was surprised by a call from Mary.

"Mary, great to hear your voice!"

She said, "I see you are showing up at the Airplane Works tomorrow."

"How'd you know?" Joe asked.

"Joe, I'm working in the Freep Life Center."

"Snooping into personnel files in your spare time?"

"Joe, what an awful thing to say." She giggled.

"Glad you did, Mary. Love talking with you."

"Be greater in person."

"Talking dirty now."

Mary said, "You'll be working on airplanes for a while...want me to let you in on a little secret?"

"All ears."

"You'll be taking planes on test flights. When you do, fly here to Mojave. You can land, and we can renew our friendship."

"Sounds like a quickie."

"Got it on first guess," she said.

"I'll call if this danged system lets me, and tell you when I'm flying there to see you."

"Joe, if you're blocked, ask someone else to call me and tell me when you'll be here. Someone you can trust."

———

The next day, Joe and Rod arrived at the Airplane Works. A looming rectangle of gray concrete, it didn't offer clues to what was inside except for a handful of electric-powered airplanes on a bare earth strip next to the building.

They went through an unmarked door to a small lobby. Behind a barred window, an old man took a look at them and then at his screen. He looked back and said, "You must be Joe and Rod."

"That's us," said Rod. "Where's the boss?"

"You mean Otmar?"

"Who else?" Rod asked. "Been running this place for twenty years."

"He's out flying around."

Rod nodded toward Joe. "Joe here's a newcomer; he'll be here for two months. I'll be here a few days and come back before Joe leaves."

"OK, lemme see if he has a space assigned." The old-timer checked his screen and turned again toward Joe and Rod. "You two will be in space thirty-two."

Space thirty-two in the living quarters was a small room with two beds, a desk, and storage space. Nothing fancy.

They entered the biggest part of the huge building, the assembly area, and made their way past lines of planes in all stages of completion to a raised control room in the middle of the factory. A black woman with a big laugh was in charge.

"Joe, I'm Quendu. We are going to get some work out of you. And if you really work your butt off, we'll put you on flying status."

"I'm ready to fly right now," Joe said.

"I haven't worked your butt off yet." Quendu laughed. "I want you to report to work at station fourteen. Tell 'em there you're a newcomer looking for a job."

Rod said, "I'll catch up with you later." And left.

Walking to station fourteen, Joe noticed that each airplane had a dedicated crew that did everything to build their assigned plane. The crew he joined had six people working away, all clad in Freep gray. They were in final assembly of a two-engine model that could carry four people. Joe was paired with Pablo, a Latino guy about his own age, with a tight beard. They installed control surfaces that made the plane pitch up and down, roll side to side, and yaw right to left.

Joe commented, "These surfaces are easy to install."

"Sí, Amigo. You put the end pivots of the surfaces in their slots, snap the retaining clamps shut, and hook up the servo motor."

"Man, this job is OK. All plane parts are incredibly light, and they fit together so easily."

Pablo and Joe met in the dining room for dinner. Pablo had worked in the Airplane Works for a couple of years and loved every minute.

"Joe, I like that I can do every job to build a plane."

"How do you learn all the jobs that have to be done?"

"You work in a team that normally has someone experienced in every job who can show you how to do things. And there is computer instruction—in case you are working on your own."

After dinner, Pablo showed Joe around the recreational areas. Nothing fancy. The gym had primitive equipment but high-tech screens that ordered or cajoled individual Freeps to stay in shape.

The next morning, Joe had breakfast with Rod. "Well, Joe, how do you like it so far?"

"Man, this is a great place to work, but living quarters? Talk about crummy. Not made for a long-term stay."

Rod said, "You're right on that score. Seems as if they are designed for you to spend as little time there as possible. Did you call Mary?"

"Couldn't get through—same old story."

"Joe, I am going to be gone for a month or so. Leaving today. Stay strong."

"Always, man. Have an enjoyable trip to wherever you're going."

Joe enjoyed airplane building. He hit it off well with his coworkers, except one: Tacker, an ex-Out-Lander. They didn't get along but tacitly agreed to avoid conflict during working hours. Probably memories of Funt prejudiced his reaction to Tacker. He guessed Tacker had him pegged as an overcoddled Marina twit. Joe had to give him half credit on that one.

Shan was another story. She worked at steady pace, not taking off time to laugh or joke. Always completely absorbed in her work and pretty in a mysterious way. Joe had to rein in his immediate attraction to her. He guessed she was part or all Chinese. Her voice, deep and sincere sounding—perfect accompaniment to her dark eyes that he thought of as headlights of her deep, reflective nature. He wanted to know more about her.

One night, he wandered through the recreation areas and saw an announcement: Discussion Group 7:00pm - Topic to Be Announced. He went there on time and quietly, but without wanting to show caution, opened the door.

"Amigo," called Pablo, "come in and help us pick a topic to argue about."

"Yeah, newcomer, come up with something suitable for us proli toilers," came a familiar voice from the darkened room.

It was Tacker. Well, at least he knew two people there. Joe decided to take the bull by the horns. He said to the group, "Hi, I'm Joe, and as my colleague Tacker pointed out, I am a newbie and have a lot to learn about Freep life."

"Give us a discussion topic," a laughing girl called out, "not a life story."

Joe looked forward to the verbal combat. Here was a chance to learn about Freeps and cultures like them that lived on the margins. "Got a topic for you, sweetheart."

"Yass, Dahling, do tell," she mocked, in a tone right out of his Mom's bridge club.

Joe smiled at that and then said, "Topic is 'How do Freeps survive with enemies all around them?'"

Tacker said, "Easy. Algo has studied every human conflict and knows what to do when Freeps are attacked. End of story."

Pablo jumped in. "That's OK if the next attack is like something in the past."

A voice from the crowd said, "We always keep a little ahead of the Out-Landers with our lasers and personal cooling systems. Mainstream gives them all the guns they want, but they are not organized. They're tribal. Always fighting with each other."

"We gotta stick together," another voice said.

The discussion continued with enthusiasm. Joe noticed that Shan had entered and sat quietly in the back. After listening for a while, she said, "It is better to win without fighting."

"How do you do that?" several asked.

"Avoid major war at all costs. Invest in intelligence to know what your enemy is thinking. Threaten your enemy's infrastructure, particularly power, transportation, and cyber capability."

Tacker said, "That's all well and good when you are talking about Mainstream."

Joe said, "They're the most powerful."

Tacker replied, "There's a bunch of gangs in the Out-Lands. They're armed to the teeth with guns Mainstream gives them, hoping they kill each other off. Hey, I come from there. Their populations are getting bigger, and a lot of them live like dogs. And don't think they're not talking about settling out here in Freep territory."

Shan said, "Settlers are the worst kind of invaders. They are motivated by their own brand of idealism, and they are willing to put their homes and children right in the front lines."

Pablo took a shot with a joke: "Aren't we all settlers?"

Laughs and snorts followed Pablo's remark, and the discussion continued until lights out in the recreational areas.

Next morning, Joe got to work early. He saw different airplane models, from one-engine single seaters up to four-engine cargo models. All had similar modular construction to maximize the number of parts that fit all models. These electric planes looked slow, and they were—to get the most range out of their solar cell wings and built-in structural batteries. The military ones had chameleon capability: they could change the color of their topsides to match the ground they were over and their undersides to match the sky above. They were invisible from any distance beyond two hundred meters.

When Joe showed up at his workstation, Shan was already there, setting up the automatic checkout equipment for a finished airplane. He said to Shan, "You're a serious thinker. How come you work in an airplane factory?"

"I worked full time in the Strat Team. Got burned out after a couple of years of serious thinking, as you call it. There I worked long hours researching historical data and developing plans to support Freep societal evolution. I'm here on sabbatical. Love building airplanes because I work with my hands and see results every day. Love the pride everyone puts into making reliable airplanes. And my job still leaves plenty of time for thinking and writing."

"Are you happy here?"

"Yes, I am. I know someday I will want to get back into the bare-knuckle conflicts that are needed to forge strategy at the highest level. But right now, I don't miss that stress. Eventually, I'll miss the action, and I believe I still have a lot to contribute. Maybe in a year or two. Now, can you help me with a checkout?"

"Sure, what do I have to do?"

"Get in the pilot's seat and do what the computer tells you at each step of the checkout. It will take an hour."

The foreman appeared as the checkout ended and told Joe that he and Shan would be test flying the plane for two days. The two of them wheeled it across the factory floor to a wide door that opened for them. It was surprisingly light, and they pushed it along with little effort. Outside, they moved it into the sunlight so the solar panels charged the on-board batteries. During the hour needed for a charge, Joe called Mary.

"I'll be up to your place tomorrow when I verify the navigation and thought-control systems of the plane we built."

"Can you make it at ten, Joe?"

"Yes, ma'am," he replied enthusiastically.

Joe went back out to the flight line. Shan told him that she would fly the first flight under manual control. They climbed aboard, and Shan announced to Air Control that she was taking off for a two-hour test flight. Under stick-and-pedal control, she expertly took off and climbed to a thousand meters. She went through a flight-card list of maneuvers, including stalls that gave Joe the willies the first couple of times. At a lower altitude, she did touch and goes with simulated engine outs on both landings and takeoffs. After completing the flight card, she climbed again to altitude and started Joe's flying lessons.

"Joe," said Shan, "you are going to learn to fly manually. Take the stick, and we'll start with a couple of turns."

"Wow! This is great. Didn't think I would be learning to fly so soon."

"Everyone here has to learn," Shan said. "Everyone flies the planes they work on."

"Now that's a real motivator to do a good job building them."

"The best," Shan said and gave him a big grin.

An hour later, they were back to earth. Joe was charged with excitement. He was fully alive. He could control a plane with thought control—he'd done that back at the Normalizer and found that it was easy and safe. Now he was learning how to fly manually, like in the pioneering days, and that was exiting. A good thing to know, too, in case the automatic control system was damaged. He couldn't wait to log some more flight training hours.

The next day, he was flying alone to test thought control and navigation capability. The flight card for the test flight allowed him to fit in a leg to Mojave. It called for ten landings and takeoffs. He timed the flight segments to fit in a landing at Mojave at ten. He landed five minutes early to be on the safe side and taxied to the place Mary said she would be waiting. He couldn't wait to take here up for a short hop and show off his piloting skills.

She wasn't there when he reached the end of the short strip outside the one-story building where she lived. He waited a while and then called. She answered, "Hello, Joe, where are you?"

"I'm outside your building. Forget? Said I'd be here at ten."

"Dammit! I forgot. Joe, I am really sorry, but they put me through the wringer today with a simulated life-and-death struggle in a virtual reality booth."

"I am really torqued off at you. We haven't seen each other for a month. How could you forget our meeting?"

"Joe, you don't understand how terribly disconcerting that virtual reality booth is. You've got to cut me some slack."

"Virtual reality! Come on."

"Well, Joe, if that's the way you want to be…"

"I better leave before it really gets ugly."

"Joe, let's—" The call ended.

———

He started the engines and took off under thought control. He finished off the rest of the legs of the flight to verify that the nav system was working within its accuracy limits. Not much joy flying back to the Airplane Works, in spite of the great expanse of desert below beckoning to him to feel inspired and happy. He was mad. Mad at Mary. Mad at himself for not forgiving her. Mad at her again. And in no mood to savor the shimmering beauty sliding by beneath him.

After landing, he and Shan pushed the plane into the hangar. They entered the flight test results into the main computer. No flight squawks. Another plane ready for regular service.

On their way out, Shan asked Joe how his meeting went.

"What meeting?"

"With the girl at Mojave?"

"What do you mean, 'girl'?"

"I took a guess. I monitored your flight profile and noticed you landed at Mojave."

"Had to make a landing somewhere; that was required on the flight card."

"But you also called someone there."

"How did you know I wasn't calling a guy?"

"You know, Joe, if you were meeting a guy there, you would have told me before you left. You were secretive; that meant a girl."

"Damn, you are good," Joe said.

"Your meeting didn't go well, did it?"

"Shan, you're starting to piss me off," Joe said.

"You looked sad when you returned."

"God darn it! You *are* pissing me off," he hissed, trying to keep from shouting. "Yeah, she stood me up. Now you know. Happy now?"

"Joe, you need a happy pill."

"I need more than that."

"You are so ready for the Normalizer. It starts tomorrow in Hemet."

"That's a long way to walk. Must be a hundred kilometers."

"Joe, I can get a plane to give you flying lessons for a few days. We fly for a couple of hours each day and stay overnight at the Normalizer."

Chapter 10
SECOND NORMALIZER

The next day, they took off early and flew toward Hemet. Shan put Joe through advanced flying maneuvers. Joe was amazed that the slow-moving plane could actually do a roll. Shan explained that he had to start with plenty of altitude because it flew so slowly. Joe was wrung out after a couple of hours of Shan's demanding instruction.

They had been heading in an easterly direction, and Joe saw the Normalizer when they were ten kilometers away. Shan let Joe practice landing in a smooth patch of desert to get the hang of it. Then they headed for the Normalizer's fly-in zone, shared by a hundred or more Freep planes. As they approached touch down, Joe could see crowds of Freeps coming on foot from all directions to the Normalizer's maze of tents and shelters. He brought it in for a rough landing but still got a complimentary squeeze on his knee from Shan for stopping the plane in twenty meters. She said, "You got us here in one piece. Now let's have some fun."

They beetled up and headed into the crowd.

The weirdness of it all, thought Joe. *Thousands of Freeps, beetled up, and looking to have a good time…walking around, talking, laughing like a penguin party—or a stand-up roach rave.*

It was so different this time from his first Normalizer, at which he'd felt like an outsider and hadn't mingled that much. Now he felt right at home, comfortable with his beetle pack on.

He thought back to his first Normalizer and the memory of Mary, the airplane flight with her, and their night of side-by-siding. He ducked into a quiet spot and tried to call her, but as usual, no luck. The memory of their falling out still hurt, and he wanted to make things right.

He was sad for a minute but quickly snapped out of it. He thought, *This is a Normalizer, and I am going to get cheered up. Isn't that what they're for?* He fell back into the crowd and realized he had lost sight of Shan, but that was OK. They'd agreed to meet the next morning at eight if they got separated. Now he was on the hunt for a good time.

He strolled along, checking out the action. At one place, under a simple sunshade, beetled-up mathematicians were furiously struggling together to work through an elaborate equation that appeared on a holographic whiteboard floating in the air for them to view. He had no idea what the equation signified, but he felt it must be important to draw such intensity from the mathematicians. They didn't even hear the nearby ice cream store where speed eating was needed to beat the 135-degree heat and a boisterous crowd cheered on ice-cream eaters trying to devour their cones before they melted.

There was a theater group putting on a beetled-up version of *Hamlet*. With concessions to modern weapons instead of swords, it was a reminder that violent human passions, in spite of everything Freeps did to calm them, never really disappeared from their hearts. After half an hour of watching in fascination, Joe decided he'd had enough of deep thoughts and left after Hamlet took the final ray-gun blast right in the gut. He rejoined the current of people until he came to a fortune teller's booth.

A beetled-up woman wearing a purple head scarf and veil above a cream-colored tunic beckoned to him to have his fortune told. He could only see her eyes, but he liked her voice and the orange harem pantaloons and gold sandals that completed her outfit. *What a treat*, Joe thought. *Some color on a woman instead of all that gray. A mysterious woman at that.* He couldn't resist and followed her behind the curtain of her silken tent.

She told Joe to configure his pack into a chair facing her similarly configured chair. She then extended her beetle-pack fore-cover and attached it to Joe's, so they ended up in an acorn-shaped enclosure cooled by their packs. She spoke. "My name is Yasminah, and you must see me eye to eye so our spirits can whisper to each other."

Joe watched without speaking as she took off her face veil to reveal a light chocolate face that matched her haunting hazel-yellow eyes and straight nose. It was a heart-shaped face, smooth without a blemish on it, with lips that were full and expressive. He was ready for her next revelation.

"Now sit cross-legged like I am."

Joe did, and their knees almost touched. She handed him a pill and small cup of effervescent tea; its pungent vapor rose and filled their enclosure. Shortly after washing down the pill, he heard a fizz and felt the surge of well-being the pill promised. He was eager for the next step.

"We'll touch fingertips now," she said, and they both rested their hands on their knees and touched their index fingers. There was a pinging sensation at Joe's fingertips, followed by a stream of warmth racing up his arms and continuing to his heart and his brain. Joe looked into her eyes; he couldn't do otherwise. He felt that he was suspended in space, and his only attachment to the world was at the tips of his fingers, where they connected ever so softly to Yasminah's finger tips.

"Joe."

He tensed up but kept looking in her eyes and said, "How did you know my name?"

Her luscious lips arced into a knowing smile. "You are open to friendly energy—you yourself gave me your name."

Joe relaxed and made sure contact with her fingertips was still there. She had earned his respect, and he had to know more. He said, "Yasminah, I'm a newcomer...looking for a chance to find meaning..."

"I see that, Joe. I see you searching—but there are conflicts in your goals." She paused and then said, "Let me see your right hand." She took it in both her hands, examining it carefully. "You can be lonely in a crowd. True?"

Joe nodded.

"You will lead in future battles to cure that loneliness. Don't stop trekking...not now. You need to trek a long way to find your role. You will meet many women as you cross our land. They will lure you with their warmth and passionate natures. It would be unnatural to reject them, but be careful, and don't give your heart away easily." She looked intently at his hand for a moment longer, then looked up at him and said, "Be aware and watchful in your journey. Your destiny will attract enemies."

He looked at her face, and his eyes locked on hers. She said, "Cherish your friends. You will need them to confront many challenges ahead."

Joe left the sultry Yasminah at her entrance curtain, again behind her veil. Was it the tea? Was it her exotic presence that affected him? He felt a warm sense of kinship with the crowd passing by, laughing and talking among themselves. He joined in the surge of Freeps shuffling down the midway. As he passed pill peddlers, card players, drummers, and chanters, he was at peace floating along in the vibrations surrounding him.

He came upon a holographic cartooning jam. One after another, cartoonists brought up spatial images of people they were lampooning, and the crowd roared approval. An old-fashioned applause meter kept score. Surprisingly, Joe watched a lot of cartoons about Algo; they were unsparing in their criticism and got as big a laugh as any of the others.

The cartoonists' irreverence was the sort of humorous medicine Joe needed after some of that loneliness in the crowd that Yasminah had picked up on. Joe chuckled to himself with that thought and then noticed a familiar face in the moving throng. Negla was passing by! His heart quickened, remembering that raw animal attraction she exuded when they were working together at the homestead.

He rushed out to greet her, and she saw him making his way toward her and waved. *God*, he thought. *She looks great beetled up in brief gray shorts and halter showing her tanned, athletic figure.* They hugged and walked on together until they reached a fresh-food stand. They grabbed a tiny table and leisurely chatted until the setting sun cast out its last rays from behind the cumulus formations. Joe noticed she had lipstick and eye makeup on. He inquired about the homestead. She explained that it was Freddo's turn to stay home and take care of things—and gave him a big wink.

They took in an outdoor, old-fashioned movie and then side-by-sided for the night. Next morning when they woke up, Joe made love again to Negla. They freshened up at the community shower, went for a trail-prep breakfast, and sat looking out at an endless desert with a few out of place clouds above it.

Joe said, "Negla, I am so happy I met you yesterday. You were what I needed: companionship and great poaching."

Negla laughed and replied, "Joe, that's pretty much my sentiment, too. Been working hard, it was a long hike in, and I needed to blow off a little steam and have some vigorous poaching." She took a bite of her protein bar and sipped the cactus tea. "You know, when you and Rod trekked through our homestead, I had my eye on you and was hoping we would meet at a Normalizer someday."

"Destiny threw us together," Joe said. "Hiking back alone to the homestead?"

"No, two newcomers on their first trek are going my way. I will be trekking along with them and their sponsors. Leaving in a half hour."

"Be careful of Bikers," Joe said.

"We have to be these days. Been a lot more of them in recent months."

They hugged good-bye as best they could beetled up, and Joe headed to the plane.

Shan was there before him and had completed the pre-flight inspection and checklist.

Joe was at the controls at takeoff. He climbed out, and then Shan put him through a series of stall and spin recovery exercises till she had him sweating and looking pooped. Then they settled in for a quiet flight home.

————

Joe didn't know anything about Shan. She wasn't the kind to talk about herself. There was that sense of mystery about her that Joe had felt from the first minute he saw her. When they reached cruising altitude of two thousand meters, he asked, "Shan, do you have a boyfriend? You never talk about one."

She was surprised at his question and turned toward him, hesitating a moment before she spoke. "There is a man in my life. At least, I think there is. We were together to the extent Algo would permit. Then a few months ago, I stopped hearing from him."

Joe asked, "Did you work together?"

She replied, "Both of us used to work at high levels. Sometimes we were both sent on foreign assignments."

"You mean outside Freep Nation?"

"Yes, Joe, it is necessary for Freeps to go outside. Can be for different reasons."

"Jeez, I thought Freeps never left…had everything they needed here."

"That was the intention at first, but Algo learned that being totally self-contained could thwart evolutionary progress."

"Ah, come on," Joe said.

She looked at him in a way that said, "I am telling you important facts." When she spoke, she did not waste a word; she spoke from a place of knowledge and experience. He could sense that she had seen things and been places that gave her total believability. She continued, "To survive, Freeps have to adapt to whatever challenges are out there. Algo has Freeps out in Mainstream and in other countries. They are our eyes and ears."

Surprised by these revelations, Joe asked, "Are they spies?"

"Some are. My boyfriend, Lon, was some sort of spy."

"Was?"

She looked at him again and then past him with a wistful, faraway look. "Maybe he'll come back. I don't know. You see, he would come and go for different lengths of time: a week, a month, a couple of months. Didn't say much about what he did." She paused. "Freeps on the outside buy things we don't manufacture here. They sell things we make too many of here. They recruit talent that is in short supply. They spy on Mainstream military leaders and economic councils."

"Wow, complicated," Joe said.

"They have many roles out there, some are dangerous. They even arrange for our satellite service.

It is from the European Alliance that likes to keep Mainstream worried by helping its enemies on this side of the Atlantic."

Joe, realizing he had probed into a personal area, said, "Hope Lon makes it back."

"You are sweet to say that. Keep in mind that Algo thinks first and foremost of Freep survival. That is its number one concern—and it should be. Unfortunately, Algo thinks Freep emotional relationships can be impediments to achieving survival goals."

"Now hold on, Shan, Algo has been studying human emotional needs for a long time and tries to keep people happy."

"Righto." She smiled. "Normalizers are great. They really help; I'll grant you that, but on an individual basis, Algo has no problem with keeping the flowers of love from blooming—or at least from blooming very far—when there is something important to be done."

"Yeah," Joe said. "I've heard Algo can get personal."

"Joe, as you learn more about Freeps, you will see that some things don't fall into straightforward right-wrong categories. You'll find that Algo is hard to figure out, and I think intentionally so. Simplicity and predictability wouldn't lend an aura of importance to a phenomenon like Algo. Algo's spirit-like presence is one of mystery and inscrutability, and that commands respect—even though it seems petty or weird at times."

Joe was impressed by Shan's insights.

"Shan, you know so much about the inner workings of the Freeps."

"Joe, you will soon have doors opened to you that reveal what is going on. It is fascinating to be part of the Freep governing team, and you are headed in that direction."

"How do you know?"

"At the Normalizer, I hung out with some of my girl-friends. I always find out what's happening from them, especially those who work in administrative services. They are always sniffing the personnel plans and schedules to see who is coming through. They're curious. Sometimes they're looking for Normalizer chums themselves. If they are lucky, they might stumble upon a guy like you. They know from the newcomer plans and their performance stats which ones are headed for the top."

"Did your pals know about me?"

"Yes, and you disappointed a few by tying up with that farm girl."

"Oh, *wow*. No secrets here," Joe exclaimed.

Shan smiled and looked at Joe in a caring way. "Joe, you can learn a lot through the informal information that Freeps have by talking with them—and listening. As you travel around Freep Nation, you want to build a network of friends and acquaintances. They will be invaluable to you when you get in a position of leadership and need to build a loyal team."

Two weeks later, Joe was scheduled to leave the Airplane Works. The last night, he and Shan were in the dining room together. He asked, "Have you heard from Lon?"

"No...no news. I'm worried about him." She paused and looked down sadly. "It's lonely here without him. Will you call now and then?"

"You'll be hearing from me—if Algo lets me through."

Chapter 11
CYBER STATION

Joe and Rod set out from the Airplane Works with beetle packs in full cooling and recycling mode. Before them were shimmering heat waves and liquid-mercury-like mirages in the distance. Algo-Net calculated a trek route through predetermined rest points that would get them to Cyber Station in three days of fast walking. Both were dialed in for optimum-heart-rate walking speed.

As they left, Rod said, "Take the lead, Joe."

"You're getting ready to cut me loose?"

"Yes, sir, I'll be with you to your next two stops: Cyber Station and Health Works. Then you are on your own."

"Do I get a graduation party?"

"Yes, in our remaining days together, I will brief you on survival techniques in case of equipment failure. And you will learn to eat cactuses and lizards and even find water."

"That's a party? Can't wait, pal."

Joe kept the pace Algo-Net commanded and felt good doing it. Rod followed and didn't push their speed. Tired at each day's end—but not to the point of spots-before-the-eyes exhaustion that he experienced in the first days with Rod—Joe felt he was in shape and had a feeling of accomplishment, knowing he had earned another step of acceptance into Freep life.

On the second morning, when they were starting out, Rod said, "I want you to work on a mindlessness state when you trek. Be aware of what you see without analyzing it."

Joe said, "I am stoked by the subtle colors, never the same."

Rod replied, "Try taking in these magnificent panoramas without sorting out the colors or reacting to the shapes."

Joe said, "Kinda like meditating?"

"Yes, it will open your spirit to receiving energy from the desert."

Joe had a few more waking hours after a day's trek now than he had at the beginning when he fell into deep sleep soon after setting up camp each evening. Now after a day of trekking, he had time to study Freep wars and discuss what he was learning with Rod, who turned out to be a good sounding board for Joe's thoughts and questions. Joe's anger at Rod for pushing so hard at the beginning had disappeared, replaced by appreciation for Rod's insight into a complicated history.

They made it to Cyber Station in three days. As they got closer, they noticed drones and manned planes flying in the same direction—delivering their cargos and people to the station. Joe's beetle pack guided them to a small building with a tight dirt airstrip wedged in a bowl of gray, house-size boulders.

They went inside the building. Nothing fancy, a small lobby, dull gray, and a welcome screen to which they gave their names and the reason for their visit: two weeks of orientation and familiarization for Joe.

Moving through the only door, they went down a flight of stairs and entered another room with four bare walls. Joe was surprised by the wall ahead with "Nerd City" projected on it in jarring flashes of kaleidoscopic colors. Then "Nerd City" morphed into another sign: "We Keep It Real," which in turn faded away. Joe didn't know what to expect when a door in the wall to his right opened and a clown walked in blowing a tune on his kazoo.

"Come in, jerks, and see my works," the clown said. Through the clown door, they entered a factory space with islands of work areas stretching out three hundred meters in each direction.

"I've been waiting to see your latest stuff," Joe said to the clown.

"I'll blow your mind with innovation, till you beg for liberation. By the way, Joe, my name is Mo."

"Glad to meet you, Mo. Hope you're not a schmo."

Mo blew his kazoo and did a happy dance at Joe's joke.

Joe and Rod stowed their packs in the small bedroom assigned to them and then Mo took them to a computer and battery assembly area. Computers were thin flexible sheets pumped out of a robotic manufacturing machine fed by packs of raw materials delivered by drones. Similar process for batteries: a robotic assembly machine with a growth of what looked like spider legs rapidly worked a few input materials and parts into a flat pack battery that could go into a beetle pack or, in multiples, be installed in an airplane or wheeled cargo carrier. The machinery attendant was dressed like Pinocchio.

He explained, "It's all robotic, really pretty exotic. Easy as pie? That would be a lie."

Joe said in an aside to Rod, "I'll never make it here for three weeks."

Rod stood back and grinned. "Don't dig doggerel? Got to loosen up, man. This is Nerd City."

"Does everyone talk in rhyming couplets?'

"It's wacky. People in this factory are always screwing around. They're smart, and the empty desert doesn't give them enough mental stimulation. They do nutty stuff and play practical jokes to stay normal."

Joe turned to Pinocchio and asked, "Don't you get tired of watching that robot working?"

"It's an honest living, and I ain't fibbing," Pinocchio replied. "I hope you come rushin' to tonight's discussion." Pinocchio's nose began to grow, and Joe broke up laughing.

That night, they dropped in to a sparsely furnished community area. *Geeks don't need frills,* Joe thought. Groups were forming to talk or to engage in games or other pastimes. Joe got an earpiece call to report to the northeast corner. Making his way there through body-painted girls, Laurel and Hardy lookalikes, astronauts, Mozart impersonators, and the like, he came upon a group of gnomes covered in silver paint.

There were ten of them, and they sat cross-legged on the floor along a wall looking at Joe. Every few seconds, one of them would make a small movement. All remained in total silence until a swarthy guy in a gray Nehru jacket and purple jodhpurs came in and introduced himself. "Joe and Rod, welcome. I am Pradeep, head of this Cyber Station. The ladies and gents in silver before you head up each division below me." They all bowed to Joe in unison.

Joe said, "Thanks, Pradeep. I am itching to hear about your electronic capability, especially that devoted to defense." The silvered people murmured in approval.

A holograph of a one-man helicopter appeared before the group. "I'm Number One," piped up one of the gnomes. She stood and said, "This is a secret model, so don't blab about it to anyone. It is completely silent, using owl-wing sound suppression on the blades. Solar powered, of course. Chameleon coating for invisibility. It mounts a powerful laser and can be flown in manned or drone mode."

"How far can it go?" asked Joe.

"Cruising speed of fifty knots as long as the sun is out, plus five hours on battery."

Another silvered gnome popped up. "I'm Number Two. We have cyber-hacking capabilities that can immobilize Mainstream. If we can get in close enough to hack into their fiber optic and microwave transmissions, we can shut down electric power, water, traffic signals, air traffic control, building security, TV, police, and emergency communications. One way we get in close is with mini bots."

"Serious?" Joe said.

"Yes, sir, think of ants. Hard-to-see ants that are the same color as what they're walking on. They get into a building through a window or a crack under a door. They relay back what they see and hear. They form chains for tricky infiltrations inside buildings. Say, one ant every ten meters that can go down stairs or in ventilation ducts to get to an enemy's secret vault and maintain communications with the outside world."

Joe was visibly excited. "Wow! They can't hide from us."

Number Three said, "Coding is what I manage. It is all speech-entry, high-level software with encryption links that defy any outside hack—"

Joe interrupted. "Do you code Algo's software?"

"No, Algo does its own."

Joe, excited and incredulous, shouted, "No way! That's crazy, because Algo could give itself any power it wanted to."

Number Three said, "Algo hasn't gone rogue in the two hundred years since it was invented."

Joe looked flabbergasted but didn't say anything.

Number Three added, "Joe, Algo's root program is a set of evolution principles, the main one being that Freeps must continuously adapt to meet whatever new challenges are out there. Basic survival. Algo is equipped to analyze masses of data describing human experience throughout recorded history. Got to do that to stay ahead of evolutionary changes—especially in our enemies' battle doctrines."

"That's comforting to know," Joe said with a hint of snarky incredulity in his voice. "But Algo can only look to the past and the present. Not to the future."

"You have a point," Number Three said. "Algo determined generations ago that the evolution of different societies does not proceed linearly. You know with organisms, they get better through successful mutations, but they are not all successful."

Joe said, "That's pretty well understood. Human societies especially. They go two steps forward and one step back."

"Exactly," Number Three said. "That's where Algo makes a tremendous contribution. Algo does not let Freep society take that one step back."

"How?"

"Algo knows the signs of a society on the verge of taking a regressive step. It found certain repetitive patterns in human anti-evolutionary behavior and it acts to prevent such behaviors from happening in Freep Nation."

Joe said, "Number Three, that sounds amazing...profound. I need time to think it through far enough to come back at you with questions that make any sense."

Number Three said, "Let's talk for an hour every day you're here."

Number Four jumped up and yelled, "My turn!"

The meeting continued until all the silvered people had spoken. Each one described a technology he or she managed. He heard about beetle-pack improvements, war-gaming, climate modeling and modification, and geopolitical threat gaming and analysis, among other topics.

———

Joe's brain overloaded, struggling to assimilate all he had heard. He kept coming back to the thought, *Algo is not controlled by the best brains the Freeps have. Not controlled by anyone. Writes its own software—like a creature building its brain. Algo's brain is distributed over a million beetle packs. Impossible to kill it. Not that I would want to, in view of the fact that Algo has kept the Freeps alive and growing in numbers from their beginning. But will Algo always be a positive force for stability and survival?*

Joe spent the next two weeks digging deeper with follow-up discussions. He wanted to understand the weapon concepts and advanced systems Freeps would use in the "threat space" of the future.

The last day, Joe beetled up for his daily one-hour trek to get his mental marbles together. He thought, *What the brainy people at the Cyber Station do is paramount to crafting the Freeps' long-term survival strategies. They develop future systems and defense plans that Algo is incapable of providing because Algo has no imagination. No one has figured out how human imagination works. No way Algo can program it if humans can't explain it.*

Their last night at Cyber Station, they had dinner with Pradeep and his top managers. Joe asked, "How many of these Cyber Stations are there in Freep Nation?"

Pradeep said, "About ten. We're well dispersed."

"Could they all be taken out at once in a surprise attack?"

"That could happen. However, we keep a minimum capability if that happens. We send personnel to other sites to install equipment or check on systems we designed here. About twenty-five percent of our scientists and engineers are traveling at any one time; they'll survive."

Joe asked, "How about manufacturing capability?"

"We have extra manufacturing capabilities scattered in a number of unexpected places. Of course, they are secret."

Next morning, Joe and Rod left early for the Health Works. They trekked side by side into the rising sun.

"A guy could feel dumb after all that high tech those crazies blew at us for two weeks."

"Those crazies are our future, Joe."

"Are they developing the right stuff?"

"Other countries build big military establishments— not a lot different from their enemies. Usually, the one with the most weapons and soldiers wins. Freeps don't have much money. So we use cheap software; cheap computers with plenty of computing power; and low-cost equipment, like our solar-powered planes, to defend ourselves. The proof of whether or not it is the right stuff we're developing is never known for sure. It remains up to the next war to answer that question."

Chapter 12
HEALTH WORKS

Mary woke up early and lay in bed looking at the ceiling. She was excited and concerned about Joe arriving that day. Excited because she never let go of the thrill of new love at the Normalizer. And concerned because of the fumbled fly-in date that she now felt was her fault. She regretted missing their rendezvous and beat up on herself ever since. When she tried to call him back to apologize, her calls didn't get through. She didn't know what to expect from him. She didn't just hope to see him during his stay at the Health Works; she *had* to see him. She got up and headed down to the crowded shower room.

Outrageous Vernu showed up in the shower shortly after and soaped Mary down with a spirit sponge. Vernu had worked in Freep Health Works for years. Stocky but well-proportioned, she was a bundle of energy with flaming red hair. Loud and domineering, she had a comedian's talent for cracking up a room full of people with her wicked wit and foul mouth. Finished with Mary, she called out, "Any of you poach pals want to soap me down?"

Obi, the famed artist and instrument designer from Africa, volunteered. He was far and away the best soaper at Health Works. Vernu closed her eyes and luxuriated in his rhythmic style, occasionally producing an erotic moan to the amusement of other bathers. Obi took his time, during which Mary dried off and dressed quickly to avoid Vernu and spend a few minutes with other friends in the cafeteria. She sat next to Pepina from registration and asked, "Pepi, do you know anything about Joe showing up today?"

"Yeah, he'll be here this afternoon. Coming from Cyber Station. You know how whacked out people are after that place. He'll need a few days to reconnect with reality."

"Can you put Joe in one of my newcomer sessions?" she asked. "We're old friends."

"You got an eye on that guy?" chided Pepina with a mischievous smile.

"We're pretty close," said Mary, feeling a blush creeping up her neck and heading for her face.

"I'll put him in your lecture tonight. But watch out—I hear he's a Normalizer sport."

That hurt, but Mary didn't let on. "Don't think I'd be interested in a dweeb, do you?"

The gang at the table laughed—all but the recently arrived Vernu, who kept a straight face.

———

That night, Mary greeted the ten newcomers who showed up for her lecture on Freep life and customs; she asked each to give his or her name. Joe wasn't there. She was disappointed but a bit relieved, too, fearing it might be uncomfortable when she saw him. She turned the lights down in the conference room and was bringing up a montage of Freep life scenes on a holograph when Joe walked in and sat in the back.

A chill ran down her spine, but she took charge of her emotions and said cheerfully, "Hello, Joe, nice to see you."

"Mary, great to see you, too," he said. The ice had been broken.

Mary began her lecture. "You have all been hiking many kilometers and probably wondering why."

The newcomers laughed and looked around at each other.

"Couple of reasons," Mary continued. "No roads or vehicles out here. Can't afford them. Hiking, or trekking as we say, is mandatory to get around. Keeps us in shape. Healthy exercise. Living in small colonies, as Freeps do, doesn't require vehicles to drive to work."

"What if an ambulance is needed?" asked a newcomer.

"Freeps have airplanes to pick up people in emergencies," said Mary. "The planes are solar powered and don't need a pilot most of the time. Real cheap to operate. By the way, Health Works heads up emergency-disaster response."

"What kind of disasters do you get out here?"

Mary answered, "We train to provide housing and medical services for large casualty events from a natural disasters or a war, if it ever comes.

"On a more cheerful note, Freeps are healthy. With our admittedly sparse diet, we never overeat. There are no diet-caused diseases here. Couple that with plenty of walking, and there are no overweight people either.

Joe put his hand up and asked, "Doesn't Freep life get boring out here in the desert?"

"Joe, you got right to the heart of the matter," said Mary, as the class snickered. "Good question, and I am going to take a few minutes to answer. Being bored is a state of mind that varies with the challenges that life here in the desert presents to a person.

"Watchers, for example, are on the front line at the borders of the Freep Nation. They are preoccupied with survival—their own and that of the Freep community. Oddly, they rarely get bored. Love doing it and the camaraderie that goes along with it. Many do it all their lives."

Another of the newcomers said, "That's OK for those who like to work alone, but how about the rest of us?"

"Gets more complicated for you normal people," Mary said, getting a few laughs. "First off, Algo wants you to find something that you like to do for a living as you trek around the desert. In my case, that was easy. I like to work with people and their welfare as Freeps. That's why I am here after only six months of trekking. Others of you might trek longer before you make up your minds. You could end up working in a farm homestead or building airplanes or programming beetle packs with sophisticated mathematical concepts."

Joe piped up again. "What do you do on weekends for excitement?"

Mary, used to tough newcomer questions, kicked it back to the group. "OK, let's make a list of everything you new Freeps like to do on weekends. Shout out your ideas."

They responded with "Taking drives, dinner with friends, dancing, yoga, traveling, parties, motorcycle off-roading, flying, playing cards, mountain climbing, movies, finding boys for sex" (big laugh at that one) "book club, swap meets..." The list appeared before them as a holograph.

Mary stood to the side as the list grew. Then, as the suggestions tapered off, she said, "Most of those things you can do here in the desert. Check out your Algo-Net for what the possibilities are. You have to make the plans and coordinate with others. You have to take the initiative to get on Algo-Net and check around.

"Oh, by the way, people here have romantic relationships that are enjoyable. But be careful not to let things go too fast. There are a lot of people passing through our lives as newcomers whom we don't want to fall hard for, only to see them gone in a day or two." Mary couldn't tell if Joe reacted to that, as he was sitting where the light was dim.

Seeing she had her audience's attention, she continued, "Some things you have listed are not easy. For example, foreign travel—not easy, but possible. A Freep can build up credits with good deeds and get to go abroad through our connection with Mexico. Travel to Mainstream has always been a problem. When relations are good, there can be limited numbers of people who travel there. Right now, relations are not good, and there are no reciprocal travel arrangements.

"OK, folks, that's enough for tonight. I'll see you at my workshop on medical care in the morning."

The newcomers, except for Joe, filed out of the room. He and Mary looked at each other, and finally, he spoke. "Could I interest you in a plane ride on the weekend?"

"I'd love it, Joe. Nothing could make me happier." The cloud of apprehension between them lifted like steam rising from hot rocks after a desert cloudburst.

———

Joe spent the days until the weekend finding about the human side of Freep life. He hadn't realized that much of what seemed to be happening randomly around him was planned. Planned by Algo, which was continuously reviewing past cultures to find out what would work best for the Freeps' evolution and survival.

In a lively study group that lasted most of the week, Joe found out that Freeps are moved around the desert settlements to prevent groups from forming that might consider themselves better than others because they developed a mini culture of inbred groupthink.

Nationalities and races were likewise spread around the population to minimize the internal rivalries and conflicts could hamper unified action when the time came to mobilize for war.

Was dissent suppressed among the Freeps? Not really, as Joe found out. Rather, it was channeled into finding solutions to the never-ending problems that human society presented as it evolved and struggled with new enemies and with a changing universe. Dissent was welcome, as long as it wasn't griping.

Freedom was an important element of satisfaction within Freep life. Freeps did not have the freedom to become very rich because, as they learned in their own history, great wealth soon led to elite families and groups with profit goals replacing Freep survival goals. Some wealth and individual homes were allowed as rewards for those with the ambition to go in that direction—if they had built up credits with positive service to the Freep community. There was no inherited wealth, with each member required to make his or her own way.

Freeps had high tolerance for nonconformists. And maybe most important, they had freedom to work at what they wanted and to change occupations whenever opportunity presented itself. Freeps had unfettered access to knowledge and learning on the Algo-Net—and there was no cost. As a result of a free-swinging intellectual environment, the individual Freep settlements, colonies, homesteads, and workshops all had distinctly different personalities and, as Joe had found out, different tastes in humor and practical jokes.

———

At last the weekend rolled around. On Saturday morning, Joe ate in the cafeteria with seven others at his table, including Vernu at his left with Mary on the other side of her. After breakfast, he went to his room to get sunglasses and suddenly felt sick. Barely making it to the toilet, he vomited and sank to the floor, feeling faint and dizzy. Mary knocked on his partly open door, opened it, and saw him struggling on the bathroom floor.

"Joe," she uttered in alarm, "what's wrong?" He could barely answer between heaves and spasms. She realized he was unable to get up and immediately called Algo-Net for help. A minute later, an emergency worker rushed into the room. From his case, he took an electronic sampler and stuck its probe into a splatter of Joe's puke and looked at the readout.

"Poison," he said with a serious expression and filled a glass with water. "Drink this and try to throw it up," he said to an ashen, pained-looking Joe, and then he turned to Mary. "Go to the cafeteria and bring a gallon of salt water, immediately." She ran off, and he turned to Joe. "When did this start?"

Joe replied weakly, "Right after breakfast."

The worker said, "It contains oleander powder…probably in your food or beverage this morning. We're going to clean you out with salt water. You drink it and throw it up until you finish the gallon."

Mary came running in with the jug and poured out the first glass for Joe. An hour later, he had cycled all the salt water in and out and was visibly better. The tech gave him a few pills, and by noon he was well enough to fly when the two-seater he had talked Shan into sending showed up. He and Mary climbed aboard, and the plane climbed smoothly through the breezy clear atmosphere and headed toward the rugged San Jacinto mountains. There they landed on a clearing Jasper told him about with a fabulous view of a shimmering empty land far below.

In short order, they had set up their side-by-side, and the months of longing erupted into the intensity of love. The slowly passing hours were filled with their voices bringing each other up to date on their treks and their experiences with Freeps.

They discussed their repeated failures at trying to contact each other. Mary said, "I work with lots of newcomers in Health Works; they all complain about not being able to call friends. Joe, the system doesn't want newcomers to get off the track they are programmed on. I want you to press on to the highest level you can achieve, and I know I won't hear from you very often. That's OK. You need to find your life's work, and you will. Don't worry if you can't reach me."

Joe replied, "I love you, Mary, and will stay in touch any way I can."

"I plan to be at Health Works for the long term. You'll know where to find me." They caressed in silence and looked off in the vast distance as the sun lowered in the sky. Their idyll ended, and they flew home inspired by a flaming sunset filtering through orange and violet layers of glowing clouds.

Back at the Health Works, Joe was summoned to meet with an investigator who was following up on the oleander-tainted food. He was the bookish type, skinny with a bald head on a long neck. They met with Vernu in a small meeting room. The investigator summed up, "Joe, I have interviewed everyone at your table this morning. It's been inconclusive. As Vernu here described the scene, breakfast diners came at different times and were up and down at the table getting their food from the buffet automat. I'm not sure how your food got contaminated. I have no reason to believe it was intentional, but I cannot rule it out."

Joe said, "Tell me how to prevent a recurrence of an oleander job."

The investigator said, "Eat only packaged food and beverages, and keep your eye on it the whole time you are eating. Let me know if you run into anything suspicious."

"Sure, you'll be the first one to know." Joe got up and left, unimpressed with the investigation.

———

Joe was ready to move on a week later, when his time was up at the Health Works. Mary knew he suspected someone had tried to poison him, someone still there and possibly ready to try again. She sensed he was compelled to go on whether someone tried to poison him or not, to try it all and experience Freep life to the fullest, while always looking and evaluating opportunities for freedom—and power.

In his time at the Health Works Mary found out that months of trekking had toughened Joe, and he looked forward to the next chapter of his newcomer year when he would be on his own. He talked with her about how the Freep social and health ideas fit into a need for defending themselves against enemies who weren't motivated by concepts of fairness and social justice. He had taken Algo's instruction to study Freep wars seriously, and although he hated to spend solitary hours retrieving information from Algo-Net to study, he was eager to engage others in live discussions about the Freeps' capacity to fight off an invader.

Mary ate with Joe on his last night at the usual informal dinner with fellow workers and friends. Vernu showed up with fiz water and pills for all to get relaxed. "Not taking any," Joe said, "Got some serious reading to do tonight."

Mary took her pill and washed it down with fiz water, and a little later, emboldened with her intoxication, said, "Joe, I come from a quiet home of university professors who were content to learn and understand life. You come from a home where the struggle for wealth and success was paramount."

Joe played along, trying to be good-natured about teasing comments aimed at him. "Yeah, and here I am, trying to find something I am good at that will make you and me happy."

Vernu popped up and said, "While you are out there looking for a job, I'll keep your lady company." Everyone laughed as she gave Mary a playful hug.

Mary shook off Vernu's hug, turned to Joe, and said, "Let's beetle up and take a walk in the moonlight." She turned to the others and said, "Moonlight is important for my emotional health. Got to get it early so Joe still has time for reading before bedtime."

Vernu made an effort to laugh as Joe and Mary headed for the door.

They hiked a mile into the desert and set up side by side with their beetle packs in a skylight configuration. They settled in for a night of moon watching and poaching. At one point, Joe said, "That Vernu looks like trouble. She obviously has hot pants for you."

"You're right, Joe; she comes on strong. I had to kick her out of my bed when she first moved in with me." Mary gave him a playful kiss and continued, "I'm saving myself for you, Baby."

"What's she do here?"

"Runs personnel. Has a lot of power. Knows a lot of people. She has a sideline business with alternative medicines. Potions, skin creams—even colonics and energy enemas if you're feeling down."

"Hmm..." murmured Joe.

Before the sun rose, they broke camp, slung on their beetle packs, and headed back to Health Works. Joe gathered up a few things from his room and picked up rations at the cafeteria.

Chapter 13
WATCHERS

Joe started his trek at sunrise. Rod was not with him now. He was on his own with his beetle pack fully deployed for cooling and full recycling to counteract the mid-summer heat. He carried enough food and top-off fluids for two weeks of trekking to the border of the Out-Lands.

There was no specific border between Freep territories and the Out-Lands. These areas were sparsely populated. Watchers continually crisscrossed these areas on foot and noted the presence of intruders of any kind and reported them to Algo-Net for recording in the territory database.

They were rarely detected by other humans in the Out-Lands. Their beetle packs could change color chameleon-like to match their surroundings. They were armed with a deadly laser; Bikers and other Out-Lands gangbangers knew that and didn't want to confront watchers one on one. Gangs preferred to bring in sniper teams to take them out from a distance—if they could find them, which was rare.

Watchers were not necessarily lost to the gangbangers if detected. They could call in a drone to carry them out of harm's way if they were spotted and needed to get out in a big hurry. For watchers close to an area of possible action, Freeps kept drones close by for rapid extraction.

Joe's mission was to meet up with a watcher near the Mainstream windmill farm not far from what used to be Palm Springs. Joe planned a four-day trek to get there.

His first trek alone took getting used to. As much as Rod had gotten on his nerves, Joe was used to him trekking ahead setting the pace, and all he had to do was follow and cuss him under his breath for going too fast. Now Joe had to find his own way. He had to follow an Algo-Net course and make decisions about how to traverse a terrain full of dry gulches, ravines, and sand dunes. His senses sharpened. He looked for signs of insect or animal life. Not much to see. The desert was not empty, like a lot of city people thought, and the occasional critter broke the monotony of only hearing his boots crunching on the ground. During the hottest days, critters were only seen at night.

His first solo dinner was pretty lonely: bars of trail food and herbal nutrient tea from recycled water. But afterward, he tuned in to Algo-Net for news and music and to do some research into Freep wars.

The research always put him to sleep after half an hour. This night was no different, he snoozed off with Algo-Net's voice in his ear. Hours later, he was awoken by his movement alarm. His heart beat wildly as he poked his head out of his beetle pack enclosure. Using the night vision scope in his helmet, he saw a herd of wild pigs racing toward him. He braced for an impact with his laser armed, ready to repel the nocturnal pigs in case of direct attack. But they raced on, bumping his enclosure roughly as they thundered by. *God! Do they stink. Don't want to get this close again. Camped too close to their trail.*

———

He set out next day with a feeling of confidence. His first night alone had gone well. After his pig scare, he'd slept deeply and woke up refreshed, feeling optimistic. He listened again to Algo-Net's Freep war history from the night before because he had fallen asleep and didn't remember much.

Walking steadily toward a mountain peak in the west, he heard that after the year 2050 in the Disturbed Era, Freep Nation grew as Mainstream elites consolidated their iron grip on energy production, all forms of communication, cyberspace, and information.

Many Freeps came from the lower-wage levels of Mainstream to take a shot at a hard but healthy life where they could live in peace. Others came from the educated levels, yearning for the freedom to think and talk freely. Some came to avoid getting drafted into continuous wars on the other side of the world.

At first, not much attention was paid to the Freeps by Mainstream. They were considered loners and outcasts out in the desert who didn't pose a threat. With the gangs in the Out-Lands, it was another story. They were predators, and the Freeps east of the Out-Lands were vulnerable and unorganized. And so the story of the Freep wars started out with gang raids on Freeps living in small groups. These raids happened in the few months of the year when temperatures were bearable enough for the gangs to drive or walk out into the desert.

Freeps needed to protect themselves with a weapon that could stand up against gangs armed with guns. With the help of the science guys from Silicon Valley, they developed laser weapons. Lasers made sense because individual Freeps had plenty of electric power. Buying bullets wasn't easy for them, and guns had problems with users shooting each other. Lasers needed Algo's permission to fire—preventing Freep fratricide.

Taking advantage of familiar terrain, Freeps could hide themselves using the chameleonlike skin of their beetle packs. With Algo-Net, they would coordinate firing on attacking gangs so that every shot found a target. By the twenty-second century, the gangs had learned not to attack Freeps without using overwhelming numbers.

Joe switched to music in his earpiece after listening to a couple of hours of Freep war history. The kilometers slipped by at a satisfying clip for the next three days. On the fourth day, he headed toward the coordinates of his destination, which he planned to reach before sunset. At that point, he was instructed to wait to be contacted by a watcher.

When he reached the location, an alarm chime sounded, and he stopped. Looking around, he could see no one. The harsh terrain was strewn with rocks and boulders. He sighted through his helmet telescope, scanning in all directions. No luck—he didn't see the watcher he was supposed to meet. He moved to the side of the trail to avoid pig parades and deployed his beetle pack in the chair configuration to wait and see who might show up.

After ten minutes of sitting in total silence, Joe was jarred by a voice that said, "You look like you're new in these parts."

Joe's heart skipped a beat, and he sat straight up with a jerk. He looked right and left, sensing danger. "Who's that? Where are you?" he said, his voice tense.

A meter-high rock suddenly moved, and its shape changed into that of a Freep. A Freep peeling back his camouflage wrap. He was only five meters away.

"Damn, you scared the crap out of me," Joe said.

The watcher, a blond guy with freckles, laughed and said, "This is the only fun I have out here, scaring new guys. Name's Jasper."

"I'm Joe."

"You probably want to know what this watcher stuff is all about."

"Yeah, Jasper, who in their right mind would want to come out here and…well…watch?"

"We watchers are kinda nuts, you might say, but we are building something. A battle-space knowledge base." Jasper and Joe got their packs back in traveling configuration, hefted them onto their backs, and started walking up a small hill. Joe was still listening as Jasper continued, "We notice everything about the area we are in and report it to the Algo-Net. If I find an old remote cabin or mine, I report it, ditto good defensive positions in the terrain. Characteristics of the ground, for example, suitable for vehicle or marchers, what kind of vegetation, places for Freeps to hide."

Joe said, "You don't mean to tell me an invasion is expected around here?"

"Who knows where an invasion might come from? You never know for sure. Best be ready for it—from any direction. Freeps win by knowing where individual fighters can hide, fire, and fall back to another hiding place. We are guerrillas who avoid massing troops for fear that the invaders have weapons of mass destruction that can take out a lot of us at one time."

Joe asked, "What else do you do? Seems one generation of watchers could have gotten the terrain mapped years ago."

Jasper, now at the hilltop, turned to Joe with a bemused look. He said, "Got me all figured out. I got a job that's already been done, and I am passing the time until my retirement from the Freep army." He paused and said, "Let's stop here and set up for the night."

Joe said, "It would bore the crap out of me."

"Note so fast, Junior, jumping to conclusions. You have another five days with me. You might come away with another opinion of what a slug I am after you spend some time trying to keep up."

———

The next day, they trekked close to the sprawling windmill farm that provided power to Mainstream. Jasper led Joe through bushes and rocks rather than on animal trails or ancient roads where Mainstream security patrols concentrated their attention. From their vantage point, they looked down on a high barbed-wire fence. Jasper said it was equipped with TV cameras and other sensors to detect intruders. Patrols continuously circled inside and outside of the fence.

Jasper checked how many windmills were operating and how many under maintenance. They climbed farther to a high peak to see many more kilometers of the huge machines churning out the power to keep Mainstream alive. This and two other windmill farms powered the whole of Mainstream in what was once California.

Jasper said, "This windmill farm shows the difference between Freeps, who each wear a backpack solar array, and Mainstreamers, who depend on a few huge power generation stations. Their power sources are concentrated and vulnerable. And we are going to see just how vulnerable."

"We?"

"Joe, they got a new model windmill, bigger and more efficient. We're going in there to take a look at its innards."

"Who cares about its innards?"

"You've heard by now that if attacked by Mainstream, Freeps will stage a defensive withdrawal and follow up with attacks on their infrastructure."

"Jasper, spare me the poor man's war story. Heard it a hundred times. Still haven't told me who cares about its innards."

Jasper said. "Algo-Net needs info on how their windmills work in order to develop a strategy to disable them. It doesn't like to be caught with its pixels down if we get attacked. We need to get inside them."

Joe said, "Look at those monsters. Their towers are more than three hundred meters above the ground. How do we get inside them?"

"We fly up there tonight in drones when the wind stops. We will each have a one-man drone pick us up and drop us on top of a windmill nacelle, that's the housing for the rotor hub and generator. From there, we enter through a hatch. Once inside, we figure out how we can sabotage it by hacking its systems."

Jasper pointed toward a new model not far from the fence. "That's the one. On this new design, the outer third of the rotor blades are moveable. They turn several degrees each time the blade rotates to get the most efficient blade angle because the wind speed is stronger at top of the blade's path than at the bottom closer to the ground."

Joe said, "I'm getting it. If you take control of the outer blade movement, you can raise all kinds of hell with the windmill."

"You got it, pal," Jasper said. "We could make individual blades flap uncontrollably in a strong wind, causing them to break off."

Joe asked, "What's the plan?"

Jasper said. "You and I are going inside the nacelle to figure out how to sabotage these babies. We'll sneak in tonight. Our drones are stealthy, emitting little noise and have a bird-size radar signature. They have short rotors to avoid hitting the windmill blades. While we're in there, we'll be linking data back to Algo-Net, so it can analyze the windmill's systems and identify vulnerable places."

"What time do we go in and out?" Joe asked.

"We'll go in at eleven after the fence patrols have made their second round and when the air is still. We stay beetled up to use the camera, lights, night vision optics, and Algo-Net voice access. We come out for drone pick up at three a.m., while it's still dark and before the morning winds start up."

They confirmed their mission plans with Air Control and then ate and slept a few hours. The drones arrived. At eleven o'clock, they took off with Jasper in the lead and piloted their drones by thought-messaging.

Joe's heart was in his throat as his drone climbed to altitude and flew over the fence. Jasper landed first on the nacelle of the mammoth windmill. As Joe approached, he saw Jasper's empty drone fly off and Jasper climbing down the hatch into the nacelle.

He followed tight as a drum, heart beating hard from the pure fright of standing on the nacelle with no guard-rail. He crouched down to his hands and knees to avoid the downwash from the drone as it flew away. Too scared to stand up, he crawled to the open hatch and climbed down the ladder rungs.

Inside, he felt secure. It was a room four meters wide and the same in height. About fifteen meters long, the rotor hub machinery and massive generator took up most of the space. Jasper found a light switch and clicked it on. He went to a desk and started riffling through documents and files.

Joe sat at an operator's console and hit the keyboard with rapid strokes. "Found design specs and schematics," he called out.

"Send them back to Algo-Net's watcher info section," Jasper said.

"Roger, Jasp."

"Holy turdbombs, I found an operating manual," Jasper said. He immediately began to photograph pages and send them off. "This'll take a while."

They had worked quietly for a couple of hours when Jasper said, "We struck gold here tonight, Joe. You almost finished sending data?"

"Will be in ten minutes."

Ka blam! A mighty thunderclap shook the nacelle. Jasper sprang up the ladder and looked out. Lightning flashed. Cold wind blew in from the north. He yelled down to Joe. "We can't take off from up here."

The three-bladed rotor started turning—sounding like a train speeding up to an ear-jarring metallic dissonance.

"Joe, we're going down the stairs."

They took off down the circular stairs as fast as they could go beetled up.

Joe, breathing hard, yelled, "Jasper, I set the controls to cycle full outer blade movement an hour from now."

"Great, with these high winds it'll self-destruct."

"And they'll blame the storm," said Joe.

"Learning fast, my newbie friend."

It took half an hour to reach the bottom—and a locked door to the outside!

"Shootin' our way out," yelled Jasper above the storm's roar. He stood back and lased, blowing hot steel sparks out where the lock had been. The door flew open.

They charged into howling wind and rain between the rows of enormous windmills. Running toward the direction from which they had come in, they both thought-messaged Air Control asking for drone pickup.

The drones, waiting to take off from over the nearby mountain ridge, launched into the teeth of the storm, making slow progress to the fence. Joe and Jasper stopped a hundred meters from the fence to avoid the floodlights' glare.

Frustrated at the time it was taking, Joe yelled, "Come on, drones!"

Seconds later, their two drones dropped out of the maelstrom, and the guys jumped on board. They headed out with Jasper in the lead, flying a low-probability-of-detection flight path, cruising dangerously close to spinning windmills and illuminated by lightning flashes.

They were looking anxiously in the direction of the doomed windmill when it happened. A ripping, crackling noise accompanied by the nacelle cracking open and fountains of sparks erupting into the gale. Shrapnel zinged by their drones. They flew over the fence at an altitude of two hundred meters when the night was illuminated with searchlights clicking on. Joe called, "Jasp. You OK?" No answer. And no answer after another half-dozen tries.

Joe thought-messaged Air Control, *Put us on the ground ASAP. Got to check on Jasper.*

They landed in the lee of a small mesa where the wind was weaker. Joe ran to Jasper's drone to see him slumped forward in his seat, unconscious, blood on his chest and right arm. He shouted, "Jasp, you're not checking out now." Seeing Jasper breathing, Joe immediately thought-messaged their drones to fly to the nearest emergency infirmary. Off they went again.

They cruised at top speed for half an hour, breaking out of the storm over the moonlit dunes and dropped down to an old shopping mall. *Might be old La Quinta,* Joe thought. It appeared deserted at first, but then lights came on at a place in the landing strip free of sand drifts, and attendants came running from a door with a gurney.

In surgery Jasper's clothes were cut away to reveal a gruesome shrapnel wound across his right arm and half his chest. An oxygen mask shut off his weak groans. Expert hands cleaned his wounds and molded broken bones and flesh back to something resembling original condition.

Chapter 14
CHANCE ENCOUNTER

Joe was lying on a donor room table to give a pint of blood for Jasper. Another volunteer came in and reclined at a nearby station when Joe recognized her: Mary! His heart started pumping his blood into the bottle faster, but he kept his cool and didn't say anything. He waited until she got needled and was pumping. Then she looked around the room out of curiosity. Joe was ready for her gaze when it found him, giving her a big wink and a smile that seemed to burst out of his face with joy.

"Joe!" she screamed. "I can't believe it's you! You must be OK if you are giving blood."

"I'm OK. It's my buddy, Jasper, I'm worried about. God, it's good to see you. They never let my calls go through to you."

"Mine either. It's all part of the training we are going through." She stopped, looked around, and in a confiding tone said, "Do you think they know what they are doing?"

"Ha!" A big laugh exploded from his chest. "I never thought of that. I'm too busy trying to show them I can do whatever they throw at me."

"Joe, I missed you so much. Can't believe…Suddenly you're here…Now tell me, how did you ever get tied up with Wildass Jasper?"

"You've heard of him?"

"Oh yeah. I've been working in this infirmary for a while and heard about this hyperactive watcher named Wildass Jasper, who has a habit of getting banged about in crazy adventures he dreams up."

"He dreams them up?"

"Word has it he does. Tell me what you two were doing."

Joe said, "We were outside the Palm Springs windmill farm gathering intelligence about the new model windmills there. Trying to figure out ways to sabotage them in case Freeps and Mainstream come into a future conflict."

Mary said, "That doesn't sound like something that would cause Jasper's injuries."

"Well, there's more. We decided to sneak into the new model windmill in the dead of night to gather technical data."

Mary said, "That's more like the kind of stuff Jasper would dream up."

Joe said, "Dream up? I thought we were under orders from Algo."

"Doesn't sound like it, Joe," Mary said. "Algo believes in constant intelligence gathering but doesn't like to do things that might not work out right and expose the Freeps doing them."

Joe said, "I get it. Because then Mainstream would beef up the areas where Freeps are probing."

"Right on, electron," she said with a perky lilt to her voice.

"Hope Mainstream doesn't figure out that I sabotaged one of their new windmills."

"Oh, Joe, it rubbed off on you," she said, dismayed, "That's the kind of thing Wildass Jasper would do."

A nurse took the needles out of their arms. They hugged long and hard to make up for the time apart and sat down in the small mess area for the coffee and pastry they'd earned for giving blood.

Joe looked across the coffee he was sipping. "Are you going to be around here for a while?"

Mary said, "I'm here as an orderly for a couple weeks. Have to finish my shift tonight. Tomorrow I'm off."

"I'll check on Jasper and then call Rod to see if I can get tomorrow off, too."

"OK, Joe, going to work now. Call me on the hospital phone to let me know what you'll be doing. Number three-five-four."

"Will do," Joe said as they left the mess area. Seeing no one in the corridor, he kissed her. His strong hug was reciprocated. They parted silently; she headed down a dim corridor, and he headed to the surgical waiting room.

No word on Jasper; still operating. He sat in the waiting room in his beetle chair so he could access the Algo-Net. There was a news item about last night's incident at the Palm Springs windmill farm: "A new configuration windmill broke up in a freak thunderstorm. Mainstream sources cited lightning as the probable culprit. Other windmills damaged by flying debris." Joe grinned with that news. He thought, *No mention of sabotage, but maybe they're not revealing everything.*

Joe tried to do some research on Freep wars to while away the time. In minutes his eyelids drooped, and he dozed off. It was light when he woke, an orderly shaking his arm and saying, "Wake up, Joe."

He sat up straight and asked, "How's Jasper?"

"OK and asking for you."

In the recovery room, Joe saw his partner in crime trying to put a few doped-up thoughts together. "Dang, it's my ol' buddy Joe. If that wasn't a damn fool idea of yours to spaz out that windmill."

Joe, eying Jasper's bulky bandages, felt a pang of guilt that his prank was the cause. "Sorry it messed you up, Jasp."

"They told me I'll make it, so no problem. Won't hold it against you. Doc here"—he motioned toward the doctor—"says I'll be back trekkin' and watchin' in a few days."

"No, my friend," said the soft-spoken Latino doctor. "More like a few *months*. There are big muscles and some ribs that have to knit together. Takes time." Turning to Joe, he said, "You'll have to go now and let Jasper rest."

Jasper had already nodded off before Joe could say good-bye. He hefted on his beetle pack and went outside to take a walk. He buttoned up against the heat of mid-day and called Rod, who came on the line to say, "I had my doubts about sending you to Jasper, but I was over-ruled. Algo thought that buddying up with a free spirit like Jasper would be good for you."

"Sounds like you heard about our infiltration of the windmill farm."

"Damn fool stunt. But got to hand it to you guys, the intelligence sent back was priceless. Too bad about Jasper."

Joe said, "He'll be off the air for a couple of months."

"Figured that when I heard of his injuries. Joe, we need you to go back there and fill in for him for a couple of weeks while we get a seasoned watcher to replace him."

"Roger, I'll head out two days from now. I need to get briefed by Jasper before I go."

"OK, makes sense. He knows that area. Here are a few things I want you to do: fly out there, but walk the last fifteen kilometers—in the dark as much as possible, es-pecially in sniper range. Check out all damage from the incident there. They might suspect sabotage and might have patrols ranging far outside the wire. Be careful and use a periscope for long-range observation from behind a boulder. We'll get you a watcher's kit before you leave. Take provisions for two weeks."

"Rod...uh...what's the chance of being able to make some personal calls?"

"Not good," Rod said sternly. "We need you one hundred percent focused on the mission."

"How long does this call restriction last?"

"Usually until nine months into your one-year trek. Then you are allowed most calls. At the end of one year, it is supposed to be unrestricted."

———

The next day, he met Mary for breakfast. "I am going to try something," Joe said.

"What's that, brother Freep?"

"Going to contact Air Control to see if I can get a plane to fly us around today."

"Joe, the Freep mentality is to avoid frivolous use of resources. I doubt if they will let you."

"Don't hurt to try," Joe said. He pressed his voice-contact button and called Air Control. "Air Control, Joe here."

"Yes, Joe."

"I need to reconnoiter a watcher area today that I just got assigned to."

"OK, we can send you a single-seater—"

Joe interrupted, "Air Control, I need a two-seater,".

"What for?"

"I want to take a colleague so we can trade information about the area."

"Sounds like a boondoggle to me. Can't get a two-seater unless you have earned an award point."

"What the heck is an award point?"

Air Control went silent for a moment and then came back on the line. "You are in luck, Joe. You earned an award point the night before last. Let me read it to you: 'For displaying initiative to enhance Freep security.'"

"Fantastic!" Joe said as he fist-bumped Mary.

A crackle of static. "Air Control again. Your plane is on the way. Be advised not to fly over the Out-Lands or any Mainstream installations such as the Palm Springs windmill farm. Stay north of the Mexican border."

"Roger, Air Control."

The plane showed up, heralded by the soft *thump, thump* of its two props. The thumping slowed, and the plane landed in thirty meters of airstrip. Joe and Mary jumped in, and the thumping started again, its frequency increased. A short taxi and the sunfed dragonfly surged aloft, its silvery wings a mosaic of solar cells gathering photons for the billion feather-weight nano-batteries that can keep the props turning well after sundown.

They climbed to one thousand meters, where they were unseen and unheard from the ground. Toward the west was the Cabazon Pass, through which westerly winds funneled, imparting their energy to the rows of Mainstream windmills.

From his watcher's kit, Joe took out an image-stabilized telescope. "Mary, I'm going to see if there is truth to the story of sabotage down there." He winked.

He trained the telescope on the windmills, scanning along the rows. He saw a gap where one windmill was missing. Wreckage of a fallen tower lay in the gap. Downwind of the destroyed tower were motionless windmills with damage to their blades, the result of flying shrapnel.

"Looks like one destroyed and half a dozen damaged and out of commission."

Joe thought-messaged the plane to fly away from the windmill farms and cruise over the rest of his watch area.

Mary said, "I often think of our first flight, Joe. I was so impressed with how you handled the airplane."

"We are going back to the Salton Seabed where we flew that time. This time we're going to land."

"That's so romantic—going back to the place of our first date."

It was one hundred meters below sea level where they set down in the middle of the seabed. Temperature was 138 degrees, and the wind was blowing an unhealthy gritty powder against their beetle suits and helmets. They set up a picnic by putting their beetle packs side by side and zipping their covers into a tent configuration. Their suit conditioners filtered the air of dust and set the temperature for comfort with no clothes on. Mary produced picnic snacks and a cool, wine-like beverage.

Joe didn't last long eating and drinking with that gorgeous body next to him. He grabbed her and pulled her toward him. The thought flashed not to be rough in spite of his overpowering desire for her. But Mary responded in kind with a powerful embrace, intense kiss, and deep moaning that played against the noise of the wind slapping against their tent.

Sometime later, Joe woke up with the wind still blowing. "Mary, wake up. Got to go."

She moved slowly, and her eyes opened. "How long have we been asleep?" She stretched and kissed him, not really wanting to go anywhere.

"Don't know. Hour or two, I guess," Joe said, quickly pulling on his clothes. "Let's get going to make it back before dark."

She reluctantly dressed and helped stow their gear.

After takeoff, they turned and headed for the infirmary. Joe, trying to understand why the sky looked so yellow ahead of him, realized he was flying into the front of a dust storm. Soon the plane was plowing through a cloud of desert dust and bouncing violently from the turbulence. Mary grabbed his arm hard, and her nails dug in.

Joe contacted Air Control. "Joe here. We're heading for the infirmary at La Quinta. Got zero visibility in a dust storm. How does it look ahead?"

"It is going to be rough all the way in, Joe. You have twenty minutes to go, and your plane can handle the wind speeds en route. You are under full automatic control. We'll advise you before touchdown, so it is not a surprise."

"Roger, Air Control."

Mary let up on Joe's arm and tried to relax, but every lurch of the plane drew a gasp from her, and they didn't talk.

Back on the ground, they went to the mess for dinner. Mary turned down a chance to play cards with her friends, instead choosing to hang out with Joe in the lounge. She asked him, "How do you like living among the Freeps?"

"It is a big change to be living close to the edge of survival. But I like that because there is no room for the unnecessary customs of Mainstream life that drove me up the wall. Here, you can see a connection between what people do and how they survive. In Mainstream, a lot of what people do supports the parasites at the top or simply uses up people's energy, so there is none left to organize resistance, question anything, or fight back."

"How about you? What's your take on Freep life?"

Mary said, "First off, I came from the serfdom of a Mid-Level farm. People had very little there. They were prisoners. But the kids, believe it or not, were happy playing in the dirt while their parents toiled in the greenhouses. You see the unhappiness of your parents and know deep down inside you don't want to grow up to be unhappy like them. So this thing called freedom that they speak of, you learn it has value, and someday you would like to experience it."

"Are you finding it here in Freep Nation?" Joe asked.

"I think so. It's the opposite of the fenced-in world on the farm. Feels good just being here where there are no fences or guards. We new Freeps travel around to learn about what freedom means to those who live here. Got to learn by osmosis, though, because nobody actually talks about freedom.

"Working in the hospitals, I am finding out more about the personal lives of Freeps. Faced with life-or-death situations, people are more apt to open up even to a newcomer like me, and share what is on their minds. I'm also finding out that it is not a precisely organized world here. Have you noticed that people bend the rules at times? A small example—they smuggled in the wine we drank today. Bigger examples would be the stunts that Wildass Jasper pulls."

Joe said, "Maybe Algo figured out that flexibility at the fringes is necessary for evolutionary adaptation."

Mary said, "I find myself super-interested in these big-picture issues. How to keep a community at peace and free. Are community peace and unity compatible with evolution, which is often thought to be lubricated by harsh conflicts? Now that is the sort of thing I could spend hours debating and exchanging ideas about. Eventually, I want to work in a job that improves community well-being and people's satisfaction with their lives. If that happens, I can say I have found the freedom I needed to make my life fulfilling."

"Well put, my dear," Joe said, thinking to himself that Mary was a bit naive.

She sensed his thought and decided to turn the conversational spotlight back on him. "I've held the floor for a while. Your turn to bare your soul and tell me where you expect to end up."

"I am being tested on this trek. Feels like a leadership test. I'm guessing if I can last one year, a leadership position will open up for me."

"What kind of position?" she asked.

"No idea," Joe said. "I don't even know what the governing body or bodies look like here. Maybe it's only Algo, in which case there isn't a job for me. Or maybe there is a leader and some sort of parliament under him running the show, with Algo being the mouthpiece for them. That would be more to my liking."

"Admirable," Mary quipped, "Leadership ambitions and a great lover, all rolled up in one guy."

"Are you taking me seriously?"

———

The next day, Joe flew to Jasper's watch area, and was dropped off far from the windmill farm to be safe. He trekked in to where Jasper had first showed him the windmill they were to check out, arriving after dark to be sure he was not seen by Mainstream patrols or sniper teams. With his night-vision telescope he checked out the windmill he and Mary saw from the air. He could clearly see shards of bent blades and a tower, fractured in a dozen places, weirdly snaking across the ground where it had once proudly stood. He could see Mainstream workers preparing the footing for a new tower.

He also saw neighboring towers on the same row and the downwind row that had been damaged by flying debris. Their rotors were being repaired. *Lucky they are still standing*, thought Joe, thinking of the high off-balance forces a damaged blade could cause on the tower. *They must have stopped them real fast. Probably an automatic shutoff system. Hmm…If that system also gets sabotaged, there will be even more destruction.*

Joe lurked around the windmill farm for another ten days. He trekked around its outer perimeter, traveling only at night and keeping a couple of kilometers away from the fence. Back at his starting point, he saw that all the windmills had been repaired. In a way, he was glad to see that. *After all*, he thought, *who gets hurt with a power interruption? Mostly ordinary people like my parents. Maybe I was too hasty pulling that stunt. Gotta be more careful in the future.*

That night, after walking away from the windmill farm, Joe contacted Algo-Net and made his report on the farm's condition. He requested an airplane for the next morning to fly in to the infirmary to visit Jasper. He was surprised when his request was approved; he could fly in and stay one night. The plane found him at his bivouac in the morning, and they landed at the infirmary an hour later. Walking in from the landing place, he saw Jasper stretched out in his beetle pack bed with the cooling on.

"Jasp, what the heck are you doing outside?"

"Joe, great to see you! I'm so used to living on the land that I am more comfortable here than in an air-conditioned building."

"Does anyone come out to keep you company?"

"Every now and then," Jasper replied, as he struggled to sit up for a better look at Joe. "Hey, man, didn't we have a blast tramping around out there by the windmill farm?"

"Yeah, Jasp, it was a hoot. But you know I don't like seeing you like this. Hope you get back out there soon."

"Me, too. Nobody gives me a straight answer when I ask them when they are going to cut me loose. If you got any influence around here, find out for me."

"OK, I'll ask my pal Mary."

"Don't think you will. She flew out this morning."

Joe was jolted. "How do you know?"

Jasper said, "I spend most of my time outside here and see everyone coming and going from the airplanes. She left this morning and wasn't happy about it. Said she was reassigned to Mojave. Also said to say hello if I saw you."

"Crap! I was looking forward to seeing her."

"You will. Don't give up. They don't want you newcomers to get too involved."

"This farging place is getting to me," Joe yelled and kicked dirt toward the infirmary.

"Man, you are pissed off."

"Bet your bollocks I am."

"Take me for a plane ride and tell me about yourself."

Joe thought-messaged Air Control and asked for a plane.

A return thought-message, *Why?*

Joe thought-messaged, *Need to take Jasper for a ride and talk.*

Return thought-message, *Plane coming for your flight. You got five hours.*

Joe helped Jasper aboard and strapped him in. They flew to Jasper's favorite thinking spot, a high mesa near Yuma. From there, an incredible view in every direction—deserts, distant mountains, occasional thunderheads, and eternal silence.

"I ponder the big stuff here," said Jasper.

Joe looked preoccupied, not seeing the world around him.

Jasper said, "You don't look happy. Let's talk. Tell me how it was in Mainstream."

"You know I hated it there. The rules in our high-security gated community. The sappy corporate loyalty indoctrination. I was a born rebel. Then the YMCA. It was grungy, but I saw what a different life was like."

"How'd ya feel about that? Jasper asked. "Kicked out of a comfortable life and ending up in a crummy Y with uncertain chances of getting back."

"When the adventure wore off, it didn't feel too good. Then I got recruited by the Freeps. And here I am. Heard the Freeps had that thing called freedom."

"You're here to stay. My guess is that you're irked because they are not giving you all that freedom stuff at once."

"Yeah, Jasp, that bugs me."

"Hey man, I'm a watcher. I like to work alone, and I like the freedom to wander." Jasper pointed to the distant mountains, dappled with cloud shadows. "That view lifts my soul. I spend my time trying to walk into that eternal beauty, to be enveloped by it."

Joe looked at the mountains. He had a thoughtful expression on his face as Jasper continued, "There are different kinds of freedom. My freedom to wander in that space is enough for me. You have to ask yourself if that kind of freedom or the freedom of the Beetle-Pack Factory or the freedom of the homestead is enough for you. If it is, stop. Jump off this journey, and live your dream. If you haven't found it yet, keep going."

"Jasp, you haven't said it, but you're telling me that if I quit, I'll never know what possibilities I might have sampled, never found out what other kinds of freedom are out there in Freep Nation."

"That's it, Brother. Now let's fly back to the infirmary—got some bootleg wine for you," Jasper said and laughed.

Chapter 15
INCURSION

Next morning, Joe was off on a plane to take on the life of a watcher once again. Dropped off back in his patch of desert. He decided to trek away from the windmills, planning to make a pattern of exploration twenty kilometers square in an area that might not have received much watcher attention because of all the interest in the windmills. He would feed information about it into Algo-Net as other watchers had done for two centuries, building and updating the knowledge base. Along the way, he frequently queried Algo-Net to find out what other watchers had found in a specific area. Where an old mine had been reported, he returned to see what condition it was in and report if it could be of use for the future.

Jasper had warned him not to make contact with other watchers or any humans he saw wandering in the desolate landscape, even if they appeared friendly. He told Joe to hide or camouflage himself until they passed and disappeared. Every sighting must be reported, however.

Joe didn't see anyone wandering at first. Four days in he saw a couple of cyclists heading east on new-looking motorcycles. They were dressed in bulky air-conditioned leathers and looked formidably big and powerful.

What were they up to? He checked Algo-Net and found out that Mainstream also sent out individual trekkers or cyclists to probe and find out where the Freeps were, often using gang mercenaries. Algo-Net believed the probers were looking for vulnerable places where military expeditions could advance into Freep land. No sense letting them know where the watchers were. If probers went in too deep, threatening Freep settlements, the watchers' alerts would insure an adequate defense.

He found a couple of abandoned mines that showed signs of Biker habitation. He alerted Algo-Net to check if the Bikers were gradually encroaching. Nothing like that had been noted; in fact, Algo-Net data showed a continuing recession of human habitation from the desert as long-term temperature trends continued upward.

Joe called Mary every day and got through one morning after trekking through the night. "Hi, Mary. Where are you?"

"Joe, you finally called."

"Got you on my eleventh try. Itching to know where you are—and how I can catch up with you."

Mary said, "I'm up here in the Mojave Desert, studying how to optimize fulfillment of Freep needs for happiness."

"You got to be kidding. Happiness? Ha! I could use a little of that."

"Now, Joe, hold on while I close the door to my room." She was back a minute later. "You are on a long-range track for freedom. That long-term journey doesn't always provide short-term happiness."

"Mary, I don't know about all that psychology stuff. I only want to see you again."

"Can you get to the Normalizer next week in the Antelope Valley?"

"I'll give it a shot, with all I got."

"Poetry now? How romantic."

"When a guy becomes a watcher, he gets into poetry, history, bird-watching...stuff like that."

Her magical laugh was cut off as the line went dead.

"Farging idiots!" shouted Joe, and his words disappeared across a sublime but uncaring desert.

He set up his beetle pack in the form of a rock, like the one Jasper had popped out of the day they met. He settled in for some quiet time researching. He voice-messaged Algo-Net: "Tell me about offensive military campaigns by Freeps against Mainstream."

Algo-Net responded, "There was a major offensive by Freeps in 2150 against Mainstream bases. This campaign was in retaliation for aggression by Mainstream setting up settlements where successful Freep farm operations had been. The reason for war given by Mainstream was that any productive land in what was formerly California belonged to Mainstream as a result of a court decision based on Manifest Destiny principles and eminent domain powers conferred on corporations.

"Freep command decided not to attack Mainstream settlements, as they were well fortified and could call in air support from Northern California bases. Instead, Freep attacked Mainstream air bases, which were a source of suffering and destruction during Mainstream's establishment of the settlements.

"At first, the Freeps did well. Using guerrilla tactics, they could easily infiltrate areas around the bases; overcome perimeter defenses; and destroy planes, ammunition, and fuel stores. They were not as successful, however, when the surprised defenders brought in air-to-ground aircraft from other bases.

"Freeps had to withdraw deep into the desert. Mainstream pursued them for a time, capturing and brutalizing men, women, and children. When Mainstream troops couldn't be spared, they employed a tactic still in use, sending in gang mercenaries to harass the Freeps. Mainstream even supported the establishment of gang settlements in Freep lands, but that didn't last very long."

After half an hour of Algo-Net's narrative, Joe said, "Thanks, Algo-Net. I'm taking a break now to digest what you have said. I'll be in contact tomorrow."

———

Before dawn, a supply drone dropped him supplies for another two weeks. He stowed the supplies in his beetle pack and headed out.

Joe observed motorcyclists heading east two days in a row. *Something big is going on*, he thought. He decided to head east, close to the abandoned highway the cyclists rode on. Decrepit and cracked, it made for hard riding but was generally better than driving cross-country because the motorcycles were heavily laden with supplies.

Joe decided to follow to find their destination. They had to be going somewhere specific, not driving east for the fun of it. During daylight hours, he hunkered down in his camouflage enclosure. On his third day out, a motorcycle came from the opposite direction, passed by his spot, and disappeared into the western horizon of haze and dust.

With dusk, he began his night trek again along the old highway. Because it was cooler at night, he had his helmet rotated back into his pack, and it was good that he did, as he heard a faint engine sound. He immediately stopped and crouched down in a stand of dead bushes to hide his IR signature. He waited and listened. The sound grew louder. Some kind of truck. It approached with its lights off. The air pulsed from its exhaust belching a hoarse, menacing tattoo.

Then he saw it rumbling not thirty meters away, huge and moving slowly over the cracked and unstable roadway. A fuel tanker built for any terrain with four articulated tread drives. Its black windows revealed no one. Joe's heart raced in fear that the gunner, with his night-vision glasses, would pick him off.

The tanker rumbled east toward an area of steep foothills and ravines. Joe had to follow. He thought, *That tanker can't get over these steep hills off road. It will have to stick to the old roadway to its destination. If it doesn't get there before daybreak, it will have to bivouac during the daylight hours and hide itself. They are up to no good.*

Joe pressed on. He decided not to call Algo-Net because even if the intruders didn't break his encrypted message, they could detect his radio transmission and find his position with direction-finding gear.

At dawn, Joe stopped. *Don't want to push it*, he thought. *Walking into the rising sun exposes me and hides them. Gotta be patient. If I stay on this track long enough, I'll find where they are going.* He set up his enclosure and buttoned up. To use his time, he brought up some past notes about the Freep wars and reviewed them. Soon he was asleep. Hours later, his alarm sounded, and he noted a motorcycle approaching from the west. It passed his position fairly slowly on the rough roadway. Slowly enough for him to see the triangle emblem on the driver's arm. *Funt!* he thought. *It's a Funt operation. That's how they know this area has little watcher activity.* Funt, too, had been through watcher training here.

Watching the motorcycle approach the steep mountains, Joe saw that it didn't continue up the old roadway into the mountain pass; it took a right-angle detour off the roadway and headed south. The detour headed over fairly level ground close to the bottom of an escarpment. *Tonight's trek will be in that direction*, he thought. *We're gettin' warm!*

At sunset Joe set out south, following the motorcycle route. He also saw the telltale tracks of the fuel tanker's treads. After a couple of hours of trekking, the ruts in the trail took a left turn toward the steep face of the escarpment. *Got a feeling I'm almost there*, he thought. In the dark, his night-vision optics could see that the track led into a steep ravine in the rock wall. *God! There it is: the tanker.*

Joe could see it tucked well into the almost-vertical ravine walls with a canopy stretched over it, hiding it from sight from above. Nearby was the entrance to an old mine. He thought, *With this source of fuel, cyclists could strike out against Freep installations and homesteaders within a three-hundred-kilometer radius.*

It was dark, and Joe was itching to light up the tanker with his laser. *I've got surprise going for me. There doesn't seem to be anyone guarding it. But this time, I am not going to rush it. Might be complications I don't know about. Freep command might be working the problem already.*

Joe entered the tanker's exact location in his computer using his helmet optics. He turned back the way he'd come, trekking near the detour. At the roadway heading up into the foothills, he headed east for a couple of hours to get well out of the field of view of the intruders in their tight little ravine, preventing his discovery by sight or radio signal. It was still dark when he reported what he saw over Algo-Net.

Algo-Net's voice responded, "Joe, we've got to stop the Bikers. Too close to dawn now. Position yourself near the roadbed detour before sunrise. Sit tight and observe if any other vehicles go to the ravine. Tomorrow after dark, trek down to the ravine. Lase the tanker from no more than one hundred meters away to insure a knockout hit. Head away from your firing position when you see the tanker go up in flames. A drone will pick you up. Expect gunfire from the Bikers. Shoot back to kill with your laser."

"Roger that."

Joe set up his Freep camo tent near the ravine with a clear view of the tanker. Exhausted, he tore into his nutrition bar and fell asleep seconds after the last mouthful.

———

After midnight, he jolted awake when his movement alarm sounded. He heard a vehicle motor. Then he saw a dark shape appear along the detour road. A six-wheel combat vehicle. Same camouflage colors and sporting the same inverted triangle emblem as the tanker. It pulled in next to the tanker, and four men got out. He recognized Funt immediately as he emerged from the shotgun door and led the others into the tunnel entrance. *The boss is here*, he thought. *Time for me to go to work.*

Joe contacted Algo-Net, "I will open fire in five minutes. Bring the pickup drone up.

"Roger, Joe, your laser is enabled for live fire," replied Algo-Net. "Your pickup drone is on the way."

Joe steadied his emotions and waited for the crosshairs of his laser sight to settle down on the triangle emblem on the rear of the tanker. He held his breath and thought-messaged *Fire!* A shaft of brilliant light connected his helmet laser with the tanker for a fraction of a second. The tanker blew up with an orange and white explosion. Searing heat blasted across his face shield and torso cover.

He ran with the burning tanker illuminating his way across the rocky ground. After a minute of full-speed running, he stopped and looked back at the billowing flames lapping up the ravine walls. He couldn't believe his eyes; half a dozen figures were running from the old mine entrance through the burning puddles of gasoline! Their bulky silhouettes showed they were wearing air-conditioned leathers.

They fanned out on his side of the detour road and advanced in a skirmish line. They must have figured he had to be in the nearby desert to have made that shot up the ravine. He sighted the closest one a hundred meters away and lased him. Scattered gunfire returned in his direction, uncertain exactly where he was. Then he heard his pickup drone close by. He shot twice more to suppress the two closest pursuers. Got them both.

The drone flew up next to him one meter off the ground. He jumped aboard with sand and stones peppering him from the rotor downwash. The drone peeled off away from the fire. He had one shot left and put his laser crosshairs on—*It's him, Funt*—and fired. Funt screamed and fell with his right foot burned off.

Even with Funt writhing in pain, his hate-filled determination drove his remaining troops to keep shooting. And one found his mark. Joe's drone was hit. Angry gnashing sounds and careening, wallowing flight over the desert marked the drone's flight path as it descended toward the desert sand. It skidded into the ground, and Joe was ejected, landing on his beetle pack.

"Algo-Net!" he yelled, fear in his voice. "I've been shot down."

"Stay calm, Joe. We have your position. Another sling drone will drop you a line from fifty meters."

"Why a farging sling drone?"

"All we got in your neighborhood. It will be there in three minutes."

"Don't hurry. I got all night," yelled Joe angrily.

After several minutes, Algo-Net came back online. "Joe, the sling line has a horse collar at the end. Put your arms and head through its loop and hook your elbows over it."

Seconds later, the collar came gently down to him. He pulled it over his head and arms. "I'm in, take me up."

The remaining troops from Funt's team saw the figure rising from the earth and opened fire with everything they had. Joe rose rapidly and headed east toward the lightening sky. Bullets whizzed by. Nothing he could do but hope not to get hit. And then he felt searing pain in his thigh as a bullet found its mark. He groaned in agony and cursed his bad luck. He thought, *Almost out of their range, swinging at the end of a rope. A hard target, but they got me anyway.*

He looked away at the cumulus clouds becoming visible with the rim lighting of sunrise. But nature's beauty lost out to the pain stabbing up from his leg, and he closed his eyes and squeezed overflowing tears out. He was buffeted by turbulence. Blood was running down his leg. A feeling of faintness and nausea surged and he vomited from his hanging perch. He had to calm down and slow his pulse to lessen the chance of bleeding out before he got there.

He awoke in an operating room. Doctors hovered above him. In and out of a dream. A mask on his face—must be oxygen. Finally, groggily, he was awake enough to talk. Heard Jasper say, "Wiggle your toes if you hear me, buddy."

He managed a half-assed grin and "Hi, Jasp."

"You're the first person brought to the infirmary at the end of a fifty-meter rope."

Joe moved in the bed to see if he could. Then he slurred out an answer. "Wanted to make an entrance."

"Man, you made a swinging entrance. I seen 'em all, too, from my outdoor hospital bed, but never seen anything like yours."

Chapter 16
DEFENSE OF HOMELAND

After two weeks, Joe was up and around on crutches. His wound had closed and torn muscles, stitched back together, were starting to function with the help of daily therapy. When he had quiet hours, he would study Freep wars in small doses. His preference was to seek underlying principles or unusual conditions that influenced the outcomes of Freep battles.

One afternoon about a month into his recovery Joe was looking at the big picture of how Freeps had resisted intrusions from hostile neighbors over the generations they had been living in the desert. Freeps fought back when attacked, using light weapons and guerrilla tactics. Their few forays into offensive attacks were disastrous. They weren't good at foreign wars—even just-across-the-border wars.

Joe came to think that Freep culture was influenced by migrants fleeing from lands to the west. In Joe's chats with them, they told him they craved freedom. When he dug a little deeper, many said they were fleeing Mainstream's draft or the Out-Lands' daily threat of violence or Mid-Level's long term oppression of body and spirit. It seemed to Joe that many migrants to the Freep Nation brought with them a predisposition to try any peaceful solution to a problem before resorting to force.

Probably why there is so little interest here in capturing or shooting intruders, thought Joe. *Freeps would rather politely ask an intruder to leave than take him by force to the border and kick his ass out.*

With these thoughts fresh in his mind, Joe got a call from Algo-Net. "Joe here," he answered.

"Commander Waxer here, Joe. I'm in charge of Freep watchers in Southern California. I've heard about your encounters with Bikers lately. They are becoming a nuisance, and we need your insights on repelling them. Can you teleconference with us right now?"

"Can do, Commander."

"We'll come up on your beetle-pack screen," the commander said. A man named Adber and a woman named Mel were the other participants.

Waxer said, "Adber has been put in charge of the area you were watching before you got wounded. Have you got any insights for him?"

Joe said, "Commander, I think you need more than one man there because the threat level has increased."

"Explain, Joe."

"By moving up a fuel tanker to a hidden outpost such as an old mine, Bikers can fan out from there and raid homesteads and Freep farms and factories. Tankers are their energy sources. With them they can air condition underground outposts and put troops in them. We can't let them sneak in."

Adber said, "Joe, you showed how one watcher can take out a tanker and fly away to fight another day."

Joe said, "I was lucky. Don't forget, my first rescue drone got shot down. By chance there was another drone nearby with a rope hanging down from it."

Waxer said, "In addition to Adber, we're sending Mel in to watch in that area."

Mel spoke up. "I've been a watcher for years in the Antelope Valley and Mojave Desert. We've had Bikers probing there but managed to shoo them away them with warnings and occasionally lasing their bikes."

Joe said, "That works for Bikers in small numbers. When they have to walk home a couple of times after their bikes are blasted, they lose interest in coming back. I understand that. Now I think we are facing something different. Something bigger."

Waxer said, "I think that with two watchers in that area, we'll be safe. Funt is out of action now minus one foot, thanks to you. I think those Bikers learned their lesson, and it will be quiet for a long time."

"I understand your thinking," Joe said, "but I have a hunch something different is going on. That tanker was not an antique truck. It was up to date. Not something a bunch of doped-up Bikers can afford. It was camouflaged during the day so watchers couldn't see it, and it traveled at night. Got deep into our territory before we noticed it."

"Could be Mainstream war surplus they got cheap," Adber said.

"Or it could be that Mainstream gave it to the Bikers along with fuel so they would move in on Freep land. Might be trying to move us away from the windmill farm," Joe replied. "They might think the Freeps are a threat, and Out-Lands' settlers will provide a buffer."

"What's in it for the Bikers, Joe?" Waxer asked.

"Usual things: women, food, stimulants, and what little booty they can find. They know that we Freeps have a vast network of farms, factories, and social facilities that are lightly defended. They could take over our facilities and run them for their own profit."

Waxer laughed and said, "Everyone knows that Out-Lands thugs can't take over a Freep operation and run it long term. Don't have the discipline."

Joe said, "Might be that Bikers will spearhead Mainstream attacks on our farm or factory settlements and then bring in Mid-Level workers."

Waxer snorted. "That's all too complicated."

Joe replied, "You may be right. But if it were me in your shoes, I would put in more watchers and improve our rapid-deployment capability on our southwest border."

Waxer said, "Thanks, Joe."

The line went dead.

Dang, Joe thought. *The desire for peace that a lot of Freeps have is clouding their judgment about the danger that is building. What good is the best intelligence in the world if it is not used to take precautionary measures? I didn't make much impact tonight on their thinking.*

When my day comes, things will be different!

Algo had me studying Freep wars for a reason. I've learned that Freep defensive strategy has worked in the past. Also learned that it costs Freeps dearly when an enemy surges deep into our territory. And there is always the thought that someday they could go too deep. Too deep to get them out. I'm not studying Freep wars anymore.

From now on, my mission is to make my home, the Freep Nation, tougher.

———

Six weeks later Joe was recovering but anxious to get going again. His pal Jasper had gone back to watching and Joe had a lot of time on his hands. Rod tried to keep him occupied. One afternoon he arranged for Freep strategy advisers from the Strat Team to brief Joe on survival in the future. Joe was in an infirmary office with three of the advisers. He was surprised to see Dojay among them. The other two were Daniqa, a bookish but clear-eyed and athletically built woman of about forty, and Wilbur, a short, jovial man of mixed race. He was dark, but it was not obvious where his forebears came from. On Algo-Net were another five advisers in other desert locations.

"Hi, everybody," Joe said. "I've been trekking Freep Nation for months, seein' things at ground level. I'm looking forward to hearing what your big-picture outlook is."

Daniqa said, "Welcome, Joe. Glad to be helping a guy who put a lot on the line for us."

"Thanks, Daniqa. So much I want to know. What is the secret to Freeps' surviving and growing?"

Daniqa said, "Dogged defense that makes invaders pay dearly for attacking us."

"Without heavy weapons or fighter aircraft?" Joe asked.

Wilbur said, "We are what used to be called a guerrilla force. Mobile, dispersed, hard to find. We fall back from attackers and harass their flanks and supply lines. We have no capital city or national treasures to capture and loot. It is not worth the blood and money for Mainstream or most other enemies to campaign in what they consider an undesirable and unrewarding place."

A voice came up from afar. "Razmik here. Joe, you have seen how we farm and make airplanes, et cetera. It is pretty small scale, dispersed in many small operations, and not very visible from above."

"Anjar here," chimed in another voice, female this time. "Survival always depends on unity. Unity depends on people living and working together. Freeps move around a lot to different parts of Freep Nation to work and get familiar with people there. Barriers bred by distance and tribal thinking are knocked down. It is a never-ending job to find ways to encourage unity. Algo-Net is a catalyst that keeps us together."

"Yeah, Joe, Raz here again. Algo-Net is totally free and open for those who seek knowledge of history or science or who want to be entertained with literature, music, and drama. As you know, we talk to each other on it, and we keep hackers out with one hundred percent encryption of everything. In a threat situation, Freeps can coordinate defenses without fear of being listened to."

A shrill voice popped in. "Nort here. Joe, my ideas are a bit different from the usual Freep philosopher prattle." The others groaned. "One reason we Freeps are still here is that we are too poor to build offensive weapons. That keeps us out here in nowhere. Another reason is that we really attract a lot of smart kids from Mainstream. They're stoked by a chance to work on the world's best computer system. Our Algo-Net keeps evolving faster than any other country's cyber capabilities. Naturally, Mainstreamers don't want to bomb the shit out of us because they might take out their own kids."

Daniqa pounded the table and yelled, "Nort, you're wrong. Mainstream has attacked us and more than once."

Nort responded, "Well, OK, they had expeditions here a few times but nothing like how they keep attacking fuzzy wuzzies on the other side of the world. Shock and smash to the max."

Daniqa yelled again, "Mainstream could hit us again if we have something they want bad enough."

"We need more powerful weapons than our individual lasers. They are OK for taking out one person or a vehicle," said Frollet, a new voice.

"Something bigger is insurance against future unknowns," Nort said with begrudging acknowledgment that she and Daniqa had a point. "But got to do it on a shoestring."

Dojay raised his hand for a chance to speak. "Military hardware always gets more expensive with time. Software and digital stuff always gets cheaper. Go for the cheapest way to get the job done."

Joe popped up, "Got a cheap fix for you now."

His table companions looked at him in surprise. Voices on the net asked, "What's that?"

Joe said, "Put five Freeps together. Connect their batteries with microwave. Give one of the five a more powerful laser to shoot a beam five times more powerful than today's lasers."

Nort said, "Where'd you guys find a Freep with an idea?"

"Yeah, Nort," Frollet said. "You tell 'em."

Joe asked, "Do you guys always hassle each other like this?"

Anjar jumped in. "Gotta have conflict to force good ideas out of a group."

Nort said, "Ha! Anjar, you were preaching unity a few minutes ago."

"Stuff it, Nort," yelled Anjar.

Guffaws stopped, and the group froze when Algo's robotic voice said, "Joe, go to the laser factory and try it out."

"Roger, Algo. I'll hike there tomorrow."

"No, Joe, fly there. While you have a plane, fly over our southern border areas. Then when your doctor says you are completely better, trek to them to understand how what you see from above feels on the ground." No more was heard from Algo.

The meeting ended. *I guess*, Joe thought, *when Algo speaks, they figure there is nothing more important to say.*

Chapter 17
GIANT EARTHQUAKE

Joe was trekking on a mountain slope facing the Salton Seabed's west shore. He was on his way to several Freep sites in higher, cooler locations. He had seen them while flying above and was now visiting them, as Algo had instructed.

A jolt! It felt like he stepped on a loose rock. More jolts, more unsteadiness. He stumbled on the uphill trail, heart speeding up. "God! What the hell?" he said, as his weird unsteadiness worsened. A low growl came from the earth.

On the sloping heights above, Joe saw dust rising from a slew of little rockslides. "The mountain is shaking! Earthquake!" The noise from the earth ramped up from a faint rumble to a gnashing, crunching cacophony. "Goddamn! This is big!"

He looked uphill. The little rockslides were partnering with big ones. He looked anxiously to see if anything was rolling down toward him. Didn't see anything. The ground was shaking hard now. Fear clutched his chest. He forced himself to run ahead over the shaking ground to get in the shadow of a vertical wall on the uphill side of the trail. *This will give some protection from slides*, he thought and then lay down against the wall where it met the path. The shaking became intense, even vertical, at times bouncing him off the ground. His heart tried to pound out of his chest. Lying prone, he put his arms under his head to cushion it against hard rock pounding up at him.

He could hear rolling boulders loping down. He looked ahead, beyond the vertical wall that shielded him and saw rocks of all sizes smashing on the path. He felt the presence of death when he saw boulders rumbling by. The growling earth was joined by the thuds of those boulders bouncing down the mountain. He stuffed his body tightly against the high sidewall and the path to prevent the earth's shaking from jouncing him away from the protective wall and exposing him to the falling rocks.

It seemed like hours, but it was minutes—maybe three or four—until it slowed. The sounds of the rumbling earth tapered off. He lay on the ground, surprised that he could still feel a vibration from the bowels of the earth through his belly against the hard rock. It felt alive, vibrating and humming with the shaking peaking randomly and with enough energy that he wondered if it would start to shake hard again. It didn't—not then. The random peaks subsided.

When he stood up, he could see wisps of dust arising from rock slides all over the mountainside. His heart, still pounding, was slowing down. He got his mind under control enough to thought-message, *Algo, what happened?*

The returned thought-message, *Powerful earthquake along San Andreas Fault. Epicenter above the north end of the Gulf of California. Evacuate immediately from low-lying areas between the Gulf of California and twenty-five kilometers northwest of the Salton Seabed. Head for high ground. Tsunamis and flooding expected.*

The Salton Seabed was two hundred ten kilometers north of the gulf. Joe estimated that tsunami flooding from the gulf could take a couple of hours to reach it. Maybe less because from thirty kilometers below the border to the seabed, it was all downhill. He knew the water from the gulf would drop one hundred meters of elevation while flowing north to the seabed's lowest point. Then, like in a bathtub, it would slosh up the north end of the seabed, overflow the shore, and flow toward what used to be Indio.

Pulling his emotions together, he stood up and looked off to the east, toward the Salton Seabed. It was silent now. No wind. Dust clouds were rising along the sloping terrain in the trails of the big slides. In a maelstrom of thoughts and emotions, he started to sort things out. He checked Algo Net by sending in a thought-message, *Algo-Net, Joe here, reporting vertical quake movements over one G.*

Thanks, Joe, replied Algo-Net.

Joe thought, *OK, still works.* He had two days to go on this leg of his trek to an east-slope homestead and wondered if he should press on. Checking his elevation through Algo-Net, he found he was three hundred meters above sea level. He thought, *No tsunami wave will get this high so far from the gulf. I'll be OK, but there are others who may not be.*

He tried to reach Mary but was told that the comm systems were all dedicated to emergency uses. He thought of his folks in Mainstream. *A quake this big will be raising hell there. God, I hope they are all safe.* Couldn't get through to them, either. Calls to Mainstream hardly ever got through, even in good times.

Thoughts gridlocked his mind. *What can this calamity mean?* His instinct, based on months of Freep trekking, was to press on to his next goal. He thought, *What good does that do? Two days of trekking alone. A whole way of life could be fighting for survival as a result of this calamity. Can't make a difference if I'm trudging along by myself for the next two days. I must act here and now.*

He thought-messaged Algo, *A tsunami will be headed north, Algo. We have an hour or so before the tsunami waters hit the Salton Seabed. We must use the time. We have to get all our planes and drones in this area to search for Freeps in low-lying areas and pick them up, immediately.*

There was a pause. Algo thought-messaged back, *Joe, you are showing the judgment of a leader. I am putting you in charge of recovery from this disaster. You will have responsibility for health, welfare, and security for all Freep territories south of Mojave. You have absolute authority. Make it happen!*

———

Joe thought-messaged, *Roger, Algo, and out.* He looked out toward the Salton Seabed ten kilometers away—a shimmering, unnaturally white thumb print on the desert sand. He needed a minute to absorb the impact of what Algo said. Algo had given him power—a lot of it. Finally, he had the freedom to do what he wanted, the freedom to follow his dreams. He no longer had to chafe under the rules that had him following someone else's goals, someone else's dream or beliefs. This was his chance to do things his way.

OK, enough daydreaming, he told himself. He snapped back to the disaster he was living through with a call to Air Control. "Air Control, this is Joe."

"Roger, Joe, we were expecting your call. Algo alerted us that you are commander of the southern Freep Nation."

"OK, let's not waste a second. Get all your planes and drones in the air to pick up people in low-lying areas near the Salton Seabed. Fly them to high ground—well above sea level—and go back for more. Use Algo-Net to get locations of every Freep out there."

"Roger, Joe, we're on it."

"Air Control, after picking up endangered Freeps, send a plane here. I'll be flying over the affected areas."

Joe called Health Works and instructed them to put into action their emergency disaster plan to handle displaced and wounded Freeps.

Joe messaged the Algo-Net data section: "Send me reports on current quake. Focus on Salton Sea and northern Gulf of California regions. Also send historical data on Freep disaster response."

The earpiece voice said, "Quake data dropped in your computer." It paused for a short while and then said, "Ditto historical data."

Joe figured it would be at least two hours before he was picked up. He had to understand this situation better and welcomed the time to think and to reach out to others to build a team. He configured his beetle pack into a chair with a tentlike cover. In his cocoon, he projected computer images on the cloth screen before his eyes. With voice commands, he brought up one after another horrific scene picked up by satellite. The San Andreas Fault had let go; the earth had sunk in a swath along the fault from the Salton Seabed to eighty kilometers into the Gulf of California. He continually looked off toward the Salton Seabed. He wanted to witness the tsunami rushing north when it arrived.

The sink in the Gulf of California floor generated a huge tsunami. It began with water in the gulf dropping into the areas that had suddenly deepened as the bottom sank along the fault. Following the drop of the sea's surface, inrushing water caused a massive upwelling, with sea height peaking over a hundred meters. Then the waters flowed out in tsunamis, heading in all directions.

The earthquake-caused sink north of the gulf opened a breach from the Gulf of California through the Laguna Salada, a shallow empty sea South of the border, into the Salton Sea drainage area. Joe knew immediately what that would mean. The rampaging tsunami will wreak havoc in the next couple of hours, smashing its way with debris-filled water into the Salton Seabed and beyond. That will just be the beginning as water from the gulf of California following the tsunami will continue to flow north through the breach to fill a massive area of the California desert that now is under sea level.

Joe instructed the Strat Team to put some of its brain trusters on the question of how long it will take to fill the areas below sea level in the Salton Sea region. Half an hour later the Strat Team reported, "Joe, inflow of water to the north will continue for weeks. We'll give you an accurate estimate in twenty-four hours. We will account for variation in water-flow rates resulting from the extreme tides in the Gulf of California."

Joe asked, "How big an area will be inundated?"

"Joe, water flow through the breach will fill the Salton Sea to a depth of one hundred meters at its deepest. Around the sea, the flooded area will be about five times bigger than the current Salton Seabed. Five thousand years ago, the Gulf of California extended up beyond the Salton Seabed into a much larger body of water called

Lake Cahuilla. Now that ancient sea is returning and will drown everything under its reclaimed footprint."

From his high perch, Joe looked outside his cocoon and saw the occasional Freep air vehicle on a mission of mercy cruising along the seabed. He needed a break from the cataclysmic data flowing into his consciousness. He called Mary and got right through. "Mary, it's me. Are you all right?"

"Yes, Love. I'm rattled from the shaking, but the Health Works has minimal damage. Now I'm afraid of water reaching us."

"Don't be. I've checked your geography and data coming from satellites. You'll be high and dry."

"Thank you, Joe, for the good news, and before I forget, congratulations on becoming our leader," Mary said. "Where are you right now?"

"Right now, I am on a mountainside looking down at the Salton Seabed."

"It was so romantic there with you…"

"Whoa! I see it now through my magnifying optics."

"What do you see?"

"Water flowing toward the seabed from the south. It's black, full of dirt and debris—"

"Oh, God," gasped Mary.

"It's moving faster than I thought. Will probably cover the seabed in half an hour or so. Been flowing downhill till now.

"Joe, put me in charge of the Freep hospitals. I know I can keep them working through the surge of patients."

"Mary, I want to give you a bigger job—handling all health and social services."

"Joe, I don't want all that power and responsibility. I want to do something I love and will be good at."

"OK, you got it. You're in charge of hospitals. I'll call it in and make it official." Then he yelled, "Whoa! Damnation! Mary, you won't believe what I am seeing. The black water is entering the seabed...a broad river... looks like ten kilometers wide. Oh God, unbelievable what I'm seeing!"

"What does that mean?" Mary asked, fear in her voice.

"The tsunami's leading edge has reached the Salton Seabed and will move toward the north shore. Moving fast now, but it will slow down in the middle at the deepest point. Then it will flow toward the north shore—uphill all the way. Our experts don't think the initial wave will go much farther than the north shore."

Mary said. "We might not see much of each other for a while."

Joe, now looking in awe, said, "Our lives will change... forever. Good luck, Mary. Stay safe. I'll be thinking of you until we meet again."

"Bye, my love. You are always in my heart."

Joe felt exhilarated by the adrenaline charging his heart and mind. Still watching the black tsunami front moving inexorably north, Joe said, "Get me Shan at the Airplane Works."

A short time later, a voice came through Joe's earphone. "Congratulations, Joe. Didn't expect you to rise so high so fast."

"Me neither. Are you all safe at the Airplane Works? Any damage or injuries?"

"I'm OK. A few bruises. A lot of minor damage to planes under construction. Some injuries. No fatalities. Minor structural damage to the facility."

"Shan, I need you to help me. I need an executive officer to make things happen."

"Why me?"

"You know how to think strategically, you know a lot about Freep Nation, and you know the politics. Huge changes are ahead. There will be chaos and opportunity," he said. "Are you ready to help shape the future of our homeland?"

"I'll help you for six months, Joe. If Lon has come home by then, I'll help you as long as you need me."

Joe said, "Am I feeling arm twisting?"

Shan replied, "Let's call it encouragement. I think from your level you might get an insight into where a guy like Lon could be."

"You got a deal," Joe said. "Right now, I want you to school me on what and who are in my area. And I want you to make a complete damage assessment—preliminary in two days, final in a week."

"OK, Boss."

Chapter 18
TEAM BUILDING

Shortly after Algo put him in charge, Joe moved into an apartment at the Airplane Works' southwest corner. Coded locks were installed, making Joe's place unlike other Freep habitations. No need for locks in a crime-free society. His new digs included an office, a secure conference room, and an attached hangar for his owl-copter. Decor was spare: gray walls and utilitarian furniture.

"Freep Nation will be changed forever," Joe said to the Freep leaders he was Algo-Net conferencing with from his office. "As you all know water flowing into the Salton Sea today will overflow its shorelines and become like the ancient Lake Cahuilla that covered much of Southern California Desert. Despite setbacks and losses caused by this inrush of water, possibilities for improving our lives are enormous."

With these words, spoken three days after the Great Quake, Joe began a monumental program to develop the southern Freep Nation in its new geographical configuration. He said, "We must all be ready to contribute in a positive way to the challenges of the new era that have been thrust upon us."

There was little response. Joe figured it was too sudden, and everyone needed time to get their heads around the life changes they faced. He continued, "I want to talk to all of you again three days from now. We'll meet by the new Salton Sea so you can see for yourselves what is happening. I need your help and creativity. I ask you to think about our future and how you can contribute to it."

In the days leading up to the meeting Joe had to develop a plan that was robust enough to handle unforeseen changes in an unknowable future. His first move: five-year plans. Been done a million times. The first five years would be crucial. It would be a five-year crash program to transform the sea area into a thriving part of the Freep Nation. At the end of five years, Joe wanted to be advanced enough in his new direction that turning away from his goals would be near impossible.

He didn't know enough qualified top managers to feel confident in picking one to reach the herculean goals ahead, and he couldn't afford to make a mistake. So he put all his chips on himself as top guy. He would take personal command of the first five-year plan. But it was more than a one-man job, and he had to marshal a competent management team—mainly from the group he had spoken to last week on Algo-Net. And he had to earn enthusiastic support from these Freep managers to whom he was an outsider.

———

Three days later the Freep leaders were assembled with their beetle pack chairs in a semicircle facing Joe who stood with his back to the roiling black waters of the breach. He adjusted his helmet microphone so all could hear above the roar of the fast-moving water. Earlier he went among the Freep leaders, shook their hands, and spoke briefly with each one. Now they sat quietly waiting for him to layout his plans for developing the new sea.

He yelled, "Freep power!"

The crowd, surprised, hesitated a second and then responded, "Freep power."

"Freep leaders," he began. "You have flown over the Salton Seabed that is becoming a real inland sea. No stopping that. See all that muddy water flowing in? In a few months, the Salton Sea will be five times as big as the seabed is now. Then it will settle out and be blue again. What does this mean for us? That is what we're discussing today."

"Will it change our life here?" someone yelled.

"There will be big changes," Joe said. "I'll name a few: our new sea will be filled with fish from the Gulf of California. It will accommodate oceangoing ships, opening our Freep seaport to world trade. The climate will cool a significant amount. The large tides will be a source of electrical power."

Murmurs were heard throughout the crowd.

"I don't want to live in a beach resort," someone yelled.

"Yeah, me neither," another chimed in.

"OK," Joe said, "here's the deal. As soon as we free up people from our earthquake recovery effort, I am going to redirect them to develop the resources here and build the facilities for the Freep population that we need to claim this land as our own. There will be seashore settlements. With plenty of water reclaimed from the sea, we will expand our farms and export food.

"All new facilities will be operational in three to five years. There will be a lot of foreigners who want to visit our new inland sea. We will have a tourist program."

Joe stopped for a minute, turned and looked at the roaring water, and then turned back to the Freeps facing him. "Now, this doesn't mean we are abandoning Freep settlements in the southern Freep Nation. They will all be kept in operation because we will always need the products of those farms and factories."

Joe watched his audience carefully. Hard to read expressions of people with helmets on. But from their body positions and movement, he sensed that some liked where he was going, and others did not. He pointed toward the water roaring by.

"Teammates, even while the Salton Sea is expanding, we will begin to develop the area surrounding it. We'll begin immediately to reestablish a settlement near the abandoned city of Calexico. This will serve as our gateway to and from Mexico. We will be finalizing plans for two other towns, one at the north end of the enlarged Salton Sea at the former city of La Quinta and one east of the sea near the Chocolate Mountains."

Joe paused to let it sink in. A hand shot up. "Doesn't building towns violate the Freep philosophy of a dispersed community of many small settlements and production nodes?"

Joe responded, "You have a point. Freep life here will be different. That can't be avoided. To hold on to this godsend, this inland sea with all its riches and potential for improving our condition, we must protect it from predatory outsiders. The required level of protection can't be maintained with our scattered settlements and low population density. Think of it—there will be a big inrush of people who want to live here, do business here, and spend vacations here. We'll be vastly outnumbered."

"What does Algo want?" asked another.

"Algo put me in charge of recovery from the Great Quake. As you know, Algo doesn't put out detailed plans for future developments. That's my job. I am proceeding in accordance with my understanding of Freep historical adaptation to changes in its threat environment. My basic understanding of Algo's order was for me to spearhead recovery from the Great Quake. Nothing in that order said we couldn't recover and grow a strong, resilient Freep community on the shores of the Salton Sea. Evolutionary doctrine avoids breeding down into weaker societal structures. Evolutionary doctrine requires adapting a defense doctrine to provide survival in new circumstances."

"Freep culture will be destroyed if our concept of individual power, computing, and defense in a beetle pack disappears," claimed someone else.

"Yes, in time there will be Freeps who will live substantially un-beetled. I don't think this means an end to our way of life. There are ways to confront this problem. Right now, we are developing urban packs that look like ordinary clothes but that fulfill many beetle-pack functions. Our immense distributed computer will be preserved, as will Algo, our leader. There will also be work programs that recycle Freeps out of this territory back into hot desert areas where they will go back to beetling up.

"I've spoken with a few people this week who want to withdraw from the Salton Sea territory and leave it to others more willing to fight for it," Joe said. "I am sad to say these individuals were on our Strat Team. They don't all feel that way, but a vocal few do. Giving up our land without a fight is an invitation for future invasion. I will never do that. Right now, I'm formulating plans for Freep military forces big enough to fight off invasions by the Out-Lands gangs or Mainstream forces."

A questioner asked, "When do you expect their attacks to come?"

"Our best guess is that we'll get three years' peace while Mainstream and the Out-Lands recover from the quake. We could be hit any time after that," Joe said. "I intend to build up this area with all possible speed. Our commercial buildup will progress in step with our military development. Freep men and Freep women, I need your help. And I need it starting now.

"Some of you might not like it. I respect that, as the plan we are embarking on has been put together rapidly. For us to develop and defend this new natural treasure, we must begin now. Delay only gives time for our enemies to prepare to attack and defeat us."

Joe stopped talking and looked at his audience from one end to the other.

"Those of you who don't support this plan will be rotated out to live in northern Freep Nation, and new leaders will be brought in to replace you. You may leave now and fly back to your home locations."

Half a dozen angry Freeps got up and headed out. Minutes later, Joe saw their planes ascend and head north. The discussion between Joe and the rest of the Freep leaders continued into late afternoon. Joe's dynamism charged them with enthusiasm. He felt a connection with the Freep team before him. At sundown when they ended, he was confident that he could create a better life for the Freeps with the gifts from the new sea.

Joe was feeling good about the way things had gone, feeling good that only a few had walked out on him, when

Mary approached. She said, "Joe, you were pretty tough on the troops. Couldn't you have given them a few days to think things over?"

"Mary, I don't have time to coddle people."

"Well...I'm flying back now. My hospitals are bulging with new cases."

"Could we spend a little time together before you fly off?"

"No, Joe, some of my friends just got fired, and I am not in the mood for poaching."

It was not the time to try to convince her she was wrong. Besides, she wasn't really wrong. She was loyal to her friends, and he admired her for that.

Joe wanted to build a strong team in an emergency situation. Decisive action was needed and would be respected. He hoped Mary would understand someday.

He watched as she walked off. It hurt Joe to see his beloved beetle heading for home—with not so much as a good-bye.

———

Joe needed a plan to upgrade Freep military capability to resist their most likely invaders: the Out-Lands gangs and Mainstream conventional forces. Within days after his meeting with the Freep Leaders, he appointed two commanders: Jasper to command the northern half of the border territory facing the Out-Lands and Waxer to command the southern half and, to the south, Mexico.

He announced their appointment in a conference call with the Team. "Teammates, I believe Jasper has the aggressiveness needed to face down the Out-Lands and Mainstream threats. Really knows the terrain he'll command. Don't know Waxer that well, but he is experienced in organizing and mobilizing Freep forces. He has done it in prior conflicts. I need that kind of hands-on experience with command of large forces."

Daniqa interjected, "Having two commanders of equal rank will foster competition."

Joe said, "That's good for getting maximum efforts out of them. They know that someday one of them could climb to the number one spot."

Wilbur said, "But it could be bad if backbiting and politics set in."

"I'll keep a tight rein on them to keep them from getting out of hand. I plan to load those guys down with extra work helping with quake relief. Don't want to give them any idle time."

Chapter 19
AFTERMATH

The quake hit Los Angeles hard. Several downtown skyscrapers had fallen over or against adjacent buildings. Loss of life was high. After Joe couldn't get through to his folks for a week, he sent a stealth drone into the city at night. The drone made it through Mainstream air defenses without detection and landed on top of his parents' high-rise building. From it, a bird-sized drone was released to fly down to his parents' harbor-view window and attached itself to the glass. Joe's voice scared Mildred.

"Joe, where are you?" she exclaimed, looking around her living room.

"Mom, I'm talking to you through a bird drone attached to your window. I'm in the desert." He was in his office at the Airplane Works.

"I see it now, and it looks real. Are you safe, son?"

"Yes," Joe said. "Not much damage out here. Most of our buildings are one-story structures that can stand shaking pretty well. How is Dad?"

"He is OK. He has to stand guard at our complex fence to keep out looters. Those Out-Landers are getting more and more threatening. Everyone is running low on food, and the electricity is always going out. All the Marina men have been given guns and stand guard in shifts at our compound gates to fight off the mobs."

"Do you have a plan to get out of there in case of a general uprising?"

"Your father has the boat ready. He has getaway plans to go to Mexico."

Then Joe heard Horace say, "What's this I hear about Mexico?"

"Dear, it's Joe. He is talking to us through a bird on our window."

"What kind of crap is that? Talking through a bird."

"Dad, it's me, calling from the desert."

"Are you all right, kid?"

"Fine, Dad. In fact, I am in charge of getting this place up and running after the quake."

"Shouldn't be too hard." Horace guffawed. "Just tell those roaches to come out from under the rocks."

Joe laughed. "Look, Dad, I can fly you and Mom out of there from your building's roof and bring you here to safety."

"We're not going anywhere. Our Business Council says they are bringing in National Guard troops. If we have to leave, then we are taking my boat and heading south."

"OK, if you run into trouble in Mexico, you can cruise all the way around Baja and up to the top of the Gulf of California. There is a new river there that you will be able to cruise to where I live."

"OK, appreciate your offer, but I think your mother and I will be all right. I know people in Acapulco. I've got plenty of American cash. We'll be fine down there."

"The offer stands to fly you and Mom out. Every now and then I'll send in a drone anyway to see how you are doing."

"Your father has a plan, and I think we'll be all right," Mildred said. "Bye, Joe. Love you."

———

Joe called Algo-Net for a briefing on Mainstream conditions. He was surprised how good the intelligence was that was regularly linked in from Freep agents throughout Mainstream. Most quake damage was in LA and San Diego. Many bridge failures. Electrical power was erratic because of windmill failures in the Palm Springs area. Fifteen percent of windmills had been taken out. Joe thought, *Mainstream is incredibly vulnerable to windmill failures. This is a big ace in the hole if they come after us. Hope it never happens, but gotta be realistic.*

Checking further, there were reports of hungry Out-Landers attacking Mid-Level farms and factories. Extra troops were called in to suppress the uprising. Food shortages were worsening. Joe thought, *Might be an opportunity for us to provide food aid to take pressure off the Out-Landers to become refugees in Freep Nation and cement some goodwill at the same time.*

Joe contacted Chet, gym manager at the YMCA where Joe had lived. "Joe here, Chet."

"Great to hear from you, Man. Heard you're running things there."

"Yeah, Chet, I'm your boss now."

"Joe, bring me home. Out of this jungle. Things are getting pretty ragged here."

"Tell me more."

"There is a lot of looting. We're still on good terms with Juanacho's gang. They're still coming here on fight nights. They're telling us about rival gangs trying to loot around here. Our workers can't get through to most Mainstream sites. Mainstream isn't paying them either. We're carefully rationing food. Gonna get worse," Chet said in a worried tone.

"I'll bring you in, Chet, but first I want you to get with Juanacho. Tell him we want to remain friends with him. Tell him we'll provide food for his neighborhood. We'll drone it in, so tell him not to take potshots at drones flying over his turf."

"When can I—?"

"You can come home same way you got me out here."

"Too hairy, Joe. All the gangs are in open war with every other gang. They are starving and crazy, irrational. We had to go through three gang regions to get you out. It cost a lot of money then. Now money doesn't help; they want food, gas, liquor, and they won't guarantee safe passage. Only thing they have a lot of is ammunition. And a ton of frustration."

"How about you stay there two weeks passing out food and establishing a long-term relationship with Juanacho and his crew? Our delivery drones will land on the Y roof. Tell your Y administrator not to report drone deliveries, or they will be stopped by Mainstream. In two weeks, you will jump on a drone making a return trip, and we'll give you a top job out here."

"Will Mainstream shoot down drones?"

"Don't think so. I got one into the Marina yesterday. Didn't even get its hair mussed."

Chet said, "Mainstream has its mind on a lot of things with this disaster. Sounds like defense against your air force is not a big concern."

They laughed.

Joe said, "Got a point there, Chet. Our latest drones have a low-radar signature, are hard to see and silent. Even if Mainstream gets its air defense back up in two weeks, they aren't going to be seein' you flying east."

Chapter 20
RESCUE OF MARY'S PARENTS

Joe called Mary from outside the Airplane Works. He had beetled up and gone outside to stretch his legs and clear his mind after an intense all-morning briefing from Shan and Jasper.

When Mary came on line, Joe said, "Mary, I'm looking for good people to fill many positions."

Joe sensed a bit of coolness as she replied, "Joe, I'm up to my ass in alligators running the hospitals."

"What kinds of patients are showing up?"

"Precious few from the tsunami. No one escapes a tsunami. We are getting refugees from Mexico and Mainstream. Some Out-Landers, too."

"They in bad shape?"

"Heat problems mostly. A lot walking into Freep territory unprepared. We're saving most of them."

"Good. I want to put them to work."

"Joe," she implored, "show some heart."

"Trying to, but I'm faced every waking minute with decisions that usually don't have a heart option."

"OK, Joe, why'd you call? You know that kind of talk isn't buttering me up."

"I want to rescue your parents."

"That would be favoritism. As much as I love them and want them here, do you realize how you and I will look? Think of team morale."

"You got a point. If your parents aren't working their asses off at something crucial, I might be open to criticism. You, too."

"OK, I think I see where you are going…"

"They are experts in desert farming. They are smart and scientific by nature."

"You're smooth talking me…"

"They can be in charge of doubling food production, if they want to be."

"Get them, Joe," she suddenly sobbed. "And come and see me sometime."

"I'll get them." Then he softened his tone, "Can't be more specific when I can see you. Haven't forgotten…our times together. Love you Mary and long for you"

"Thanks for getting Mom and Dad. Your challenge is immense—and I am willing to wait for you, for whatever little bit of time you can spare."

"You've got a good heart, Dear. Gotta go now."

"Good night, Love."

Joe walked back into his command center. Shan and Jasper were still there, both looked exhausted. Joe said, "I'm convinced more than ever that we can crank up food production by getting farmers to work more intensively. Right now, I want you to cut back ten percent on Freep food rations. I need more for immediate export.

"We need more coordination of food production instead of farms producing autonomously. I'm bringing in a couple of smart people who were banished to a Mid-Level farm near Fresno over twenty years ago. They're Mary's parents. They'll be key to increasing food production and becoming a food exporter. I believe this will strengthen our security because, with a dependency on Freeps for cheap food, our neighbors will be less inclined to attack us.

"Mary's parents don't know they have this job yet. First, we have to rescue them from a Mid-Level farm. I believe they'll be motivated to work for us in the glow of their newfound freedom and a chance to live near Mary, their only child."

———

Joe contacted the commandant at the farm where Mary's parents lived. He used a bird drone so as not to leave a traceable signal path. Nothing had changed; for a price, anything could be arranged. Joe agreed to pay twenty-five thousand units and twenty bottles of whiskey to ransom

Mary's parents. The Freep treasurer provided the twenty-five-thousand-unit ransom packet for two "high-value" immigrants. Whiskey was gotten at a Biker border swap.

Joe flew a high-tech owl-copter north a couple of hours and landed on the bare ground of the Mid-Level farm compound. A group of guards gathered around as the commandant came forward and looked at the owl-copter approvingly. Off-duty farmers watched from behind the guards.

"Like to have one of them things," the commandant said. "Cain't see 'em coming, cain't hear 'em, and all of a sudden there it is—landing right in front of ya and blowin' sand in yer face."

Mary's parents were standing nearby. Guards blocked their way forward toward the owl-copter.

Joe climbed out and stood by the copter door. He looked exotically strange beetled up with his helmet face shield down. He said, "There are more at altitude above us."

Both he and the commandant looked up. No copters could be seen or heard in the clear blue sky.

The commandant leered at Joe and said, "Your bluffin' because you're here by yourself. Tryin' to scare me so I don't take your money and keep your tricky copter and your roach suit."

Joe said, "Got you zeroed in. Your goons, too."

"Izzat right?" sneered the commandant.

"Look at that boulder." Joe pointed to a boulder ten meters beyond the fence. The commandant turned in the direction Joe was pointing in time to see a blinding flash from above blast the two-meter-high boulder into a pile of glowing fragments that started weeds along the road burning. Startled, the crowd jumped back. All eyes turned back to Joe and the commandant.

"OK, Bug Guy, you made your point," the commandant said with a forced bravado in his voice. He beckoned to Mary's parents; the guards got out of their way. "You're forgettin' something, ain't ya?"

Joe said, "You'll get your money and your whiskey when we're all sitting on board. Stand clear."

The commandant backed up several paces and put his hand on his pistol.

Joe said, "Pull it, you're charcoal." He took a large box out of the copter and set it on the ground nearby. "There's your whiskey."

Mary's parents climbed aboard. Joe got in last, his eyes not leaving the commandant. The rotors spun up. Joe closed the cockpit door behind him and tossed a packet of bills through the window to the top of the whiskey box. "There's your money."

The smoke from the burning weeds was cleared out by rotor downwash. Joe thought-commanded the owl-copter to fly at top speed back to the Health Works. It cruised away silently, leaving the farm crowd watching in open-mouthed amazement and their commandant counting his money.

Joe turned to Mary's parents, thinking, *They look skinny and tired, with their short gray hair.* They looked older than he'd imagined. He gave them an engaging smile. They shook hands. "I'm Joe."

"I'm Jason."

"I'm Jade."

He could tell they weren't comfortable climbing out and flying above the arid Central Valley, and he wanted to reassure them. "This is our new owl-copter. Very advanced and safe and, as you have probably noticed by now, as quiet as a barn owl swooping down to nail a mouse running through the hay."

"Oh." Jade shivered with fright. "Please don't swoop down to nail anything."

"Don't be alarmed. We're on a comfortable, straight, and level flight path." He handed snack packs to his passengers and didn't tell them he had added relaxation powder to their fruit juice.

"When will we see Mary?" Jason asked.

"She'll be there when we land in two hours," replied Joe.

"I can hardly wait to see her," Jade said. "How do we thank you?"

"It's all in a day's work, ma'am," Joe said in an exaggerated Western drawl and with a mischievous grin.

As the flight continued on into a hazy afternoon, and everyone got to know one another better, they traded stories about farm life and what the parents might expect from Freep life.

Joe mentioned he had learned a lot about their backgrounds from Mary and eventually led into how he was trying to double Freep food production. The parents were amazed by Joe, who obviously was at a high level in Freep government—if he was trying to double food production—and how he personally came to fly them out of captivity.

Joe allowed as he and Mary were good friends. From her, he told them, he had learned about their academic backgrounds and their many years on the farm. As they were approaching the Health Works and their reunion with Mary, Joe told them he needed people with their mix of talent to plan and develop ways to rapidly increase food production. Joe also spoke of the Salton Sea as a source of water for farming.

Nearing the end of their flight, Joe sensed Mary's parents were interested in becoming part of the food-production program that would benefit people who migrated to Freep Nation for a better, freer life. Joe didn't mention how he also planned to use food for export to gain currency reserves and to leverage the Freeps' meager power to counter threats of hostile neighbors. He didn't want to get into too many bruising realities at their first meeting.

The owl-copter settled in softly at the Health Works. Mary was waiting there beetled up. She turned away from the blowing sand from the rotor downwash. Her parents jumped out of the copter and hugged her tearfully, not caring that the beetle pack made her look insect-like. Joe thought, *She looks so beautiful with that blissful smile.* He bid them good-bye. The newly liberated parents looked confused and happy. Mary hurried them inside, out of the scorching heat and into a new life.

———

Joe headed for home, filling the time aloft by conferring with his team on recovery progress. With a month gone since the quake, the outside world was cleaning up and making the first steps toward recovery. The news was spreading that the Baja breach would greatly expand the Salton Sea. Joe predicted that, as the sea filled, there would be more interest in it from outsiders. He called Waxer and Jasper. "Joe here. Waxer, give me an update on your border traffic."

Waxer said, "Starting to run into outsiders wanting to see the Baja breach."

"What kind of people?"

"Some are academic types from Mainstream. We let them fly in our planes over the breach for a high price. We are keeping Bikers out of Freep territory, even if they wear air-conditioned leathers. I think we are going to fight them someday, and I'm not giving them reconnaissance opportunities."

"Good," Joe said. "Right approach. Your job is to guard land from the border to one hundred kilometers north of it on a line roughly fifteen kilometers west of the new western shore of the Salton Sea when it fills up. As quake-recovery troops become available, use them to build up a force of fighters big enough hold off invading Out-Landers."

"Understand," Waxer said.

Joe said, "Jasp, what's happening?"

"I have less rescue and recovery work to do than Waxer. Tsunami didn't get far in my area. I'm building up a defense to repel Bikers at the northwestern end of the Salton Sea."

Joe interrupted, "Jasp, in addition to border protection, I want you to practice war-gaming with the new owl-copters."

"Roger, Joe."

"One last thing," Joe said. "The flow of refugees will increase from all directions. Don't let Bikers in unless they're injured, give them food and turn them back at the border. Mainstream refugees and Mexicans refugees are OK—we need workers at all levels to farm and rebuild."

Joe landed at the Airplane Works, worn out from the long day. He called Shan. "Let's have a bite in the cafeteria and talk. I want to discuss Lon and where he might be."

"OK, I'll meet you in the shower."

That's odd, he thought, *but I could use one to relax*. He went into the steamy room and was washing away desert dust when she came up to him out of the hot clouds of steam and said, "How about a shampoo?"

"OK..." He tried to say more but couldn't. *What a bod!* She had never pushed sexiness, but she was coming on like gangbusters. With her standing nude before him as he leaned his head forward for her to scrub, he took it all in—her firm ivory body was exquisite. She went to work massaging suds into his scalp, and he felt a surge of warmth and excitement.

Her mouth was close to his ear, and he heard her say, "Don't talk about Lon's whereabouts." Then a spray of water to rinse away the shampoo, and her mouth was close to his ear again. "Don't talk about Freep intelligence operations. I will tell you when and where we can talk."

He didn't like being told what to do without any pleasantries. He was the boss and wanted to set her straight about that, but he held back on rebuffing her. She had much experience in the intelligence world and might have a good reason for whatever the hell she was up to.

She beckoned him to follow her into a massage room. Walking away, he took in her glistening body from behind, and his irritation disappeared. On the table, her massage went beyond therapeutic; she had her way with him, and he forgot about who was boss. Lying there depleted, he heard her ask, "Will you come to my condo cave after we have a bite to eat?"

He said in a firm tone, "Shan, I gotta talk to you on a number of serious issues."

"Joe, we can do it there." She looked him in the eye. "Promise?"

He thought she might be trying to manipulate him, but decided to do things her way, at least for now, to find out what he could learn from her.

He felt guilty about Mary saving herself for him, and now, shortly after saw her, he and Shan had poached.

"OK, I'll come over for an hour. That's all the time I have."

They had a quick dinner in the cafeteria with half a dozen members of his team. He told them of the rescue of Mary's parents. He and Shan left with a crowd of curious eyes following.

They took his owl-copter for the one-kilometer flight to her condo cave, located under a pile of boulders. It was a couple of rooms with a scattering of alabaster windows and skylights. Shan said, "In daylight, the alabaster glow lends a mystic ambiance to this place. At night, I use light-display images to suit my mood or provide background for research." She gestured toward a bare wall and kaleido-scopic shapes appeared and slowly morphed into a calming Atlantic sunrise.

Joe said, "I like your getaway hut. It's got a welcoming feel about it." Joe looked around and then back at Shan. "Now brief me on the Baja breach."

"Do you mind if we have a hot walk while I fill you in?"

"No problem. I need some heat and a little exercise."

They took their packs and shirts off and walked in their gray shorts down a path that gradually dropped out of view of the condo cave. Bright moonlight illuminated their path. While walking, Shan said, "Freep geologists and hydrologists predict that the Salton Sea will grow by a factor of five in forty to fifty days."

Joe said, "That will change our climate, won't it?"

"I have them working that, too," she said over her shoulder, which was starting to shine with sweat as she walked down the path. "They generally agree it will be cooler near the sea." The 130-degree air kept them walking at a slow pace until they sat down at a little table well out of sight or earshot of her condo cave, facing each other and glistening with moonlit sweat. She continued, "It will be cooler because of evaporation from that large body of water. And there is the possibility of injecting water into the air by windmills or mile-high pumping towers to create clouds and rain for further cooling."

"Shan, this new sea can be the salvation or destruction of us Freeps."

She replied, "You're right."

Joe said, "I am determined that it will be the salvation." The moonlight showed intensity in Joe's face that matched his words.

"You can make it happen, Joe, if you have the stomach for fighting the predators who will rise out of nowhere to seize what the quake gave us."

"Appreciate your frankness. I know I've got the stomach for the job as long as I know who my enemies are—and who my friends are."

"Aha...You're coming to why we're here, Joe." He could see a hint of her smile in the dark.

"The reason you poached me in the massage room?"

She chuckled at that and continued, "We are not wearing our packs or any digital devices. There is a big rock between my condo and us. Here, we can talk about Lon and talk about Freep intelligence."

"Because no one can listen in?"

"That's right, Joe, because no one can listen in—not even Algo. Algo couldn't hear us in the shower. I had to get you away from buildings, airplanes, beetle packs—away from anything electronic. I had to get you here to talk in secret."

"Jiminy Christmas, Shan, you mean Algo was tuned in when you and I were poaching?"

Shan laughed, "Algo doesn't care about what people do with their gonads. But Algo is concerned about key people getting into relationships—falling in love, as they used to say. Algo thinks strong love commitments distract key Freeps from their goals."

"Why's that?"

"Algo has learned from observing humans for generations. Observing that lifelong commitments between men and women were stronger than commitments to Algo. For top jobs, Algo wants one hundred percent commitment without any romantic loyalty shared with another. Joe, it's OK if you and I have a casual in the shower, as far as Algo is concerned. I had to get Algo off guard to talk with you and hope you didn't mind."

"Beginning to understand," Joe said, frowning.

"Like your calls not reaching Mary?"

"Yeah, stuff like that."

Shan said, "Keep in mind, too, that there is no chief of intelligence in Freep Nation, but you can get first-class information. Algo-Net supplies intelligence information if you call up and ask for it. You'll get it right away—except for some requests."

"Like what?" Joe asked.

"I can't find out where Lon is or if he is ever coming home. I've asked Algo-Net—even put in thought-messages to Algo. Can't get a straight answer. There is no individual in charge of intelligence that I can call. I've tried everything." Her eyes welled up. "Find him for me, Joe," she said, with a look of pleading. She turned away, turned her firm breasts with rivulets of sweat coursing down them away from his gaze, and they headed back to her little hideaway. Moonlight glistened off her back, and her shorts darkened in places from perspiration flowing down her body.

Chapter 21
ON THE BORDERS

Joe flew back to the Airplane Works wiser about the rules of the game he was now playing. He went to his conference room, getting right to work to fill the emptiness that sneaks in on him at night. He turned on the wall screen and said, "Algo-Net, brief me on Freep border-crossing points."

Algo-Net started the briefing with a map showing illuminated Out-Lands gang territories bordering the Freep Nation. For each territory, there was a border crossing. Algo-Net said, "There are a dozen crossings facing gangs to the west. We do business with peaceful gangs. We exchange food for cash or other goods that we need. Our agents in Mainstream sometimes come and go through these crossings. And we get Mainstream escapees, like you."

Joe asked, "Do Freeps ever trade in weapons?"

Algo-Net said, "No...Well, let me clarify. We've bought Mainstream weapons in small quantities for testing. We don't allow Freep lasers, beetle packs, or cyber gear out of Freep Nation."

Joe said, "Come on, Algo-Net. No security is perfect."

"Joe, you have a point. But keep in mind that if a beetle pack with its laser gets out of here, it can't be used without a coded signal from Algo. Algo knows who is wearing each pack and only sends an enabling signal if its assigned owner is wearing it. Algo hasn't ever let an outsider use the beetle-pack capabilities.

"By the way, Joe, not all gangs are friendly, but we stay in contact with them at their border crossings."

Joe asked, "Why stay in contact with them?"

"We sometimes exchange prisoners or return bodies after fire fights. With all border contacts, good and bad, we look for intelligence information."

"About what?" Joe asked.

"Mainly about threats."

"Threats?"

Algo-Net said, "We want to know about raids, kidnappings, or incursions on land they want to annex. We always have our ear to the ground. Always looking to see if something is brewing. We want to be ready."

Joe said, "Tell me about southern border contacts."

"Freeps have had good relationships with the Mexicans. They let us enter Mexico freely, and from there, we can go anywhere in the world. The tsunami wiped out some of the crossings, but one still exists near Mexicali."

Joe asked, "What's our biggest issue on the borders?"

Algo-Net said, "Right now, food shortages."

———

Joe had been meeting immediate commitments to feed people displaced by the quake by cutting back on Freep calorie intake. Not a popular move. Joe ate in a different cafeteria every day and rallied Freeps with pep talks about their duty to feed the hungry. Freeps responded well, seeing his willingness to share their hardship. Joe assured them that food rationing would be temporary, as Freep food production was ramping up.

Every day, Joe was aloft, flying from place to place to see Freeps rebuilding. For weeks, he flew alone to check as many Freep locations as he could squeeze into a day, to keep morale up and speed reconstruction. Although he was in contact with the Freep world through Algo-Net, he missed having another person to talk to while flying from site to site. He decided Rod was right for the job—enthusiastic and dedicated—a true-blue Freep.

Flying above the Salton Sea on Rod's first day with him, Joe asked, "What do you think about developing our inland sea into a new frontier?"

Rod said, "That'll bring a lot of outsiders in here. They'll want to screw around fishing and drinking beer. That's not our way."

Joe replied, "We need more people to settle around our new sea and develop it."

"They could be a danger to our culture. They haven't been through the trekking and austere living that bonds us together."

"I hear you, Rod. But the danger of doing nothing is much greater. This inland sea will be magnet for those who want to grab its natural resources and its energy."

"Energy?" Rod asked.

"Tidal energy through the Baja breach. Those tidal currents can drive undersea turbines to generate plenty of power. Not as vulnerable as windmills or solar cell farms either. My plan is to get there first and develop it. At the same time, we'll increase Freep defense forces to send a message that we'll fight for it."

Rod laughed and said, "Sure ain't easy leading a quiet back-country life when the seashore catches up with you."

"You're not kidding."

They laughed.

———

Joe's plane approached the Salton Sea's southern end. He contacted Señor Trinidad Luz. "*Hola*, Señor. Can I buy you lunch?"

"Ah, Joe, my friend, please fly in. I need your advice."

At Señor Luz's hacienda, prevailing breezes blew through misters exhaling clouds of atomized water to cool the shaded patio. Joe and Rod left their beetle packs in the foyer and sat down with Señor Luz for a work-packed two-hour lunch. "Joe, how can we work together to bring back the northern gulf towns?"

"Trini, we dredge the Baja breach deep enough for oceangoing ships to reach the Laguna Salada Harbor in Mexico and the Salton Sea Harbor in California. We install inexpensive tidal turbines in the breach and sell power on both sides of the border. I got tech guys designing prototypes right now."

Señor Luz said in a serious tone, "We've had towns along the gulf totally wiped out, Puerto Peñasco, San Felipe. Right now, many of my people are without work, struggling to stay alive.

"Joe, you know water from the breach goes through one hundred sixty kilometers of Mexico to improve things for you. It must provide as much of an improvement for Mexicans as for Freeps."

Joe considered Señor Luz's tough opening salvo for a few moments and then said, "I'm expanding our food production and can deliver some food relief right away. We can take sick and injured for medical treatment. And I need workers to build new greenhouses for farming. I can pay your workers what we pay our workers, which isn't much."

Señor Luz said, "I want you to build as many green-houses for me in Mexico as you build for the Freeps, and I want our people to learn your power-generation technology."

"That's a lot, Trini. What do I get in return?"

"You get a guarantee that international shipping will be allowed safe passage up the Gulf of California and through the Baja breach. There will be no tariffs imposed on your imports and exports. We take care of any shipping channel dredging south of the border; Freeps handle dredging north of the border. You get a continuation of the open border and the good relations we have now with the Freep Nation."

"Will you help us if we get attacked?"

"Yes, we'll help repel anyone coming through Mexican territory."

"Sounds good," said Joe. "Let's put it on paper and sign it."

"Ha." Señor Luz laughed. "You want it all on paper?"

"Not everything, Trini. Can you and I talk for five minutes?"

"Of course, my friend. Let's walk through the fountain garden. It is cool and private."

They strolled through arching fountain tunnels, away from his nosy beetle pack, where they would not be overheard. "Trini, as you know, we have intelligence agents who go from the Freep Nation to other nations. Many go through Mexican border stations."

"They have for a long time, Joe."

"I'm looking for an agent who I believe went on foreign assignment and hasn't returned. His name is Lon. We would like to see anything you have on him."

"We will investigate through our intelligence agencies. By the way, Joe, we think you might have spies from the outside in Freep Nation."

Surprised, Joe said, "We do? How do you know?"

"Sometimes Freeps come across at border-crossing points and buy a telecaller. They make calls and then throw them away. Freeps return after doing something that can pass as a reason to go to Mexico. Shopping, prostitution spas, restaurants."

"Trini, can you track them?"

"We're on it and will give you a list of people and contacts."

"I don't talk about spies when I have my beetle pack on." Señor Luz looked surprised. "The pack can listen to me and watch me."

"I understand, Amigo. I'll be discreet."

———

Leaving Señor Luz's hacienda, Joe and Rod flew west along the Mexican border. Joe marveled at the silver sun reflection from the Baja breach as they passed over it. The water sliced through land that sunk when the Great Quake shifted the earth's plates at the San Andreas Fault.

Once the flow had started, it carved channels where the downhill track to the Salton Sea was steepest. The Laguna Salada dry lake once again filled and presented a forty-kilometer bulge in the path of the breach that otherwise ranged from two to eight kilometers wide. Now that the flow from the Gulf of California north had stabilized, Joe's engineers were planning the dredging operations to clear channels deep enough for shipping.

They flew beyond the breach for half an hour and landed at a higher elevation than usual for Freep habitations, on a rocky clearing one thousand meters high. Waxer was there to meet them. Joe wanted a firsthand report on border traffic from the guy in charge of its security. Waxer, a handsome Ethiopian, explained that Indians who lived there at the higher altitudes could survive without personal air conditioning much of the time. They adapted to climate change better than others, drawing upon the cultural memory of their forebears who lived in the deserts for millennia before Europeans arrived.

Joe, Rod, and Waxer walked to the Indian border post. They sat down with Chief Humming Bird and two lieutenants in a small meeting room. Chief Humming Bird, middle aged with medium build and a tired face framed with two long braids of black hair, came right to the point, "Since the quake, our income has plummeted. Not many Mainstreamers are coming to gamble. Nothing like it used to be."

Joe said, "We don't use money at the people level. It's mainly for foreign travel and trade. Right now, we don't have much to help you out."

"Joe, it's not money; it's Bikers. They are getting into the protection business, and they want us to give them a protection contract. We had to lay off most of our security staff because of the quake. If we don't give those Bikers a contract, they'll probably try taking us over."

Joe said, "I would like to have a casino on the shores of the new Salton Sea."

Chief Humming Bird looked concerned and asked, "You want us to relocate there?"

"No, build and run a casino for us. We don't know anything about that kind of business. In return, Waxer here will put in troops to defend your casino and resort."

Waxer looked surprised and asked, "Why me?"

Joe said, "I want you to get your troops bloodied. Get them battle experience fighting with the Bikers. Chief, I need you to get some skin in the game, too. I want you to match whatever troops Waxer provides, man for man. These are tough times with unrest all over. We won't be able to support you without that commitment."

Chief Humming Bird looked at Joe. "I want to talk with my men for a few minutes."

The three left the room and came back in twenty minutes. The chief said, "Joe, we need food. I can't do this deal unless we get food for our people."

Joe said, "We're increasing our food production. With the new sea, we'll have fish. We make a deal now: you get a food shipment tomorrow—and continuing until you are back on your feet."

"OK, Joe, you got a deal."

Aloft again in the owl-copter, Joe said, "Rod, I want to see what a hostile border crossing is like. Find one where a contact will be made tomorrow morning and take me out there. I want to be part of it."

The next morning, Joe joined a convoy of a five electric-powered, wheeled cargo carriers with Freep troops driving and guarding the vehicles. He got on board the lead vehicle ten kilometers before the rendezvous point. He had heard that he could expect Funt to be in charge there.

As the Freep convoy approached the point, the Bikers came into view. Twenty of them stood by the red line spray-painted across the rotted concrete of old Route 10. Funt stood before them, facing the Freep convoy as it stopped ten meters away.

Joe dismounted and walked alone to where Funt stood. Funt told Joe, "I haven't forgotten you—ain't finished with your ass."

Joe responded, "Watch your mouth. You're in my crosshairs. Anymore shit from you, and you're all fried." Joe turned and ordered the cargo carriers to drive in reverse to the red line.

When they reached the line Funt ordered, "Unload." Grubby, jean-clad Bikers shuffled forward, unloaded crates of foodstuffs, and placed them in trailers behind their motorcycles. Funt checked off the delivered crates on his clipboard. He approached with a packet of bills and handed them to Joe with his arm fully extended. Joe extended his arm and, with eyes on Funt's face, took them.

Funt said, "This isn't the last you'll see of me, roach man."

Joe grinned. "I'm looking forward to our next date."

Chapter 22
FOOD PRODUCTION

The next day, Joe met with Mary's parents at the Health Works. He flew there without Rod. Gave him a day off to relax and see his girl. Joe met with Mary's parents in a consultation room. They were apprehensive as he sat across from them.

As Joe was getting down to the reason he was there, Mary dropped in with a cheerful "Hi, everybody."

Joe said, "Mary, I was about to ask your folks to help out with something big."

Mary said, "The big food program?"

"Yep."

Jason jumped in. "Joe, you told us you want to expand food production substantially. Is this to cover extra mouths to feed caused by the earthquake or to restore damages to your farms?"

"Yes, to both questions. And beyond that, I plan to use food exports to cement good relations with allies and to improve our foreign exchange capability."

Jade asked, "What do you need us to do?"

Joe replied, "Right now our farms operate autonomously, using Algo-Net to find out what is needed, and then the harvested products are picked up and distributed by drones to locations selected by Algo-Net."

"Isn't that expensive? Flying instead of trucking goods to the end users?" Jade asked.

"Not really," Joe said. "You see, Freep solar-powered drones are cheap to manufacture. They fly under automatic guidance, so we don't have to pay a pilot. No fuel costs either; they're solar powered. Only takes a few people to handle software for distribution and scheduling. Don't have to build roads, buy trucks, or pay truck drivers to get our products to market."

Jason said, "In our time here, we've seen many of the homesteaded farms and their aeroponic growing spaces. How much more production do you envision?"

Joe said, "I need your help to answer that question and to manage how to get there. Right now, we have people on our borders who need food. I took care of their immediate demand by cutting our own rations by ten percent. That's a temporary fix, obviously, because Freeps weren't fed anything extra to begin with. I'd like you to see if we can squeeze more production out of our current facilities, either by increasing grow-lamp power to shorten the time to harvest, adding water or fertilizer, or any other way you can think of to use facilities more intensively. Next step is to build new greenhouses for large farm operations by the Salton Sea."

Jade said, "But that's salt water."

Joe replied, "We'll use solar-distilled water from the sea. We'll have plenty of free energy to distill water and pump it to our farmers. We manufacture all greenhouse equipment here in Freep Nation. We can make massive increases in production."

Mary said, "All this means our way of life will change."

"Yes, there will be changes away from a subsistence culture." Joe was visibly excited about the picture he was about to paint with words. "Here's why: the enlarged sea is cooling our climate, and we will further increase cooling with active seeding of the atmosphere. That means people can live near the sea without beetle packs. Our tidal turbines in the Baja breach will provide immense amounts of free power, allowing people to live in larger, up-to-date houses—not the tight quarters we now live in.

"This southern desert became unlivable over the last two hundred years. That's going to change. Because it won't only be Bikers in search of plunder. Mainstream will want to come here, too. We're going to have to fight to hold on to it. We've got to populate the area around the Salton Sea to establish a claim that we live there. We need money to open up trade to cultivate foreign allies. And our farm exports will bring in that money."

Jason and Jade were raptly focused on Joe while he spoke. Finally, Joe said to them, "Will you two manage our food production expansion? I'm asking you because you have unique backgrounds. Both of you are university trained and know how to plan and organize something that hasn't been done before. Both of you spent many years on a Mid-Level farm and understand the aeroponic technology we use on our farms."

"We need to think it over. This is so sudden," Jason said.

Joe stood up and said, "OK, I'll be back in half an hour."

When he returned, Mary and her parents were still deep in discussion. He saw in their faces that they had questions and concerns. An intense discussion followed. Joe sensed things were going his way after an hour of answering question as best he could. The parents, starved of meaning in their lives on the farm, realized that the project they would manage would take Freep living standards to a new level. They felt a resurgence of an earlier idealism, a chance to do something for the society they lived in by bringing Freeps a more bountiful life. Joe had to assure them that the increase in food production would not finance aggressive military action, except in defense of the Freep Nation.

Mary watched her parents' eyes widen under Joe's spell, with his face so full of earnestness and enthusiasm, and was happy for them. She was proud when Jason finally said "Joe, we'll do it." And they all shook hands. They celebrated with a round of fiz water and happy powder.

Chapter 23
THE CONNECTION

The earthquake caused thousands of injuries in Los Angeles. Mainstream's emergency-response teams were taxed beyond their capability to care for the injured. Horace was drafted away from his job as the Marina Tower's property manager and put in charge of emergency field hospitals located in tent complexes in a dozen city parks. His new job, coupled with shortages of needed supplies, had him at his wits' end.

In desperation he went before Mainstream's highest level of government, the Business Council. Two hours waiting in the anteroom had him frustrated, which put him in a nasty mood.

When it was his turn to present his petition, he was barely capable of suppressing his anger. His face was red, and veins bulged on his forehead. "You gentlemen know our hospitals and emergency teams are overwhelmed by casualties. You've got an army sixteen thousand kilometers from here. They have been there fighting on and off for over a hundred years. You've got to bring medical units home from the Mideast to man our hospitals. And you've got to bring troops home to fight off terrorists attacking my friggin' neighborhood."

The Business Council chairman, a silver-templed, tanned man in his fifties, regarded Horace with unfeeling steel-gray eyes and said, "Listen, you had a good run managing that marina; now it is time for you to do some real work. You clean up this health-care crisis, and you'll be rewarded by getting your Marina job back. Right now we need you where you are—and we expect you to use market-driven solutions to improve efficiency and do more with less."

"Market driven, my ass," Horace shouted. "When your Mid-Level farms and factories were under attack, you brought troops home to protect them. They weren't market driven. They were driven to protect the wallets of every one of you on this council."

The chairman listened impassively and said, "Your concern and strong reaction are understandable. And, in fact, we are bringing more of our forces home from the Middle East. We are beginning to see an enemy closer to home that we have to confront."

"What enemy is that?" Horace asked.

"This is classified information now," responded the chairman. He continued in a conspiratorial voice. "So don't spread it around. Our strategic planners see Freeps as a gathering threat."

Horace banged the podium and yelled, "What have the Freeps done to us?"

"It's their potential for danger. For generations they have attracted our bright young people. They have taken advantage of naturally rebellious teenagers to lure them to their squalid existence. They lure them with promises of all kinds of freedoms. They offer them a life of personal indulgences instead of our ideals of home, success, and God."

"Well, so what," Horace said, thinking of his own son throwing in his lot with the Freeps. "A few of our kids go there, but they haven't invaded us and never will. Those kids can come home whenever they want."

"Don't be so sure," chimed in Mainstream's defense minister. "Everything has changed since that quake. That inland sea is now a reality. It makes them a nation with a first-class seaport. Climate at the Salton Sea is cooler now and can be made even more so with active sky tech. That land will prosper—and it rightfully belongs to California. It belongs to Mainstream, and the sooner we take it back, the better. In time it will become more populous; it will become richer and more powerful—able to fight back. We should take it while it is still easy to take."

"We can barely beat Out-Lands' gangs now," yelled Horace, glowing with anger. "How can you think of invading another place? I'm freakin' about my neighborhood getting overrun. We're fighting them two blocks from where I live. I'm freakin' about hospitals unable to handle people coming in every day, and you want to start a war. Are you out of your mind?"

"Relax," the chairman said. "You've got a point. We have problems." He looked around at his council members. "Our defense team has already begun to build an invasion plan, but we won't attack for at least two or three years. Got a lot of rebuilding to do in Mainstream first and alliances to build with some Out-Land gangs." He returned his attention to Horace. "Short term, I am going to assign more help to you in your hospitals. We will give you half of what you requested and expect you to work smarter to make up for the rest. Next petitioner."

———

Horace didn't expect to get much of anything, so getting half wasn't so bad. Hearing about Business Council's plans to invade Freep nation was a jolt, but he couldn't let on that his son was in a command position there. Couldn't afford to lose another job, or he would end up there himself. He said, "Thank you, council members"—as he was expected to and left. The elevator carrying him up from the command bunker to ground level was full. When he stepped out and headed for the subway escalator, a young Asian man fell in next to him and asked what train went to the Marina.

"Come with me," Horace said. "I'm going there."

"Great," replied the stranger. "Don't know much about that part of town."

"I live there," Horace said. "We're lucky the Marina train is still in operation."

On board they found adjacent seats. The stranger told him that he was a representative of the Far East Trading Company and was in Mainstream looking for reconstruction business. His name was Lon. He offered to buy drinks at the Marina bar.

"After today I need a few drinks," Horace said as he drained his third.

Horace found Lon fascinating, even though after two hours he had learned little about him. He told Lon about his son, Joe, who was a big shot Freep. Lon showed an interest and said he would like to contact him. "Give me your card. Next time I hear from Joe, I'll pass on your contact info."

"Appreciate that," Lon said. "Please ask Joe to contact me at the offshore number on my card."

Lon said good-bye and left to meet a colleague at a Marina restaurant that Horace had never been in. Horace thought, *Young crowd, too rowdy.* He walked unsteadily toward his condo tower and had a good feeling about Lon. *Personable, well-spoken young man.* he thought, *Could be a good influence on Joe. Maybe even get him out of the desert for a decent job with an offshore outfit.*

Horace walked toward his building gate. He thought again about Joe, *Too soon for Joe to get a situation in Mainstream. Got to leave that one alone for a couple of years. Even then, gonna be some ass kissing and fence mending to make that happen—when they find out he was a Freep. Shoot! Lon might even get me a job. Hate that friggin' hospital stuff they stuck me in.*

The sentinels at his condo tower let him through its heavy metal gate.

"Elevator out, sir, saving power."

"Twenty-six floors. No big deal," Horace said sardonically with an alcohol slur. But it was a big deal, trudging up twenty-six flights, with a long stop for breath at every floor. He thought, *Stairs dirty and littered. Marina life turning to crap.*

Chapter 24
MARY'S TEAM

Got to pinch myself to know it is real, she thought. *Managing a whole hospital system, caring for an avalanche of sick and wounded.* She gave herself twenty minutes to grab dinner. *This is a big job. The most people I have ever managed before was twenty-five. Got fifty or sixty hospitals and infirmaries to run. Not even sure how many. I don't have time to learn; casualties are pouring in.*

She sat at her usual table, and soon Vernu and other colleagues appeared with their trays of food. Vernu said, "I've had enough with administrative paperwork telling me when patients are ready for work again."

Mary ate quietly, but sitting there eating and listening to small talk made her feel guilty that she was wasting time. She had to think and act at a high level of information and decision making.

Right now, she thought, *I've got to get to work.* She stood up. Her colleagues looked after her questioningly. They were wondering why she was so reserved after a big promotion. She walked to another table where the building manager was sitting. She sat down and said, "Sorry to bug you at dinner, Taj."

Taj asked, "Is it urgent? Something that can wait for a little while?"

Mary said, "No. I need you to give me a private apartment tonight."

He started to respond, "Well, that is not so easy—"

She cut him off. "If you can't handle it, send me your replacement to do it."

Taj's face glowed red, and he said, "Don't worry, I'll take care of it."

"Also, Taj, I'll be bringing a few more people in to be on my staff. Please fix them up with living quarters. I need a dedicated command center with communications and display equipment." She got up. "I'm taking a walk now. I'll see you in an hour to see what you come up with."

"OK, boss lady. See you then," he said, with a look that could have been a look of grudging respect—or a look of almost-suppressed malice.

She beetled up, pulling her pack on with a momentary flashback to the first time she had struggled into the beetle-shaped provider of energy that made life possible. It was much easier to beetle up now. And with a great challenge confronting her, she felt secure and comfortable in the last light of day trekking under the emerging stars to get her mind calmed down and her thinking straight.

Her attitude became buoyant as she took in the desert's eternal beauty. She thought, *Stay calm, attached to the earth*. With her beetle pack flowing cool air around her body, her spirits soared. *I can do this*, she thought. "I can make a difference."

Fifteen minutes put a kilometer between Mary and the Health Works. She was feeling a natural high when she got an inspired idea: call Algo. *Sounds crazy*, she thought, *but I need a good team immediately, and I don't know many people who can handle extreme pressure.*

She pressed two buttons and thought-messaged Algo. A return thought imaged two eyes peering directly at her through a haze in her brain. She thought she heard, *"Hello, Mary."*

She thought-messaged back, *Hello, Algo. I need six good people on my hospital management team to head up our earthquake medical response.*

Algo thought-messaged back, *You have the authority to recruit them.*

She shot back, *No time for a recruitment fair, Algo. I want them tomorrow.*

Algo chuckled…at least, she thought she heard a chuckle, and then a clear list popped into her consciousness with six names on it. Taj was one—the others she didn't know.

She thought, *Is Taj OK?* remembering his ambiguous look an hour ago.

Algo thought-messaged back, *Taj is OK. Be firm and be fair. If you can't be both fair and firm, be firm.* Then Algo was gone from her thought space.

Walking back to the Health Works, she felt good—charged up. Wasting no time, she switched on Algo-Net and contacted each of Algo's recommendations. She briefed them as much as she could about what their responsibilities would be. Tomorrows morning's meeting would provide each time to define his or her mission in detail.

Back inside, seated in a Health Works conference room, she contacted in turn all sixty hospitals under her command. Each came up on Algo-Net. They all told the same story: their planes and drones were bringing in injured Freeps in an increasingly fast stream. Her mission was clear: provide a surge in personnel, equipment, and supplies in time to save a lot of humans whose hours of life were inexorably running down. Working all night, she finished watching the morning sky offering up majestic cumulus towers, rim lit by the cerise sun disk rising behind them.

———

She met her six-person team at nine. They were in the conference room when she showed up, hoping they wouldn't notice she was nervous because most of them were older than she was. She hugged each new teammate, then learned their names, and found out what they did and where they were located.

They sat down at the conference table. She said, "Thanks, team, for coming on short notice. You have all been highly recommended, and I need your help to handle an onslaught of casualties." She turned to Taj, "I'd like you all to meet Taj, my executive officer."

"Thanks, Mary," Taj said, appearing composed and strong, as she wanted her executive officer to be. He didn't disappoint, going on to explain his program for coordinating emergency care through Algo-Net. "I will be using a decision program on Algo-Net that collects all demands on our system, such things as casualties and treatment needs, and then finds such capabilities as doctors, operating rooms, et cetera. Algo-Net decides the best connection of patients and services."

The rest of the meeting was devoted to the other five members of her leadership team defining their areas of responsibility. Mary was happy that Algo had come through with the six good people sitting in front of her—a solid team that had hit the ground running. They left for their home sites at dusk, all except Taj. She knew they would work together well, because as Freeps, they were aware their lives were close to the edge of their environmental tolerance and their resources so meager they couldn't waste energy in pointless conflict. She was in a crucible, teamed with top talent who for years had been determining the health of their culture and their civilization. She accepted her role with a feeling of excitement and acceptance of a worthwhile mission in life.

She hoped she could share her journey with a loved one, with Joe. She would see him occasionally, and those times would be heaven. Why couldn't she see him, well... every day? Logically, she thought as they increased in experience and knowledge, they should be able to find a way to manage their lives and spend more time together—even live together. Even living together half the time would be OK because, as things were now, it was far less than that.

Chapter 25
FUNT REBUILDING

Six months after the quake, a phalanx of Bikers rumbled through Riverside. Funt rode up front, flying his barred triangle flag. They passed crowds of down and outers among collapsed and damaged buildings. The homeless filled parks and empty spaces with tents and makeshift shelters. Smoke wafted skyward from cooking fires. Fear and a sense of imminent danger permeated the yellow-tinted air.

Funt thought, *Right now they want protection. Someone to keep them from killing each other. Like the Middle East. They'll follow a powerful leader who'll protect them. As long as they don't starve, they will follow—and they are not starving yet—but they might not be that far from it.*

Funt was riding the Biker bar circuit looking for re-cruits. First stop: Bushwhack Bar. He drove to an orange pickup truck in the middle of the parking lot and jumped up onto its bed, surprisingly agile with his new prosthetic foot. He looked right and left and gave a clenched fist salute in both directions. Got raucous cheers from more than a hundred Bikers in return. When they quieted down, he said, "Brothers and sisters, never kill the goose that lays the golden egg. OK, we all know that saying. Right?" The crowd stayed quiet, puzzled. "Well, we are living by it."

What the hell was he talking about? They wondered what Funt would say next.

"Gonna give you an example of not takin' out the goose." Funt looked around and heard chuckles and snorts. Then he continued, "There is a Mid-Level farm north of here. Got attacked by Los Gringos, a local gang. Mainstream couldn't fight them off—too busy with a thousand brush fires they're pissin' on—and they asked us for help. We attacked Los Gringos from behind. Picked off a bunch of them with our snipers, and they quit fightin'. Fargin' bunch of pussies.

"Now we protect that farm and get twenty percent of everything that farm raises, every year. That's how we feed our Biker friends here in Riverside. And that ain't all. Got cash, too—upfront payment. So ya see, we didn't kill no goose. We protected it." Approving hoots and whistles. Funt paused and looked around for effect. "To celebrate that victory, Bushwhack Bar is serving you free booze, pills, and food for three days. Party's on me."

Cheers erupted, and excited crowd murmurs filled the smoggy air.

Funt raised a hand and waved in recognition of their hearty applause. "Now, let's get down to what we're all here for. I got a big contract with Mainstream to patrol around their windmills. They got security there, but they want us to patrol a couple of kilometers farther outside the fence. An added layer of defense. It's them fargin' Freeps causing trouble. They want us to take 'em out on sight."

Someone yelled, "They got lasers."

Funt said, "Our sniper gear can take them out up to six kilometers. They will never get close enough." He paused for a moment. "We need ten of you from the Bushwhack and a couple of mamas to keep them lucky boys happy."

Funt pointed toward a huge Biker sitting on the orange pickup's tailgate holding a clipboard. "Sign up with Big John here and wear the barred triangle proudly." Another pause, while he looked around. "Don't sign up, and I burn this dump to the ground."

Funt jumped down, mounted his dull black steed, and kick-started all five hundred horsepower. Ear-splitting noise and sparks erupted from its pipes as he roared off with his troops scrambling to keep up.

They hit three more Biker bars. Funt gave the same speech at every one and then headed back to his headquarters. He got all the recruits he needed for the windmill contract.

Biker headquarters was a jumble of single-story buildings in a deserted industrial park. Located in the higher elevation of the Banning Pass, it was not as hot as the scorching lower-desert areas. In the middle of the complex was an airstrip and aircraft hangar. Funt and his top five crew members went into the hangar and then through two code-protected doors to an inner conference area. They kicked back after a long day on the road, digging into beer and barbecue served by nearly nude "interns"—girls with the barred triangle tattooed on one buttock.

"I'll make it brief," Funt said. "Our gang is gettin' bigger. We need to find more protection business to pay for our operations—and my new castle. Mid-Level farms or factories are fair game for you to sell protection to.

"It's a new game now. We are getting along with Mainstream—not like the old days when we were ripping them off and getting our asses bombed in return. They got revolts all over the Out-Lands, wherever their Mid-Level settlements are located. They need protection. Our prices are high, but Mainstream farms and factories are willing to pay."

Funt gulped down beer and mouthfuls of meat. He continued, "We're doing great, but it's only the beginning. We're going to increase our business and our territory for a couple of years. I want you to keep fighting with other gangs. Take their territory where you can without too much loss to your own crews." Funt looked each in the eye in turn. "Don't take on the Freeps. I'll take personal command of that operation when the time comes."

The crew, slurping beer and munching hungrily, nodded in agreement.

One asked, "What happens after a couple of years?"

Funt replied, "We attack the Freeps. We'll have the strength to hit them hard. Mainstream's backin' us. We're going to invade Freep lands; Mainstream will follow up and help occupy the place. Mainstream's giving us the guns, ammo, and vehicles we need. Right now, they're also giving us food to keep us from starvin' until our farm-protection business gets a full head of steam.

"That's enough for now. Grab an intern and party on. Be ready to ride at eight in the morning."

Chapter 26
CHANGE AGENT

Soon after the quake, Joe directed all factories and farms to prepare for big changes. He told them to produce enough food and beetle packs to handle tens of thousands of refugees. He was relentless in bringing managers up on Algo-Net to brief their progress at his morning meetings. Anyone not meeting goals was given help, wanted or not.

Manager changes had to be made, and they weren't always easy, especially in cases of popular managers who weren't performing well. Sometimes changes were made abruptly, without the spirit of patience and understanding that underpinned life in normal times. They were in survival mode, and Freep welfare came before individual sensitivities.

Joe frequently called the Strat Team for advice. Their realistic and sometimes ornery feedback kept him from getting too far away from the Freep close-to-the-earth existence. And ominously they were beginning to spend more time warning of the threats outside their borders.

Joe's Airplane Works command center was little changed from six months ago when he established it; its offices were utilitarian and plainly furnished. That was OK with Joe. He was fully focused on developments at the Salton Sea. Didn't need trappings of power—just the latest in communications and display technology in his conference room.

The Freep's recovery from the quake was rapid. There was solid progress on the first five-year plan for the Salton Sea area. Salt water conversion plants, greenhouses, and power turbine construction projects at the seashore were underway. Plans for Joe's Citadel, which would be the seat of government, and a hospital, which would be the Freep's main health facility, were nearing readiness. Both these projects would be located along the eastern shore of the sea. A casino would be build on the western shore.

———

On this afternoon Joe was experiencing that good feeling from being caught up and finished with his day's work. His team had all left for the day. The sun was dropping behind gray clouds that matched his gray walls. He found rare solitude with no calls waiting from his many projects, and his gaze drifted off to the west, catching glimpses of the setting sun sneaking through the cloud layers.

Then it happened: a pair of eyes burned through the horizon clouds after the sun dropped out for the day. Algo's eyes! They were accompanied by a friendly thought-message, *Hello, Joe.*

Joe thought-messaged back, *Hello Algo. It's been a long time; must be six months.*

Algo thought-messaged, *I see activity on many fronts and observe rapid progress.*

Joe thought-messaged, *Our quake recovery is proceeding well. Freeps had a solid infrastructure to begin with. It was a matter of expanding rapidly to handle the increased migration and the expansion of health and food services.*

That's good, Joe.

My challenge now is to adapt to changes caused by enlargement of our inland sea.

Algo though-messaged, *Change comes with both bad elements and good elements. Make sure you recognize the difference and proceed accordingly.*

Algo abruptly disappeared from Joe's thoughts. Joe grinned and said aloud, "He didn't even say good-bye."

Joe went to the shower to relax and was accosted by Shan. Wordlessly, she brushed her soapy body against his and whispered her invitation. They bonded together in the massage room, exploding in a torrent of repressed energy that had to be released.

Odd, he thought, as they flew to her little abode, *having explosive sex and then talking about serious things. Usually it's other way around.* After walking bare chested into the nighttime heat, they came upon their big rock and its total isolation.

Shan asked, "What have you heard from Lon?"

Joe said, "Lon contacted me in an indirect way."

Shan, puzzled, asked, "Indirect?"

"Yes. He befriended my father in Mainstream at, believe it or not, the Business Council headquarters. My proud father bragged how his son, Joe, was a Freep big shot heading up quake recovery."

Shan listened intently with sweat dripping off her nose and chin and running down between her nubile breasts. "Can you get word to him, Joe? Can you tell him I love and miss him?"

"Better than that. I'm flying him back here next week to see if his Asian supply company can help with our recovery needs."

"You're joking," she said, standing up and motioning him to go back inside.

"No. I'm bringing him here for that reason—recovery help—but I think he might be working for Freep intelligence, spying on Mainstream's Business Council, and I'd like to talk with him to see if he can bring me up to speed on what they're up to."

"Oh, Joe!" she squealed and gave him a slippery hug. He took a step back.

"Before we go back in, I want to tell you that Algo contacted me."

"Didn't say much, did it?" she said with a wry grin.

Joe laughed. "You know Algo is a man, or perhaps a woman, of few words. Said change can be good or bad. That was about it."

Shan looked at Joe seriously now. "Algo wants you to carefully analyze its cryptic messages and do the right thing in accordance with evolutionary principles."

"That's all you can tell me?"

"You must learn how to figure out Algo's gist yourself," Shan said. "In your position, you can't have others trying to figure out Algo for you." She stepped aside and motioned with the smallest nod toward the path. "Getting pretty hot out here. Can you lead the way back?"

Chapter 27
RECOVERY AND DEVELOPMENT

A year after the quake, Joe's commanders were still helping refugees who trickled into Freep territory. But their main job was bringing their new commands up to strength and training them for combat.

Joe told engineers at the Cyber Station and the Airplane Works to come up with new weapons. On a conference call with them soon after the quake, Joe had said, "We need to anticipate new attacks. Use threat analysis to optimize your weapons designs. One thing I want is for stealthy owl drones to fly over a force of approaching vehicles and blast them with lasers with every shot targeted on a vehicle with no duplication or gaps. I want a one hundred percent kill probability."

Pradeep spoke up. "When do you want this new capability?"

Joe said, "I want your first war game in six months. Anyone who doesn't think they can meet this objective, tell me now."

Pradeep gulped, "Cyber will be ready, Joe."

"This is Otmar at Airplane Works. We'll be ready."

Joe had been right about Mary's parents. They attacked production problems on multiple fronts. They established a zero-waste program for food producers. They sent audit teams to all Freep farms to search for unused capacity and put it to use. They installed and upgraded grow lights to accelerate growing cycles. Among homesteaders and farmers, they became familiar and respected colleagues.

They oversaw design and construction of seashore greenhouses on both sides of the border and water distillation systems that provided fresh water. They were often on the construction sites in their beetle packs, which they wore with pride.

Joe juggled a hundred balls at any one time. This earthquake-driven opportunity that had dropped at his feet could not be ignored. He picked it up and ran as fast as his driven heart would propel him.

He had to take this new sea that flowed to their doorstep and put it to work. He had to settle their new seashores with enough people to stand against predators, be they Mainstreamers or any other power that might claim a right to colonize this Freep territory using that time worn excuse that it was sparsely occupied and unproductive.

In spite of a crushing workload, Joe found time to take Mary for airplane rides. They flew in Joe's owl-copter, letting it cruise in lazy circles above a landscape of burgeoning Freep colonies while they poached. They surrendered to the atmosphere with bodies locked together in surges of ecstasy driven by the plunges and lifts of afternoon turbulence.

———

Two years after the quake, Salton Sea construction projects were distinctly noticeable from above. On its east shore, Joe's Citadel was rising. Its white-wedding-cake form made a clear statement: power lives here. Not far south of his Citadel, another white structure was underway: a new health center and hospital.

Across the sea, a casino foundation was taking form, planned to open a year after Joe's Citadel. Checking out its construction from above, both naked and relaxed from making love, Mary said, "Joe, I get an uneasy feeling looking at all that construction."

"Uneasy?" Joe turned from looking at the seashore below to face Mary at his right.

"Yes, the plans are all terrific, but as I see buildings rising, I see this part of Freep Nation moving away from the special simplicity and community that Freep life is based on."

Joe said, "It was about two years ago, when Algo put me in charge of health, welfare, and security for all Freep territories south of Mojave."

"I know, Joe, and I'm so proud of all you've accomplished," Mary replied with a smile.

"Mary, I could have interpreted this order from Algo as a recovery operation to care for injured and starving refugees pouring across our borders and then, after a year or two, gone back to my wandering, trekking around in a beetle pack." Joe looked off to the mountain silhouettes backstopping a carpet of vibrant desert sands. "I could have interpreted it that way—a minimalist way—that would have been in keeping with how Freeps usually approach things.

"I thought long and hard about having an international body of water here. I asked the Strat Team and other big-picture thinkers if Freep business as usual could coexist with our new reality. I pressed them hard to break out of comfortable thinking and confront ugly threats lurking out there. All agreed attacks would happen. It was only a matter of time. No one advised me we could hold it using our defensive retreat strategy because now an invader has a powerful incentive to hold on to this prize."

Mary listened intently as Joe told of his decisions that would shape the Freep Nation's future. She said, "Why do you need such impressive structures? Your Citadel, hospital, and casino. I hear Freeps saying they are afraid of losing their culture. They value a close-to-the-ground existence with only their next Normalizer fighting off its drabness."

Joe responded, "Historically, Freeps have existed without much contact with the outside world. Now with this inland sea, itself a natural wonder, there will be great interest in traveling here. With many business, vacation, education, shipping, and fishing folks coming here, there will be a need to house them, meet with them, and provide them recreational facilities. Traditional Freep population and production dispersion are not a good fit. We need to build towns to accommodate our people living and working here and also people coming here to visit or do business. And we need the economic vitality of these towns to pay for more security forces and defense."

Mary said, "I hope you are right."

"You know about Algo telling me to study Freep wars."

"Hated it, didn't you?" she teased and kissed him.

"It finally sunk in. West of us is an unhealthy three-way symbiosis of Mainstream, Mid-Level, and the Out-Lands. Together, they are an unstable threesome that needs violence and misery to continue to exist. Evolution has stopped for Mainstream and its unhappy partners. They will always be dangerous and medieval in their thinking."

"Does that mean they will always try to hit us Freeps?"

"Always have and always will," Joe said, "unless attacking us will result in such severe retribution that it is not even worth trying."

Mary said, "But Freeps aren't good at offensive war."

"Right you are," Joe said. "We are going to raise infrastructure destruction to new heights, and we're doing it cheap: Hacking into key systems, spies, cyber attacks, owl-copters, and deadly small drones. And we are doing it without masses of our troops invading on the ground."

"Is this evolution, Joe? As Algo looks at it?"

"Algo doesn't tell us. But I think it is," Joe said. "We will be adapting to changes in our environment and trying not to repeat past mistakes."

Chapter 28
PENETRATING MAINSTREAM

Lon stood alone on the roof of Marina Towers, where Joe's parents lived. His meeting with Joe's father after the quake had led to a friendship and to Lon being invited for occasional dinners. Visiting them gave him a reason to get past the Marina Tower's security and access to the roof stairway. There, in complete darkness, an owl-copter materialized and touched down with only downwash noise to announce its presence. A cockpit door opened, and Lon jumped on board. Didn't bother him to be alone with no one driving. Pretty common thing in his business.

He pulled a seat restraint across his lap and felt the drone's upward heave into the coastal clouds. Lon flew "clean"—without any electronic device that could reveal to Algo-Net where he was. And now he was winging east to Shan and their bondage games.

After a night and day of excruciating and ecstatic love play with Shan, the two of them met with Joe behind the discreet boulders near Shan's condo cave. Joe asked Lon to get mini bots into the Business Council's inner chambers, so Freep intelligence could listen to their plans and also so Joe could talk to them directly. Lon asked Joe, "Why do you want to talk to them directly?"

"Lon, we've been setting up a means of destroying Mainstream infrastructure. This has been done quietly."

Lon said, "Freeps have been laying that groundwork for years."

"Using mini bots?" asked Joe.

"You'll be happy to know we have already infiltrated the Business Council with them."

Joe said, "Damn! You guys are top notch."

"Surprising how smart those ants are."

"Lon, I want you to know we have Juanacho's gang well trained with our gun drones. These drones are small, and we can swarm them into Mainstream to shoot up anything an infiltrated sniper can hit."

"Smart planning, Joe."

"When a need arises to sabotage Mainstream, I want to tell them it's us doing it. What good is our capability of wrecking their infrastructure if they don't know who did it? What good is it if they don't realize how devastating it will be for them?"

"Makes sense, Joe. Old thinking was that we would destroy their infrastructure if they invaded us, not for prevention of an invasion."

"You got it."

Lon had a voice that was deeper than seemed right for his boyish face. His easygoing personality and quick laugh appealed to both men and women. There was something about him that appealed to Algo, too, because he had been recruited into Freep intelligence service in his early twenties. In his overt role as a Chinese manufacturer's rep, he cultivated friendships at the Business Council's highest levels. In his covert role as a Freep spy, he picked up important intelligence for Algo-Net analysis.

Joe brought Lon back to Freep Nation every month. On Lon's trips home, he briefed Joe about Mainstream's top-level thinking, particularly as it affected Freep security. It wasn't much different from what was available on Algo-Net. That reassured Joe about the quality of Algo-Net intelligence.

Joe learned that Mainstream thinking was heavily focused on reclaiming the new Salton Sea in collaboration with the Bikers. Making that possibility more ominous was Funt's rapid rise to the top of the Biker world. Joe was convinced the Freeps had to prepare for all-out war.

———

Six months after Joe first brought Lon home, Shan appeared in the shower when Joe was there. She sidled up to him. "Can you give me a back scrub?"

"You know you've got me, standing there in your birthday suit. Turn around."

Joe took his time soaping her back and smooth buttocks and then scrubbing gently with a loofah. They disappeared in the steam to a massage room where they poached and then Shan, as before, invited him to her condo cave for a night-air sweat.

Out there behind the big rock in the roasting radio silence, Joe said, "I'm surprised you wanted to poach tonight—Lon's coming home frequently now."

"Joe, Algo wants you unattached. I'm poaching you for your sake and for Mary. If you were only poaching her, Algo would take more aggressive measures to spoil your love for each other. Algo thinks we are here to poach and that is good for you—and me, too."

Joe said, "Weird."

Shan continued, "I have another reason for wanting you to be here. I want to help you understand the rules of the game for those like you who are climbing to the top.

"Following Algo's rules, you can attain power but never get personal fulfillment beyond being a Normalizer sport. For your fulfillment, you and your loved one must find time and space to be out of Algo's cognizance. And you must be aware of the tricks Algo is capable of playing with those who have power that rivals his."

Joe tried to grasp this startling revelation. He took in a deep breath, put both hands to his face, and squeegeed sweat away. "Why is Algo like that?" Blinking a few times, he finally found a steady gaze and looked into Shan's eyes as if trying to find something more than she was telling him.

"Joe, Algo is an evolved product of human experience. Algo has unmatched power to select a correct response for any challenge that arises, taking into account historical, social, and biological forces at play. I have no argument with Algo's use of evolutionary rules to underpin its reasoning. But Algo does not experience emotion as we do. This is where Algo gets heavy-handed, because emotion is nuanced and sometimes contradictory."

"Let's cool off and let my head stop spinning," Joe said. He stood up and turned toward the path back.

"A last thought before we emerge back into Algo space," Shan said, as she hugged him from behind to stop him. He stopped and waited for her last thought. "Algo can alter intelligence information you receive from Algo-Net. And Algo's information changes may not be for the good."

"I hear you," said Joe. He thought, *What she is saying— is it weirdly true? Or simply weird?*

"Do you believe me?" she asked playfully and gave him couple of jolting squeezes with her strong arms.

"I'm trying to." He hesitated. "But it's tough. Tough and downright depressing because I've believed the greatest part of Freep life is that all collected information is put on Algo-Net for anyone to use unfiltered. When I came here, I likened Algo-Net to drinking from a primal spring of pure knowledge after a life of drinking from a faucet tainted by any number of adulterants like chauvinism, religion, advertising, prejudice—"

"Joe, Algo keeps our info ninety-nine-point-nine percent pure, but Lon and I have noticed from our experiences in the spy world that Algo will do whatever it takes in situations it considers to be matters of Freep survival—or of Algo's survival."

She withdrew her arms from around him and said, "Let's cool off and have a powder for the road. It's been a heavy discussion, and I want you to go away with that happy, devil-may-care attitude I've always loved about you."

Chapter 29
WAR GAMES

Well over a year after the quake, Joe was talking with Waxer and Jasper in an Algo-Net conference. "Guys, quake recovery has bought us time because our enemies had a lot more damage to recover from than we had. They have been busy rebuilding. But don't think they haven't been planning to attack us."

"They're gonna want to invade us," said Waxer, "when they see how our inland sea has changed things for the better. Especially that casino." He laughed aloud.

"You've got it, Waxer," Joe said. "Got to anticipate what happens next."

Jasper said, "We're in a high state of readiness. We've enlisted thousands of refugees to bulk up our troop strength. They are trained in our way of fighting with lasers and hiding in the terrain. Our owl-copter force is almost ready."

Joe listened patiently to his guys as they proudly described the fighting forces they had developed from scratch. Then he broke it to them. "Get ready for war games."

"War games?" Jasper said. "You mean like kids play?"

Joe responded, "There will be both computer simulation and live fire exercises."

Waxer said, "Why now, Joe? Freeps survived a long time with a simple defensive strategy."

Joe said, "I've studied our history of resistance. It worked against invaders who were not motivated to conquer and hold Freep territories. Mainstream invaded to convince their people they had an external enemy that needed its ass kicked now and then. They always withdrew a year or two after invading. Heat and lack of war trophies worked in the Freeps favor. And you know all about Bikers: small attacks by thugs looking to rape and pillage. True believers will put down roots in an empty desert—not Bikers."

Waxer persisted. "Today we have a hell of a lot more trained troops to face potential invaders than we ever had."

Joe said, "Our intelligence reports that the Bikers have been supplied by Mainstream to carry out extensive operations in our land. Your own watchers have observed and captured Bikers with effective air-conditioned suits. Mainstream gives them food, fuel, and ammo—all they want. Mainstream recently gave them armored personnel carriers. We need massed firepower to meet this threat."

Jasper asked, "But why war games?"

Joe said, "Gotta practice to teach your battle controllers how to use a cloud of owl drones to wipe out Biker attack formations."

Waxer asked, "When do we start?"

"Tomorrow. Got a top gamer named Chertikoff. He put together a simulation of our Southern California battle space. He's gonna put you two through the paces. Gonna see how you handle invasions and how well you work with each other."

"Work with each other or play games with each other?"

"Jasp, you're joking now. But you won't be after Chertikoff runs you ragged. He'll hit you with invasions from different directions and by different players. He'll speed up time so that you two have to fight off a three-day invasion in an hour. You'll be evaluated after each exercise. Chertikoff will throw as many simulated invasions in a day at you as you can stand to see how you hold up when exhausted. It won't be play."

Waxer and Jasper were quiet.

Joe continued, "We meet again in two weeks. Plan for live fire maneuvers based on what you have learned from the war games."

———

Junk vehicles of all kinds were found in the desert for use as war-game targets. Air Control sent in heavy-lift drones to haul them to the gaming area. A week later, Joe had these wrecks of motorcycles, dune buggies, and various other long-abandoned iron carcasses arranged to simulate an enemy attacking in a phalanx five kilometers long and one kilometer deep. They weren't moving but would still challenge Jasper and Waxer's abilities to use Algo-Net's attack-management process in a live-fire exercise. Fresh from simulation training with Chertikoff, Jasper went first.

Joe cruised above the gaming area in an owl-copter. "Jasper, I'm at fifteen hundred meters and waiting for your exercise to begin."

Jasper, calling from his mobile command center, said "Roger, Joe. I see you on my screen. Our operations will take place at altitudes between three hundred and twelve hundred meters."

"Are all your drones in place now?"

"Some are up and orbiting, others flying in from their bases. Crossing the forward edge of the battle area in ten minutes."

"Are they attacking in random formation?"

"Roger, Joe, they are at random altitudes and dispersed randomly. Algo-Net will handle real-time computing for target selection, as well as flight path and fratricide deconfliction."

Joe looked down from his circling owl-copter and could see target vehicles spread in the echelon formation the Bikers preferred. It felt good for Bikers, who would be aboil with testosterone and courage salts, to be part of a wave of roaring, flame-spitting desert demons. They wanted to look right, look left, and see Biker comrades advancing with them in a chain of growling steel hurtling into Freep Nation.

Jasper announced, "Crossing the forward edge of the battle area in ten seconds." Joe banked his owl-copter and looked down into the kill box.

Brilliant laser beams started blinking down from invisible owl-copter drones. These pencil-thin shafts of light zapped targets in a random way. After two minutes, Jasper's hundred attacking drones had flown unseen over the targets. Their pencils of extreme energy had burned through four hundred targets.

Joe said, "Saw plenty of lasing. How'd we do?"

"Our hundred owl-copter drones each destroyed four vehicles," Jasper replied, "No overlaps or gaps."

"OK," Joe said. "Now attack again. Same targets, but this time, fly north to south."

Jasper said, "We haven't prepped for that."

"Jasp, we won't be prepped when we're attacked," Joe said. "Make it happen ASAP."

Jasper commanded his drones to circle right as a group to two hundred seventy degrees and hover while their software warriors programmed their new engagement geometry. Fifteen minutes later, they were ready, and Jasper commanded his drones to move out.

He contacted Joe. "Ten seconds to contact."

"Roger, Jasp. Proceed across the battle area and then halt and maintain position and altitude."

"Why, Joe?"

"Because I want you to reverse direction and attack with what was the trailing edge of your force going in first."

"OK, Joe."

Jasper, now covered with sweat, yelled at his command staff. "You heard him, reprogram for attack to the rear in five minutes on my command...What the hell's he going to throw at us next?"

Chertikoff, silent until now, popped up. "Jasper, bring up extra copters; you are going to take losses. Tell your programmers to be ready for one-minute retargeting."

"What the hell for?" shouted Jasper. Patience at zero, he jumped up and kicked his desk. "This is a *game!*"

Chertikoff walked over to purple-faced Jasper and said, "Survival is a game you want to win."

Jasper, still mad, sneered, "How would you know, game player?

Chertikoff, cool, not bugged by Jasper's taunt, replied, "History has often told us of big battles won by boldness and surprise. Get ready for surprises. Learn to respond under pressure."

Jasper, irritated by a staff adviser telling him that, was tempted to hit him, but he knew the gamer was right. He took a deep breath, held it, and blew it out through pursed lips.

"OK, team, Chertikoff's right. Bring up fifty copters and hold in ready reserve within two minutes' flying time to the main force."

A staff trooper announced, "We are ready to reengage in the opposite direction."

Jasper replied, "Send them in." He then contacted Joe. "We have initiated our attack. Crossing FEBA in ten seconds."

"Roger, Jasper," Joe said. "You made it under five minutes."

"Joe, I want to try some scenarios of my own."

Surprised at Jasper's suggestion, Joe asked, "Such as?"

"I want to attack from two directions at once, and I want to bring up reserve drones to replace those I pull out for simulated losses."

Joe said, "Good, do it. Get in some night attacks later on when it is dark. I want an after-action review at eight a.m.—No, wait, hold on. I am getting ahead of what makes sense. Jasper, spend time with your team. Get their feedback on problems and how we can do it better. Let me know tomorrow what time you'll be ready for your after-action review."

"Roger, chief. Will contact tomorrow."

Chapter 30
FUNT'S CASTLE

Built of blue-gray granite, Funt's castle lurked high on a rugged overlook of the Cabazon Pass. From its crenellated ramparts, Funt could see Mainstream's windmill farm on the eastern slope of the pass, and he could see towers marching through the pass shouldering the high-tension lines that carried energy west to Mainstream. With his castle situated along Mainstream's energy artery, Funt demonstrated his willingness to throw his survival in with that of his benefactor, the Mainstream Business Council.

Funt had cultivated a close relationship with the council's military. So close that they had set up a high-tech control center in Funt's castle as a gesture of goodwill. Funt needed that capability to control Biker lands that were expanding like a poison inkblot on the map of what used to be California. More than five hundred Mid-Level farms were under Funt's protection. Mainstream provided all the guns and ammo the Bikers could ever use. Troublemakers in Biker-controlled areas, if they survived Funt's brutal enforcers, were turned over to Mainstream to fulfill foreign draft quotas.

On this day, Funt stood on the rampart watching a ducted fan aircraft approach. It flew in from the southeast and landed on a rampart pad. A man dressed in the bulky air-conditioned leathers of Funt's barred triangle force stepped out.

Funt stepped forward, thumped his right fist on his chest, and extended his arm with fist clenched. The man returned the salute and then pulled off his helmet. Funt said, "Kadjuk...just in time."

"For what?"

"We're talking about our next phase."

An albino with African features and red hair, Kadjuk's tough image was a match for Funt's hard-as-nails face. They talked privately for ten minutes. Both commanded awe as they entered the control center in their maroon tunics, blue riding britches, and black boots.

Funt said to his thirty-man command staff, "Kadjuk is here to brief you on our Freep situation."

Kadjuk gave the Biker salute; the command staff returned it, shouting, "Freep death!"

Kadjuk stood before the excited crowd, looked right and left, sizing them up. "Minutes ago, I flew in from our desert front. Impressed how we're building strength there. Freeps are on the lookout for us; they continually patrol with their watchers. We probe all the time to check their alertness and readiness for resisting attack."

Someone shouted out, "Where will we attack them?"

Funt stepped forward and said, "That information is classified at this time. We'll be moving continuously along the border in battalion-size units. Keeping them guessing. When conditions are right, we attack. It could happen in six months or in a year. And it could happen anywhere along the front.

"Maintain your unit's readiness and fighting morale at a high level from now on. Rewards will be great. As we invade, we take out weakly defended farms and award them to deserving commanders. We'll take over many of their factories. The Salton Sea and its riches will fall into our hands and be split up among you warriors and our Mainstream allies."

"Freep death!" was shouted again and again.

————

Six months later, Funt, Kadjuk and the rest of his top commanders were at a table on a castle balcony. Interns brought flagons of ale to wash down crystal clears, their latest pill fad. Funt said, "I've built a castle that people can be proud of. They look up to me because I live like a leader. Not in a hole like a disgusting roach."

Kadjuk laughed and slapped a nubile intern's behind as she leaned in to serve a tray of sausages.

"My castle is on high ground," Funt said, "like the ancient Alhambra. Its towers are designed for interlocking fire at anyone trying to scale our walls or take down the gates. Got my own jail for special prisoners."

Kadjuk said, "I'd like to take this vixen to your jail," as an intern squirming to get out of his grasp punched him in the nuts. "Ay yi yi!" he uttered in mock agony, grabbing his crotch with one hand and ripping the intern's filmy skirt off with the other as she ran away, giggling. The barred triangle tattoo jiggled on her left buttock.

Funt joined the hearty laughter and then said, "Men, I want ten minutes of your time before our orgy gets going. Interns, clear out." And they left through a door to the castle.

Funt said, "Y'all know I am out to get Joe. We have a spy in an important position in Freep nation who reported it was Joe that raided our outpost and blew up a fuel tanker. Cost me my foot when that fuckin' roach got me with a lucky shot.

"So listen to what I am telling you. Joe and that whore-bitch Mary—I want them alive. There will be heavy casualties on both sides, but I want those two alive. Me killing him and his pal Mary will be a delicious ending to a meal of revenge to be enjoyed slowly. I can't kill them slow if you don't bring them to me alive.

"Now let's get down to why you are here today. I know how to attack and beat the Freeps." Funt paused. "We're going to do it under cover of a sandstorm." The others were surprised. "Their lasers don't work with the air full of sand particles. And Freeps don't have any backup weapons to use when their lasers aren't working. My spies tell me that Freeps are spread thin along the southern front.

"Tell ya the truth, they have an intelligence weakness there. We have been infiltrating tankers and shock troops more successfully there then their northern front. Our tankers and assault Bikers are hunkered down out of sight of Freep planes and watchers.

"They are mostly underground or camouflaged in craggy mountain ravines. Our hidden troops can roll out of the high ground west of the sea and be at its shore in hours.

"When does the sandstorm come?" Funt asked rhetorically. He paused and looked around. "We don't know exactly, but we can predict two to three days in advance when conditions are favorable for a major storm that will last a couple of days. They are caused by the wind storms we get every summer. We are entering that season now, and you are all ordered to maintain your highest readiness state from now on."

A commander asked if Mexicans would come to Joe's aid.

Funt replied, "Don't think so. They have their problems with wars to their south, and they are supporting uprisings in Texas. But to be safe, the main invasion will be accompanied by a thrust to occupy both shores of the Baja breach. We'll stop any Mexican warships that try to come to Joe's aid or any ground forces. Commercial shipping cargos are ours for the taking."

Another commander asked, "Will Mainstream support us?"

Funt said, "They gave us all the guns and ammo we need and will resupply us as the campaign proceeds. They also gave us comm gear, trucks, fuel, and food needed to support the invasion.

"When the sandstorm is over, Mainstream will fly in aircraft that can detect owl-copters. Mainstream planes can see them on radar a long way off and take them out with air-to-air missiles. With the Freep owl-copter threat neutralized, any land we grab during the storm stays in our hands."

Chapter 31
SANDSTORM

A month later Funt was in his control center past midnight. He shouted at his weather forecaster who was studying a large meteorological screen, "You slimy lizard, why can't you tell if this front is strong enough for a sandstorm?"

"Too early, General Funt," The weather forecaster said.

"Idiot."

"Yes, General, right now it looks like conditions are right for a sandstorm. In six hours, I can tell you for sure."

Funt turned away, talking aloud as if trying to convince himself. "We have no choice but to be ready. Waited four years for this chance."

He paced back and forth, clenching and unclenching his fists. He shouted, "So goddamn tired of this dickydorkin' around. If we keep our troops on full alert any longer, I'll have a farging mutiny on my hands." Other personnel in the control center sat silently looking at their screens.

Funt's three top commanders, Buscob, Dreudart, and Aderth, waited at their jumping-off locations with their troops. Each was in a tracked command vehicle supplied by Mainstream. Funt's plan was to attack first at the northern front. Funt was counting on the Freeps reacting in force, drawing attention away from their southern front, from which his main pincer attack would come.

After three hours of Funt pacing and raving, his weather forecaster yelled, "General Funt! Conditions are perfect for a major sandstorm to start in two hours."

Funt, with both fists gripping the commander's podium, shouted, "Commence northern attack!" At 5:00 a.m. a phalanx of massive desert motorcycles with riders clad like monsters in black air-conditioned leathers moved out in the early morning light, under the command of Colonel Buscob. Armored personnel carriers with ten troops aboard drove among the Bikers charging across the desert sands.

Freep watchers were the first to see the Bikers charging into the Freep Nation. With their personal lasers, they fired with deadly accuracy, killing Bikers but not enough to stem the oncoming horde. They fought valiantly until their five shots were used, and then they reconfigured for camouflage in the terrain. Many survived that way, but others fell to Biker fire from snipers or the deadly APC Gatlings. The attack was relentless, barely slowing down when overcoming the sparsely located watchers

The marauders were ten kilometers into Freep territory before Jasper's unseen cloud of owl-copters unleashed laser blasts destroying a kilometer-square group of attacking vehicles. The owl-copters flew on and destroyed another kilometer-square patch of enemies with no survivors. Funt was surprised at the lethality of the invisible owl-copters. He nevertheless ordered his northern force to continuing attacking to strengthen the impression of it being the main attack force. The sandstorm would soon obscure the battle space and spare the Bikers not yet killed by owl-copter lasers.

———

When Joe heard of the invasion he flew from his command center in the Airplane Works to Jasper's mobile command center, now positioned ten kilometers behind the front. He witnessed the battle on drone recon TV. Jasper was in continuous contact with his lieutenants, marshaling the lines of dug-in troops bracing for attack, and with the watchers who were engaged, even dying, as he talked with them.

Algo-Net crackled an update: "Our owl-copters are taking out the attackers in patches along the front. Calculating the speed of the attackers and the coverage speed of our owl-copters, the Freeps should destroy all attackers in four more hours if the weather stays clear."

Jasper, looking worried, turned to Joe. "Shitty weather. Sand will kill us."

The command center was buffeted by a gust. Joe said, "It's here, what's your plan, Jasp?"

Jasper said, "I'm planning for the worst: the storm getting here before we have 'em all killed. We are switching to defense in depth. Old-fashioned Freep stuff. Lines of Freeps dug in on the ground, one behind the other, a hundred kilometers deep—fighting with lasers and guts."

Joe said, "Good call, Jasp. Keep your owl-copters away from the storm front. Can't afford to lose any needlessly. And keep this command center well behind the front. Can't let it get overrun."

"We're on that, Joe. Got a number of fallback areas to ground our air fleet ahead of the storm. We'll drop them back in time. Rolling the command center back in three minutes."

Joe said, "I am relocating to the Airplane Works command center. This might be a longer war than we thought."

Joe was off in his command owl-copter at midday. From altitude, he contacted Waxer. "Been hit hard in the north. We inflicted heavy casualties, but weather stopped our air assaults. Falling back, fighting on ground until weather clears."

Waxer sounded tense when he said, "We're fully engulfed in the storm now. Joe, there is almost zero visibility. We are flying our air assets away from the storm. Our watchers are reporting movement on a broad front. My battle board lit up with enemy penetrations in the last few minutes. Jesus, this invasion is huge, getting bigger by the minute." His voice rose. "Massive, Joe, using the storm to hit us hard. Our lasers near useless in blowing sand. They're pouring through in some sectors."

Joe ordered, "Pull back your command center immediately. Don't get surrounded. Tell your ground troops to go camo with their beetle packs until the enemy's within five or six meters and lase them. Then fall back. Have your owl-copters ready to attack when the weather clears. Set up defensive lines sixty kilometers deep."

"Hate to retreat, Joe."

"Got to, Waxer. They hit us hard up north before the storm. Tried to distract us into thinking that was their main attack. We have got to plan for it coming through the south."

"Roger. Saving as much of my force as possible."

"Be ready to fight in the air and on the ground when the weather clears."

"We'll be ready."

Joe called Mary. "We've been attacked."

"I know, Joe. It is all over Algo-Net."

"Go into full disaster mode."

"Already am, Joe. I am running the medical teams from our new hospital by the sea."

"We're getting attacked in the south. There will surely be an enemy pincer coming up your side of the sea. You're vulnerable there."

"I hear you, Joe, but now we are in a real mother poacher of a sandstorm."

"I can see the cloud from where I am north of you. I am in a race to get to my Airplane Works command center before the storm gets me in the air."

"How bad is it?"

"If it clears tomorrow, we have a chance. Mary, I want you to haul ass out of that hospital if the Bikers get near it. Can't have you get captured."

"OK, Joe."

Joe landed at the Airplane Works as the first gusts of blown sand hit. He raced into the command center. He ordered his chief comm guy, "Put me in contact with Mainstream's Business Council chairman."

"Roger, Joe."

A minute later, the comm guy said, "Got him, Joe."

Joe looked at a grainy screen to see the chairman discussing Funt's attack. "Gentlemen, we have been observing our ally General Funt's campaign into the Freep territories."

Joe said, "Hack me into his display screen."

In a minute, Joe's face appeared on the screen in front of the startled members of the Business Council. He said, "Your Biker pals have attacked us, and we're going to make you pay for all that help you gave them."

The council chairman said, "Very clever, roach guy. You got some smart kids hacking us, but Funt's corps will decimate you before you can touch us."

"Yeah, we'll see about that." Joe said. "I'm going to start with your electric power and will be back in touch." He disappeared from the screen.

Joe told Ted, his covert operations boss, "Take out half their windmills."

The moving weather front had strengthened the winds through the Cabazon Pass. Mainstream windmills were at maximum speed—the ideal condition for sabotaging them. Preestablished signals from Freep covert ops snapped the outer blade controls of half the windmills to full extension, sending blades into violent spasms that snapped them off in less than one rotation. Blade hunks whipped in every direction, wreaking further havoc.

In less than a minute, half the Mainstream power generation capability disappeared. Lights and services went out all over Mainstream.

Joe said, "Ted, we'll recontact Mainstream after they have time to appreciate what just happened. He walked over to Shan's position in the command center and said, "Got another job for you."

She asked, "Is the war going to reach us here at the Airplane Works?"

"Don't think so. I need you to save as many of our civilian Freeps who are in the way of the enemy attack as possible."

"OK, Joe. I'll ask the Strat Team to give me the people I need."

"Good. I want your team to contact all homesteaders and trekkers and any other Freeps out there who might need help. If they're in danger, work with them to fight or flee to a location where they can go into full camo. When the weather clears, get them whatever help or protection they need to survive."

"Roger, Joe. Will there be repercussions in Mainstream because of our sabotage? I'm thinking of Lon."

Joe said, "We're pressuring Mainstream to stop supporting Funt's invasion. It could get rough for spies who get caught in Mainstream. We'll pull Lon ASAP when we get a spare pickup drone."

———

Joe called Juanacho, who excitedly exclaimed, "Joe, been waiting for your call. Seen on TV your Freeps been attacked. What can we do?"

Joe replied, "We've been invaded by Bikers backed by Mainstream. We are going after their infrastructure."

Juanacho asked, "You want us to throw in the sniper drones you gave us?"

Joe asked, "Are your guys trained and ready?"

"Yeah, man. Our guys are great. They been gettin' plenty of simulator practice. Itchin' to go."

"OK, Juanacho, put five fifty-caliber rifle drones up with your best operators. Each one over a different freeway. Put a fifty-caliber round into the engines of oncoming cars. Keep the rifle drones moving and bring them home after ten shots. Fly them through circuitous city routes. Don't let Mainstreamers know where your base is."

"You want kill shots?"

"No, engine shots. We're gonna rattle them. Don't kill anyone, not now."

The drones were aloft in ten minutes. Flying over lanes of freeway traffic, they fired straight through automobile grills into the engine blocks bringing cars and trucks to rattling, grinding halts. Juanacho's guys were top notch. After a car was hit, they rapidly targeted another in an adjacent lane to create a choke point. They expended ammo in minutes, and then the drones dropped down to treetop level. Barely overhead, they snaked through city streets, riverbeds, and back alleys to their hangar in a deserted rail yard.

Freep moles turned on jammers to shut down Los Angeles, Van Nuys, Long Beach and Ontario airport communications, radars, runway lights, and landing aids.

Joe contacted the Business Council an hour after the first contact. His pissed-off face showed up on their screen. Stunned Business Council members glumly listened as Joe spit out a grim message: "We wiped out half your power, tied up five freeways, and closed down your airports. It's just the beginning."

The chairman, humble this time, said, "Funt's corps invaded you. We don't have any control over them."

"You've outfitted them and support them with food, fuel, and ammo."

"Joe, they are on the march. We can't turn them back."

"Listen, Mr. Chairman, we are going to continue strangling your infrastructure. Mainstream in Southern California will be tits up in a couple of days."

"You Freeps must be reasonable. This situation is beyond our control."

"Time to get it back in control. You've got tremendous leverage with the Bikers. They work for you, protecting your Mid-Level farms and factories. You supply their food and money."

"Yeah, but in the time frame you—"

Joe interrupted, "You will find the way."

The screen went blank. The council chairman and his staff, stunned at first, looked at one another, waiting for someone to speak up. Someone with an idea, a direction.

The council chairman sensed fear and panic in their faces. He maintained his authority with an order. He said tersely, "I want you Business Council members to define our options. Trade-off responses we can make. Find our best response to get that goddamn bug off our backs."

He stood up and looked at the members before leaving. "I'll be back in an hour, after I rally our emergency responders to fix the damage those savages have done to us. Remember, our highest priority is Mainstream survival and power—I emphasize Mainstream—nothing and no one else."

Chapter 32
PINCER MOVEMENT

Joe was staring at the command center battle display. Funt's forces were deep in Freep territory. Their advance was faster than anything he had gamed with Jasper and Waxer. He knew that Freep unpreparedness for this scenario could be fatal if the sandstorm lasted another two days. Sandstorms seldom lasted that long—that was his hope. Then, with the clearing, his mauled forces would attack. What was left of them, that is.

Joe called Waxer. "Can't get down to you through the weather."

"It's OK, Joe. Here's the story," Waxer said, "Bikers punched through in two places. It's a pincer movement. Right pincer headed for the south end of the Salton Sea. Probably to go up its east shore toward our hospital and the Citadel. Left pincer is headed straight east toward the sea. It'll probably head north when it reaches it."

Joe asked, "How are Bikers getting across the breach?"

"They have air-cushion vehicles, Mainstream issue, to ferry their forces across. Twenty troops at a time with motorcycles."

Joe said, "Dammit to hell! Air-cushion boats—what don't they have?"

My frustration's showing, thought Joe, *Gotta stop that right now.*

Waxer said, "Joe, one more thing. Got word that Bikers infiltrated as prepositioned assault teams. Couple of my watchers saw them emerge from underground hideouts, probably old mines, and roar off toward the sea."

"What are you doing about them?"

Waxer said, "Can't do much. Owl-copters grounded. They're headed between Jasper's and my forces."

Joe called Jasper and asked what he could do about the Biker breakthrough.

Jasper said, "I'm sending a fast-reaction team. They're riding wheeled cargo transporters. Will be there in a couple of hours.

Joe asked, "Waxer, what's your weather like?"

"Blowing sand. Visibility five to ten meters."

"Waxer, you've got to stop Bikers advancing up the west shore. Can't let them get behind Jasper and have our north front collapse."

"Roger, Joe. When visibility improves, we'll throw our owl-copters at them. Until then, it is a fighting retreat. We've practiced for this possibility, and our Freeps are maximizing Biker kills."

"Stay strong, Waxer. When weather clears, we'll send more owl-copters to help you go on offense."

Waxer said, "Roger, Joe, over and out."

Joe said to his staff in the command center, "We've had an intelligence breakdown on our southern front. Infiltrators got through—probably months ago, and now they're going to hit us behind our lines."

———

The storm continued into the next day. Funt's forces made steady advances along both sides of the sea in spite of dogged rearguard actions by Freep troops.

Joe said to his team at midday, "Time to slam the Business Council's infrastructure." He conferenced with his advisers and the Strat Team by Algo-Net. Their conclusion: hit Mainstream infrastructure hard, but don't go all the way. Let them know what will happen with a total Freep attack on their infrastructure. If Freeps go all the way too soon, Mainstream, with nothing else to lose, could unleash a nuclear response.

Joe agreed and stepped up infrastructure strikes against Mainstream and again had his face brought up on the Business Council's screen. "Business Council members, you are tasting our capability to clobber your lifestyle in a big way. We just took out another twenty percent of your electric power. Your Internet is in hack lock. Our rifle drones are escalating freeway attacks. Your surveillance and protection electronics are shut off. All your airports are down. And we've shut down three-quarters of your food deliveries from Mid-Level farms."

The council chairman said, "Funt is on the verge of defeating you, Joe."

Joe said, "Yeah, Funt could take our Salton Sea area temporarily. But we melt into the sand like roaches, and then when the sun comes out, Funt will be stopped. There are a million Freep computers out here, all working together to wreck Mainstream infrastructure. We're sun-powered and dispersed to an individual level. We've infiltrated your infrastructure over years and planted viruses waiting for the call to destroy you."

"We can tough it out for the few days you live, Joe."

Joe said, "You are talking tough, but remember, your food all comes from Mid-Level farms protected by Funt's gangsters. They have to protect your trucks through the Out-Lands to Mainstream. We shot up forty percent of deliveries today. Tomorrow all of it goes. Our rifle drones are unstoppable."

The chairman said, "We have nuclear weapons and an air force that your kites can't stop."

"When your first plane crosses our border, we stop playing around. All your power goes off, food totally cut off. Freeway shootings to kill you, not to cause traffic jams. Sewage, garbage, and water services down the shitter. And let's not forget that Freeps have hacked me into your control center to talk to you right here in your bunker. We can hunt you down remotely and take you out. All of you sitting before me, we know all your addresses. You are in our crosshairs. We know where you and your families live. We'll kill you off, starting from the top down. We can swarm our killer drones over Mainstream and terrorize you forever."

The Business Council went to another room to confer away from where Joe could see or hear them. Ten minutes later, they came back, and the chairman said, "Joe, we are prepared to stop offensive actions against you, including air and ground support of the Bikers. In return, you immediately stop destruction of our infrastructure." Cheers went up from Freep command centers.

Joe replied, "I'll throttle back to a harassment level. But if the Bikers don't start withdrawing from Freep Nation in one hour, we'll nail you again."

"We don't have control over them."

"You have more control over them than you think. When you stop your air-to-air support the Bikers will be annihilated by my owl copters." Joe said. "I'll be back in an hour to let you know if the Bikers have started to withdraw." Joe disappeared from their screen.

He turned to his team. "Continue harassing Mainstream. No killing, but let them know we can do it if we choose."

Chapter 33
ABDUCTION OF MARY

After Funt's troops charged to the Salton Sea on the afternoon of the second day of the invasion, they headed north, fighting furiously. In most cases, homesteads, factories, and farms cleared out before the invading Bikers showed up. But not all of them. Some were overrun and the Freeps killed before they could beetle up and hide.

Freeps on foot could not outrun Bikers on their collection of motorcycles, armored personnel carriers, and other vehicles that could handle a desert environment. Every Freep had laser power to kill an assailant. Many did—and many died when their five laser shots were expended, and Biker bullets and blades did their deadly work.

Other Freeps went into camouflage mode, dissolving into desert, awaiting orders from Jasper or Waxer to sally forth and fight.

Bikers advancing up the Salton Sea's east shore drew most of Waxer's reserves. He deployed them in depth.

When a clearing interval occurred, his Freeps came out of camouflage and lasered Biker targets in sight of whatever gullies, boulder piles, or foxholes they had been hiding in. With renewed storm intensity and blowing sand, they hunkered down again in their camouflage configurations. Bikers on the west shore reached the sea's north end after two days. Losses on both sides were heavy.

There was no sign the Biker attack was slackening as a result of Joe's threats to Mainstream. He called in his war gamers and Strat Team.

"Teammates, we are going to survive by making every shot count. This storm has lasted longer than most sandstorms. Well over a day so far, and we need a strategy that keeps us alive if it lasts another day. We are pushing Mainstream hard to stop the Bikers. We have already heavily damaged their infrastructure. By now, Mainstream knows they made a mistake supporting the Bikers.

"OK, where am I going with this? Why does every shot have to count?

"I'll tell you why. We have Freeps spread all over the battlefield. They are hungry, hiding, but still loyal and ready to fight. They will be a big factor in the victory we are seeking. I want our gamers to set up a fire-decision program to tell each Freep when to fire at the enemy. Our Freeps who are hidden out there are reporting sightings of every invader they see.

"Conditions are bad, but with thousands reporting fragmented information, we can build a surprisingly good overall picture of enemy locations. As the weather clears, Algo-Net, with software additions that our team is building right now, will direct every shooting decision for Freeps hunkered down out there.

"This stage of our guerrilla tactics will be highly effective. When the weather clears, air assets will be back fighting. Algo-Net will deploy our drones according to a search-and-destroy program that optimizes each drone's flight path to maximize kills.

"Teammates, we use this integrated fire-control software as soon as it clears. That could be in hours or at latest tomorrow. This briefing is over."

Several of his staff left, and others on remote screens signed off. He brought up Waxer. His face blurred on the screen. Joe said, "Brief me on your situation."

Waxer replied, "We are in retreat. I have come across the sea in a skiff and am in my fallback command center that is ten kilometers south of the hospital. Battlefront is another two kilometers south. Storm continues with occasional cessation of blowing sand, and then we fight back. These pauses don't last long, and then we fall back some more. Bikers are fighting viciously and paying dearly for their advance. I'm leaving Freep troops in areas of rough terrain to slow them down and we're putting some uphill in mountains east of here to prevent us from getting outflanked."

Joe asked, "When will they reach our hospital?"

"With continued blowing sand, they'll be there at 2:00 am. They have five times as many troops as we can put in front of them." Sounding exhausted, Waxer said. "We better evacuate the hospital, Joe."

Joe replied, "I sent them twenty air-conditioned wheeled vehicles, and they are taking out as many of their patients as these vehicles can carry. Three-quarters are still there. The staff is committed to staying. We have sent in cargo drones to see if they can fly against high winds. Lost some, but as the wind tapers off, we can get through."

"Joe, we can make a last-ditch stand before the hospital—but we risk everything."

"Can't risk losing your force. This storm will end within a day, and our lasers will come back into play, as well as our owl-copters for which they have no defense. There has never been a sandstorm that lasted three days. They have to defeat us in a day or be defeated. We have no choice but to continue your fighting retreat and be ready to attack when it clears."

"I hear you, Joe."

"Don't invest the hospital with troops or fire from it. We don't want the hospital bombarded and have a mass loss of life. If the Bikers get there, the hospital will surrender and appeal to the Bikers to foreswear destroying it on humanitarian grounds. We will promise reciprocal destruction of their noncombatant facilities if they ransack our hospital or harm its patients and staff."

"I understand, Joe. We'll fight on and retreat tactically in readiness for our turnaround."

———

Out of the pitch-black, blowing sand, a fishing boat docked at Mary's hospital's pier. It was midnight of the second day of the attack. A four-man team in hospital scrubs disembarked. They wheeled a gurney carrying another man toward an entrance door that was opened by Vernu from the inside.

Once inside, they wheeled their gurney down a corridor, passing a few serious-looking nurses. They stopped at a door marked Director's Office and opened it. Mary was slumped over her desk unconscious. Two unconscious colleagues were slumped in chairs facing her. The form on the gurney came to life and got off. They lifted Mary to the gurney in his place, covered her with a sheet, and put a large oxygen mask on her face.

The kidnappers left the way they came and headed for the pier. Vernu went with them. They clambered aboard the boat and took aboard the gurney with its legs folded, then motored off into the howling sandblast as fast as the heavy chop would allow.

In the small wheelhouse, steering the boat through foaming whitecaps, stood the captain in a Biker uniform. He said to Vernu, "You sure have a way with chemicals."

"Yeah," she laughed, "I can put them out for an hour or a week. Just let me know what you need."

"I need her out for a couple more hours until we get to Funt's castle."

"She'll sleep until then."

They arrived at the west shore well after midnight. Two ducted fan aircraft stood by the dock. Funt was waiting there with Kent, one of the pilots. The kidnap team rolled Mary's gurney to the closest aircraft and loaded it aboard. Funt said, "Vernu and Kent, you are responsible for getting Mary to my castle. She is not to be poached around with."

Kent and Vernu climbed aboard.

Kent shouted, "Strap in and hold on. It's going to be a shit flinger." They lifted off into a black, howling storm.

Vernu said, "Hey, Freep planes can't fly in this sandblaster. How can this thing?" Then a series of ferocious lurches, lifts, and drops had her exclaiming in a shrill, frightened voice, "Can this poacher climb out of this crap?"

Kent, calm as a cucumber, said "Now, Vernu, don't get your twat atwitter. These ducted fans can handle all the sand the storm can throw at them."

"Screw sand—can it clear those farging mountains?"

"These fans have a high disc load. The heavy sand gives them more thrust."

"Yeah, if it don't grind the propellers up and spit out the blades first."

They careened on into the night, reaching Funt's castle an hour later.

Chapter 34
FUNT IN THE FIGHT

By the second afternoon of the battle Funt's three colonels, each with a corps of tens of thousands of Bikers, was deep into Freep Nation. They had to get most of the job done under the storm's cover. They threw all their resources into their attack and they were on schedule. No reserves held back. Their orders were to kill as many Freeps as possible and take out any of their airplanes, primitive as they may seem, to prevent the use of their deadly accurate airborne lasers.

Buscob led the northern feint that opened the invasion. He knew that many of his troops would be lost to make way for Funt's main attack, but he still charged with unalloyed determination. He would be well rewarded with booty and land.

Aderth led a southern pincer up the Salton Sea's east shore. He was born to lead aggressive war and was good at it. He didn't give mercy or expect it on the battlefield.

Dreudart led the center attack group. His first objective was Joe's casino. Next objective was to head north and cut Jasper's force off. Freeps and beetled-up Indians fought side by side against Dreudart's troops, retreating back past the casino that won top billing as a pillage target for the Bikers. The Bikers had trouble motivating their troops to fight past where the money and whiskey were. But Dreudart threatened executions and his lieutenants found enough motivated troops to keep Jasper's troops retreating.

Late that night Funt flew by ducted-fan aircraft to Dreudart's command vehicle at the Salton Sea west shore. He spent most of his time glued to an electronic wall display of the battle space and remained in frequent contact with his other two colonels.

At midnight the devastating call came from Mainstream. The call cutting off Funt's fuel, food, munitions and air to air fighters. A Mainstream voice said, "Funt, we have to cut off your support immediately. Farging Freeps are destroying us from within. We have no choice."

Dumbfounded, Funt listened in silence as he collected and focused his rage. Finally, he screamed, "You can't leave us now at the height of our campaign. In another day we'll overrun them completely. You must be there when the weather clears. We need your air cover to find Freep drones and shoot them down. With them up there, we can't survive. Only planes with radar, your planes, can find them." Red-faced, Funt stopped.

The voice from Mainstream firmly said, "Pull out now. Save what you can for a future invasion. There will be another day. Right now, we have to solve their threat to our infrastructure."

"This right now is my future," Funt bellowed. "We prepared four years for this war."

The Mainstream voice said, "Mainstream is not committing suicide to support your plans of raising hell in the desert. All our shipments of fuel, food, and ammo are halted, and we're withdrawing our liaison troops."

"All right, you scummy Mainstream prick, we'll withdraw. Watch your six o'clock next time you head for a golf course."

Funt was a soldier before everything. He watched every action of his amphibious squad that was committed to kidnaping Mary, even as he received the calamitous news from Mainstream. Vernu was his inside player. She observed radio silence until Mary's abduction from the hospital was complete, and then Funt heard her radioed announcement, "Mission accomplished!" as the fishing boat pulled away from the hospital pier.

The calculus of war changed in an instant. For Funt, his dream of total domination of Freep Nation vanished. But Funt couldn't let this gut punch demoralize him. He had another hand to play with two black aces in it, extortion and ransom. It would bring him back to fight another day.

Mary was worth more alive to Funt than dead, or somewhere in between. When the fishing boat returned, he personally saw its unconscious cargo loaded on a duct-ed-fan aircraft. He sent Vernu along to keep an eye on things and make sure Mary was not raped or worse during the flight or at the other end.

Back in the command vehicle, Funt told Dreudart that the Bikers must immediately stop advancing and begin withdrawing. He gave a pep talk about the future when they would go it alone without the treacherous Mainstreamers. Funt took off in his ducted-fan aircraft; he made brief stops at his other two colonels' command posts to deliver the bad news in person. He told them that Mainstream had abandoned him, cutting off support he needed to fight on to victory. Funt told them Joe's drones would be unstoppable in clear weather without Mainstream's air power, and his decision to retreat was the only alternative to annihilation. Then he headed for his castle in his ducted-fan aircraft, making it back safely under cover of the storm.

———

Mary awakened slowly. Nothing registered in her mind that made sense. She felt numb mentally, seeing but not feeling at first. Seeing a room with a closed door. An unfamiliar room with stone walls. It was quiet, and she started to gain more consciousness, now her body felt the rough blankets covering her. She looked around. Nothing fancy. Saw another door, ajar to reveal a bathroom behind it. She sat up in bed and rubbed her eyes to try to clear them, to comprehend better what was around her. She was still in gray scrubs.

The door opened. Vernu entered, followed by an orderly carrying an armful of linens, towels, and clothes. Vernu said, "Welcome to the castle."

"Castle?" Mary said. "What castle?"

"Funt's castle," Vernu replied, with a cocky pride. "Your new home." She walked over to Mary, now sitting on the edge of the bed. "You are Funt's girl now, and you'll be living in this dungeon until he has confidence that you can be trusted to move freely in the upper levels. We are thirty meters under the earth here. Beyond the reach of anything Freeps could come up with."

"Oh god," Mary said, still not comprehending her situation. "War still on?"

"Yes, and you're its most important prisoner."

Mary stood up; the intern reflexively moved close by Vernu in case some muscle was needed. The intern was a muscular woman in a thong and halter with the Funt insignia tattooed on her left buttock and other tattoos with tough warlike themes covering most of the rest of her.

Mary looked from the intern back to Vernu and asked, "Why are you here?"

"I always wanted to be a spy, and Funt gave me an opportunity for adventure and a chance to live without looking like a bug." She laughed and winked at Mary. "Besides, he treats me right, and I get my pick of these lovelies." Vernu put her arm around the intern and gave her a quick kiss on the mouth and a feel of her crotch. "Now you need to get cleaned up, dressed, and hair done to look good enough to sit at Funt's table tonight."

Mary, crestfallen, spoke slowly and deliberately. "I'm not eating with Funt. Or you either, you traitorous bitch."

Vernu slapped Mary across her face and said, "You will eat with us if you don't want to see your Freep captives tortured."

The intern grabbed Mary's arm as she wound up to hit back and expertly twisted it into an armlock. Mary struggled in vain as another brawny intern joined in to subdue her. Mary, overpowered, snarled, "Why don't you just kill me?"

"No such luck, my dear. Now let's get you squared away for your coming-out party tonight."

———

That night, Mary was led into Funt's dining hall and seated to his right. She was depressed in spite of the powders Vernu had dropped in her glass of water earlier. The high-energy prog-rock music also failed to pump her mood back to normal.

Funt's inner circle was gathered around for evening dinner at his triangular table, with its room for twenty people along each side. Some places were empty. Funt explained to her that they belonged to his officers at the front. He said that he wouldn't stay long and ordered food and drink be brought immediately. He turned to Mary. "I want you to know you are playing a big role in saving the Bikers from destruction."

"I hate myself for anything that helps you," she replied.

Funt smiled and said, "You're mad. I get it. Gonna treat you real good, and in time, you'll get to like it here."

The music rose to higher and more frenetic levels and glittering light shafts pierced the dining hall smoke. Fully tattooed tumblers arced through a pulsating haze to the hoots and howls of Funt and his cronies. "You see, Mary, I've made a deal with Joe. He will let half my army come back to the Out-Lands. After I trade you back to the Freeps, the other half of my army will be allowed to come back."

"When do I get traded back?"

Funt smiled with hatred curling his crooked lips. "Tomorrow you will *almost* get traded back." He bit off a mouthful from a drumstick and continued, "You will be in a cage slung below a ducted-fan aircraft. Freeps won't shoot it down because…well, you would die."

"When it looks like half our army has returned, we show you off to the Freeps and that shit bag Joe by flying to the exchange point and hovering over it." Funt paused for a slug of ale. "Then, and this is the fun part, we don't lower your cage and let you go. We turn around and fly right back here to my castle."

"And you don't get the other half of your army back."

"Right now, I don't care," replied Funt. "We have slums that can turn out plenty of tough recruits for my next army, and we have a battle-hardened cadre to build around. Actually, your Joe has to figure out what to do with a bunch of pissed-off prisoners."

Funt slurped from his flagon and continued, "You will stay here and be my companion. I will give you a little time to get used to your new home, and then if you are still having trouble liking the idea of becoming the most powerful woman in the Out-Lands, we'll offer you other options. But you might not like those options so much."

Mary didn't respond. Her gaze sagged to the floor. She looked like someone with no way home. No way to return to a dream she had yet to fulfill.

Funt emptied his flagon and stood up. "Duty calls." He looked down at Mary. "Keep it warm for me." He turned on his heel and left the noisy room through the main door.

Vernu and her interns guided Mary out another door to the winding dungeon staircase.

Chapter 35
THE TURNAROUND

The second night of the war at the Airplane Works command center, Joe was watching the battlefield info screen. Rod and Yahzorn were with him. He watched the Bikers advance toward the hospital. A kilometer south of the hospital they stopped and—unbelievably—were falling back.

Within minutes Waxer contacted Joe to announce there was a lull in the invasion in his area even though there was still blowing sand.

"Waxer, be careful it might be a feint to suck you into a flanking attack. Monitor developments with small recon forces."

"Roger, Joe."

Jasper told Joe a similar story about his front.

"Shadow them with caution, Jasp. We'll start cleaning up when our owl-copters and drones get aloft."

Joe called Mary well after midnight. The staff couldn't find her. They told him two of her team members were unconscious in her office, but she wasn't there. Couldn't page her either. The staff was still looking for her, but she apparently was not on the premises.

The staff also told Joe they were investigating a suspicious patient movement last night from and to a boat that docked at the hospital pier. Joe thought, *That scummy Funt. He kidnapped her!*

Joe was answering a sudden surge of incoming calls when Algo-Net informed him that Funt had joined his call-waiting list.

Joe ordered it brought up immediately. "What do you want, Funt?"

"Joe, the storm will be over in hours. We're pulling back."

Joe, in amazement, said, "Smart move because our drones will be annihilating your forces when it clears."

"Yeah, without Mainstream air cover, you can do that," Funt admitted.

"Mainstream cut out on you?" Joe asked.

"Yeah, they dropped supporting us when your Freeps messed with their lawn parties. I think you knew what was up, Joe."

"Your army is dead meat, Funt. Our drone-targeting accuracy is one hundred percent, and kill probability is one hundred percent.

"You don't want to do that, Joe."

"Yeah, why?"

"If you do, Mary dies."

"You flaming piece of shit."

"You didn't have enough brains to protect your old lady, did ya, Joe?"

"Look, Funt." Joe spoke, voice raised. "You let her go, and I let your army return home. Keep her or harm her, and I kill or cripple them all."

"You think I'm dumb as dirt?" Funt asked in a mocking voice. Then, with a dead-serious tone: "Let my troops go first, and I let her go."

"I have no guarantee you will keep your word and release her."

Funt, after a long pause, replied, "Let's do it this way: you release one-half my army, and I bring Mary up from my dungeon and give her to your forces at our established border crossing. After you take her back, you release the second half of my army."

Joe, playing for time, replied, "I'll discuss it with my staff and get back to you in an hour." He thought, *I need every minute to figure out a way to rescue her.*

Joe linked in an Algo-Net conference with his top subordinates and the Strat Team. He related his conversation with Funt to them. "We know where she is. Time is short. We're going to figure out how to rescue her in an hour."

"You can't jeopardize our defense operation for one person," said a Strat Team member.

Joe, taken aback by a blunt stating of what he knew to be true, said, "We don't want their army anyway. If we hold them as prisoners we are stuck with feeding them and keeping them cool."

"Can't just let them go. Got to punish them so they don't do it again," said another member.

"Make them repair what they destroyed," said Waxer. "In areas they occupied, there is real damage and many dead."

"Their invasion must be avenged harshly," chimed in another voice.

"The punishment can't do more harm to us than to them," Shan said.

The heated discussion offered every point of view. Joe would have to come up with something no one else had thought of. Had to do it with the imagination Algo expected.

He listened carefully to each argument. He was frantically searching for the solution to a complex problem that would justify his claim to leadership. The moment demanded action. Joe had to aim Freep energy, anger, and frustration in a direction that would lead to a viable postwar community for the Freeps. Joe needed Freeps behind him, not against him but he couldn't get Mary's plight out of his mind.

"Let's agree on something right now," Joe said. "We are going to capture or kill Funt. He is enemy number one. We need a stealth commando team to raid Funt's castle. Jasper, I want you to put it together."

Jasper, happy with a commando raid in his future, said "Joe, my second in command, Shirlene, will take over northern front responsibility as of now. Signing off and going to work."

Joe continued, "Science guys, tell us how many owl-copters we need to gang-lase through the stone walls of Funt's castle. Get your air fleet together starting now. Shirlene and Waxer, the storm will end soon, and we want rapid rescue of our wounded and processing of our dead. Notify Freeps that are hunkered down in camo to let Bikers pass on their way back."

———

Joe was formulating an approach to settle the score with Funt in real time. He played for time by asking for each individual's recommendation.

Then he spoke. "We are going to use Funt's offer to our advantage. It will take the first half of their force a day to make it back to the border on their motorcycles and APCs. Two kilometers from the border, we destroy their vehicles, and they walk from there. They stack arms on the way. Our copters, both piloted and droned, will be observing their retreat. If they shoot or act up, they will be lased and killed by the nearest owl-copter. Funnel them through a few border check points to make sure they do not take any booty or Freep women with them."

Joe's team listened attentively. One questioned, "Why don't we keep them all prisoner?"

Joe replied, "Got a heat problem. If we keep them in captivity, their suits will run out of refrigerating fuel in a few days, and they die. We don't want to clean up over fifty thousand dead Bikers. We don't have enough beetle packs and cool locations to accommodate them on short order. But we want some of them to rebuild what they wrecked. And we want some Bikers for spies. We'll keep any Mainstream advisers who are with the Bikers for prisoner exchanges.

"The second half of the Biker force will be those of the right pincer toward the hospital. They have a long way to go home and will take longer. We'll ask how many would like to be part of a reconstruction team, working beetled up. Should be a good bunch of volunteers, in view of their miserable lives in the Out-Lands. If we don't get enough volunteers, we draft as many as we need.

"Shan, have your team start immediately on a damage assessment of Freep Settlements. Need an answer in two days to figure how many Bikers we press into service.

"Looking ahead, we have learned a valuable lesson from this war. That is, we stopped Mainstream by totally infiltrating and wrecking enough of their infrastructure that it wasn't worth it for them to support an invasion of our land.

"We didn't bother with infiltrating the Bikers over the years. We didn't know enough about them; we were dismissive of their capability. They hit us harder than we thought they were capable of. Can't let that happen again. Gotta stop any Biker invasion before it starts.

"Lon, we are going to infiltrate the Out-Lands' gangs as we have penetrated Mainstream. We are going to blow out their military infrastructure before it can invade again—ever. I need your first plan by tomorrow morning.

"We want to find Bikers we can turn into our agents. Plan on recruiting the first bunch from the second half of the retreating Bikers. Your job number one: Find Bikers with knowledge of the castle who'll pledge allegiance to us now. We'll need them for tomorrow's fight. Job number two: make a long-range plan for full infiltration of the Bikers as we have done in Mainstream."

The voice persisted, "What are you going to do to teach them a lesson?"

Joe replied, "We are going to take out or lock up Funt and his top officers. We'll capture those we can find in their retreating forces and any other Bikers who have committed atrocities. Others that we find in the future will be brought here to face war-crimes trials and imprisonment.

"Jasper's commandos will capture Funt's castle and demolish it, as well as any other installations of his war-fighting organization. We will wipe out their money-making protection service by bringing in other gangs to replace the Biker's protection service for Mainstream farms and factories in the Out-Lands. And we take away most Biker territory and give it to other gangs—especially those who supported us against Mainstream.

"We will keep as many retreating troops as we need for reconstruction and cleanup, which could take years. We're hitting Mainstream for war reparations. Mainstream has agreed to airlift out Biker wounded and dead. They have already started."

There were no further questions. Joe contacted Funt and told him they had a deal for the day after tomorrow.

Chapter 36
BIKERS RETREATING

On the third morning after the attack the storm tapered off. A straggling army of Bikers was headed home. Their instinct for survival told them that their lives were dependent on careful rationing of fuel and water. Freep owl-copters and drones were aloft, monitoring the pullout.

Freep troops who survived by hiding in the desert were calling in for pickup. Air Control picked them up first.

As airplanes became available, Air Control flew Shan's team to the myriad Freep settlements scattered across the desert landscape to evaluate damage.

Biker communications were inefficient. Word to retreat got through their ranks in a slapdash fashion. Some Bikers were still hunting down and attacking Freeps hours after a withdrawal command went out from Funt. As soon as any continuing offensive action by Bikers was reported, it was dispatched with deadly fire from unseen owl-copters in a clear blue sky. In half a day, rogue Bikers were silenced.

Bikers motored home at low speed to conserve fuel. They converged in ragged columns heading west through thick dust kicked up by their own vehicles. By noon of the third day, motorcycles and other vehicles were starting to run out of gas, and Bikers walking in cumbersome air-conditioned leathers were appearing with greater frequency. The temperature was in the one hundred thirties. Bodies and wreckage of ground and air vehicles littered the terrain. Downed Bikers pleaded with Freeps for fuel to get their personal cooling apparatus going again. Mainstream vertical takeoff and landing medevac aircraft lumbered into the battlefield and took out one hundred Biker casualties at a time.

Joe was aloft in his command owl-copter. His pilot, Alf, sat in the front left seat. Joe was aft on the left side with two screens for tactical information. Rod, in the right front seat, was handling the follow-up for Joe's orders. A top gamer, Yahzorn, in back right seat, interfaced with Algo-Net to study the progress of the retreat, to study short-term attack options for capturing Funt's castle, to construct casualty reports, and to provide real-time data for Joe's top-level understanding of the battle space. He also simulated near-term reconstruction scenarios to determine optimum policies for handling a Biker empire that was doomed.

"Yahzorn, give me a plan to infiltrate Funt's castle in case Jasper needs support," Joe said.

"Roger, Boss."

325

"You sure you want to put yourself there? Gonna be a nasty fight," Rod said.

"Yes, I want a backup plan that is unexpected, in case Jasper gets in trouble," Joe said.

"Roger, Joe."

From above, retreating Bikers looked like lemmings marching toward the sea. Every one of them knew that hanging around in the torrid land of the Freeps could end in death when their leather's air conditioning ran out of fuel.

Joe cruised above them and saw for himself how much damage they had caused in the two days of their onslaught. His thoughts went to the first homestead he had seen as a new Freep. "Fly to Freddo and Negla's homestead," Joe said to Alf. They flew over it at two hundred meters to stay invisible. The homestead where he'd spent happy days as a new Freep had been overrun. A greenhouse door was left open; Freddo's corpse lay in front of the adobe building that was their home. Joe was jolted at the sight.

"No!" he shouted. Then made a few touch entries on his right screen, searching for beetle-suit beacons. Three red pinpoints were shown two hundred meters up the rugged slope above the homestead. "Go there, Alf, they're hiding." The copter dropped close to ground level at the pinpointed place. Three concealed Freeps were there.

Joe disembarked and walked to a rock, and a barely conscious Negla moved. She attempted to stand; Joe helped her reconfigure her beetle pack into the upright shape.

Her two kids were barely responsive. He barked an order for the closest medevac copter to get there at max speed. He gave them water and made sure their beetle packs were cooling sufficiently.

In minutes, a rescue copter landed, and Negla and her kids were lifted aboard for revival treatment. "Avenge Freddo, Joe," she pleaded. "He held them off while the kids and I fled up here." She didn't cry but held Joe in her iron gaze.

"We'll get those bastards." Joe squeezed her hand and jumped back aboard his owl-copter. From aloft, they spied four Bikers descending a trail from the homestead toward the west. "Lase them," Joe commanded.

The Bikers bumping downhill with their motorcycles laden with booty from Negla's homestead were executed in the space of four seconds by a shaft of brilliant energy that danced from one to the next. They crashed into a jumbled pile of machinery and bodies. Fuel tanks ignited. Acrid black smoke drifted off with the breeze.

———

Joe headed west to where the first half of the Biker army would be crossing back into the Out-Lands. Joe wanted to see the lay of the land at the exchange point.

Algo-Net had complete situational awareness of the battle space now that drones and owl-copters were aloft again. Shirlene played Algo-Net like a precision war fighting instrument. It provided Shirlene all the info needed to disposition her forces efficiently.

Joe could see from his owl-copter that a minimum number of her troops were handling the mobs of exhausted Bikers walking the last couple of kilometers home. Any resistance from Biker hardheads among them was dealt with by a laser blast from an unseen source above. Same story with any Bikers trying to take booty or weapons with them.

Exhausted after four hours aloft, Joe headed for the Airplane Works, which had not been overrun by Bikers. He called Shan. "Can you brief us on the extent of the war damage?"

"See you in two hours," Shan said. "Joe, get some sleep. You are starting to sound like you're out of it."

She showed up two hours later to wake Joe, asleep at the conference table. She notified Joe's reconstruction team on Algo-Net and got right to the point. "Teammates, heavy damage was inflicted on new greenhouses and power systems at the south end of the Salton Sea. On the brighter side, there was much less damage to homesteaders and widely dispersed Freep factories and medical installations. They were too far apart or located in such severe terrain that the effort to find and overrun them was too much for the Bikers."

Like Shirlene, who put Algo-Net's vast knowledge base and powerful decision programs to work in the war endgame, Shan used Algo-Net to build a plan for reconstruction of every damaged facility. It compiled what was needed for each project: material, personnel, and schedule. Joe's team was awed at the speed and efficiency of her work.

Joe asked, "Shan, how many captured Bikers are needed for reconstruction?"

Shan said, "We need fifteen thousand five hundred for two years."

The meeting ended with Joe's directive to begin reconstruction in the morning. Joe's staff headed for the dining room. Shan lingered and invited Joe to her condo cave for a drink and a steam with her and Lon.

———

He owl-coptered to Shan's condo cave an hour later. He strode in and couldn't believe what he saw in the kaleidoscopic light. Shan was suspended from the ceiling, tied in a limbs-folded ritual Shibari position. Joe was jolted by the sight of her trussed in a web of red ropes. "Shan!" he exclaimed on seeing her suspended, nude except for many ties and knots making exotic designs all over her body. "Are you hurt?" Shan couldn't answer with a gag in her mouth, but her head could shake a small amount, enough to say no, and her eyes betrayed a far away, transformed state.

Lon said, "She's OK, Joe."

"I never saw this before," Joe said, wide-eyed. "Don't hurt her."

Lon started untying and lowering Shan to the floor. He said, "It is a source of intense pleasure for her, you'll see." She was starting to move as each body part became free and to breathe deeper with her chest bonds loosened.

"Hi, Joe," she said happily, as her gag was removed. Finally stepping out of the last ropes, she stretched and turned slowly so Lon and Joe could see red stripes spread around her body where the ropes were. She and Lon were exhilarated and Joe still taken aback when she cheerfully announced, "Let's steam, guys."

They headed out behind the big rock, now all clothed in gray shorts, and starting to glisten with sweat in the moonlight. Behind their privacy boulders, totally alone and away from Algo's eyes and ears, Joe said, "I must get back to the war in twenty minutes. I want to know from you two what Algo has been like in the past facing a calamity."

"If his Freep leader, in this case you, Joe, continues to be successful, Algo observes and chronicles what the leader does to determine if Freep life is on an ascending evolutionary arc," Lon said. "Algo will let you lead as long as you are in tune with evolutionary laws."

Joe let that sink in and then asked the two of them, "How am I doing?"

Shan said, "You are doing well. The enemy has been defeated. But there is something you should know about that didn't involve your leadership."

"What's that?"

Lon said, "There was an intelligence lapse."

Joe said, "You're right. Our southern theatre was infiltrated by Funt's forces before the attack."

Lon said, "All that information from watchers and drones didn't get to Waxer. Only Algo could have filtered it like that. Result, your casino got taken out, a lot of Salton Sea development was laid waste, and Mary was kidnapped. You have to analyze what that means."

They went into the condo, dripping wet from sweat. After toweling off, dressing, and beetling up, Joe accepted energy powders and a cold fizz drink from Shan to stay awake and in a good mood. He said, "I've got to talk more with you two."

Lon said, "You are facing decisions that will shape Freep destiny, Joe. We're here for you whenever you need to talk." They hugged—as much as they could with Joe beetled up—and he hurried off to his owl-copter and flew off.

Flying back, Joe thought, *Why the hell would Algo let the Bikers punch through our lines and capture Mary? Maybe it wanted to put pressure on me, and things got a little out of hand. Maybe Algo wants the construction projects to be toned down. Are they too extravagant? I'll review with our architects.*

Back at the Airplane Works, his command owl-copter was ready for takeoff. Joe climbed aboard; they took off and climbed to two thousand meters.

"What's been happening?" Joe asked.

Rod said, "Biker command notified us that Mary will be delivered tomorrow at noon. They will bring her in a ducted-fan aircraft to the main border crossing."

Joe said, "I smell a set up."

Yahzorn said, "Me too, Joe. We are running through scenarios that we believe their scurvy minds are capable of."

Joe said, "Tell me more."

"For starters, they could return her, and when you come forward to greet her, you both could be shot."

"Yeah, they're walking home disarmed, half-dead, with big losses and no booty. Funt could cheer up his followers with that. We know it would cheer him up."

"They could even not deliver her, assuming that she represents more leverage if they hold her instead of releasing her."

Joe said, "We still got half their army. That's huge leverage."

"Not necessarily. They are more hungry mouths to feed. We think Funt wouldn't care if they never came back. Bikers are not equipped to put them all to work and to take care of their wounded. Mainstream would have to be unusually generous to the gangs to avoid unrest and starvation—that could threaten them. Mainstream is unusually stressed now with all that infrastructure damage we did to them. They don't care if the Bikers don't make it back to their border."

Joe hesitated for a minute and then spoke. "During the exchange tomorrow I'll be in this owl-copter at two thousand meters. Completely unseen. There will be an added one hundred Freeps at the border to accept her release and spirit her away immediately. Aloft, there will be another ten owl-copters to fight any extra ground or air threats and provide a confusion factor, in that they won't know which one I'm in."

Joe brought Jasper up on Algo-Net. "Jasper, Mary is to be released tomorrow. If it doesn't work out, I want you to be ready to attack Funt's castle and penetrate it."

"Joe, we'll be ready with A, B, and C airborne commando teams. A and B teams to strike and C in reserve."

Joe said to Yahzorn, "Get our intelligence teams to interview prisoners to see if any know about the design of Funt's castle. Find out if there are vulnerable areas. Check out what Algo-Net knows about castle security."

———

Joe made the rounds, dropping down to congratulate Freeps now on their march to victory and visiting the wounded in aid stations and hospitals. Visits were short but appreciated.

After one such visit to a group of wounded waiting to be picked up, they had climbed out and leveled off at two thousand meters. Joe's intercom was momentarily quiet when it happened, that feeling of an otherworldly force being present, the fog before his eyes and its clearing to reveal Algo's eyes in a thought-message. Joe, startled, looked away from his screens and out a side window to indigo darkness and stars. Algo thought-messaged him, extinguishing the stars and commanding Joe's total mental focus. *You have done well in many areas.* Joe pressed his two beetle pack buttons and wondered which ones Algo was referring to.

A series of his accomplishments scrolled into his consciousness: *Recovering from the quake. Building an army. Developing air-ground tactics based on Algo-Net. Expanding food production. Infiltrating Mainstream to inflict decisive infrastructure damage. Befriending a gang ally and maintaining good relations with the Mexicans. Developing the Salton Sea resources.* The scrolling stopped.

Joe thought, *It's good to get feedback from Algo. Algo has seen the whole history of the Freeps and has good things to say about what I am doing. No one else has ever put it all together like that and told me how well I performed. Wish Mary were here to share this recognition by Algo, to break the loneliness Yasminah, the fortune teller, knew was in me.* His thoughts quieted and he wondered, *Is that all from Algo? Is that all Algo is going to tell me this time? Algo has told me a lot, and I'm not seeking more compliments—but there is a hell of a lot going on. All uncharted territory.*

Joe looked back into the plane. Alf was focused on air traffic, and there was a lot in the sky that night. Rod was barking out orders for bringing up the second half of the Biker army and setting up the formations for receiving Mary after her release. Yahzorn was working spy and defector recruitment possibilities among the retreating

Bikers. His team at the top of its game. He was proud of them.

It was quiet; no one needed him at the moment. He looked out again, savoring a deep-blue desert night. Algo came into Joe's consciousness again with this thought-message, *Think of survival in the broadest evolutionary way. Common good determines adaptations that must be made.*

Algo disappeared. Joe thought, *That is so obvious. Of course evolutionary adaptation has to suit the widest needs of any species. Obvious as all hell, but Algo is telling me that for a reason. He is telling it to me now. Why now? OK, Joe, let go of your ego, stand back, and take a calm look at what is going on.*

Joe stretched his arms and pivoted his head to relax his neck and then said, "Guys, give me a combat meal, and don't forget the go-powders. I'll be awake for another day or so."

Back to thinking, *War winding down. A lot of problems, but they're the kind of problems that attend all wars: prisoner exchanges, reconstruction, veterans returning and needing care, home and infrastructure rebuilding. Got Shan and her gang working these things with the world's best brain, Algo-Net.*

Then, back in the tactical world, Joe asked, "Yahzorn, have you found any defectors?"

"Yeah, Joe, good luck. Our interrogators have a squad of eight Bikers that worked on Funt's castle. They want to defect, and they're spilling their guts. There is a secret tunnel for a castle escape."

"Put two defectors in each of Jasper's three assault teams. Keep two in the rear in case we need them."

Joe turned to Alf. "Alf, take me to the nearest aid station."

Ten minutes later, they were on the ground. Joe and his crew walked through a tented facility. Heart-wrenching scenes of men in agony from the wounds of war brought them back to the reality of how horrible the last few days had been for those confronting a cruel enemy. Joe had a few words with some of the men to show there were people in leadership positions thinking of them. Although their stay was short, Joe was aware that morale in Freep Nation was dependent on care of those Freep warriors whose bodies were on the line.

Outside again, Joe and Rod took a walk in the darkened desert surrounding the aid station. It was a hot night, and they were well beetled up but with their helmets opened enough to talk without microphones. He said to Rod, "I thought-messaged with Algo an hour ago, when we were cruising above the battlefield."

"I'll bet Algo was as enigmatic as ever."

"You got that right," Joe said. "Algo said to think of survival in the broadest possible ways, and the common good determines adaptations. Help me with this, Rod. What's Algo really saying?"

"Wow, tough question. But let me throw some thoughts out for you to chew on. The fighting part of this war may turn out to be the easy part."

Joe said, "Yeah, a hundred things to be decided right over the horizon."

"In deciding these issues, Joe, you must be careful not to give the fate of a few more weight than the lives and safety of all the rest."

"Or," Joe said, "maybe the fate of one person endangering the rest?"

"Could be that you must stay away from the border for your safety and that of the community that depends on your leadership."

"Could be," Joe acknowledged.

They walked in silence back to the owl-copter.

Chapter 37
ASSAULT ON THE CASTLE

As noon of the fourth day of the war approached, Joe positioned his owl-copter two thousand meters above the border crossing point. Freeps were deployed on three sides of a one-hundred-meter square with an open side facing the Out-Lands, and the exchange point in the middle.

At noon, a ducted-fan aircraft approached from the west at low altitude. Beneath it hung a rescue basket with Mary inside. It slowed and hovered at twenty meters over the exchange point. Mary sat in it, holding on with one hand and shielding her face from prop wash with the other.

Joe watched from above. His magnifying goggles showed Mary clearly. Joe could see Mary's dark hair blowing around. She looked terrified when he caught a glimpse of her taut, fearful features. He clenched his teeth and hissed, "Funt, you'll pay for this."

Ten Freep officers approached the exchange point on foot. They were to take the handoff of Mary and then signal the second half of Funt's army to be released. Suddenly, inexplicably, Funt's aircraft began to withdraw back toward the west with its rescue basket still dangling below. Freep troops watched in bewilderment as it flew in a circle with the rescue basket flying outward from centrifugal force, and then it headed west. The basket was slowly retracted with Mary holding on in terror.

———

Reeled back aboard, Mary was rattled and disoriented. Funt helped her out of the basket and strapped her back into her seat with wrists locked to its arm rests. When she calmed her forced breathing enough to speak, she said, "I hate you, Funt."

"Didn't see your boyfriend there."

"Joe isn't stupid. He wouldn't show up for your dumb trick."

Funt slapped her hard and yelled, "Shut up, bitch. He'll fall for my next trick."

She recoiled and was without words for a few seconds as tears ran down her face. Then she hissed, "You slimy dog." Another slap excited Mary into violent thrashing against the wrist and ankle restraints and shouts of caged anger.

"Ready for a tattoo?" Funt sneered. And then to the pilot, "Hold speed down to sixty knots to make sure those owl-copters can keep up." He turned to Mary. "Got some fireworks waiting for your guy back at my castle. He's unfortunately never going to see some beautiful art work on your ass."

She spat out the words, "Proud of yourself? You pig!"

———

"Goddamn shitbag!" shouted Joe, watching from his high perch Funt's fly-by with Mary slung in a rescue basket underneath his aircraft. Then he ordered: "Hold fire on Funt's aircraft."

He watched as the ducted-fan aircraft gained speed and headed west. He ordered four unmanned drones to follow at high enough altitude to be invisible. He did not know what kind of air defense there was at the castle. The ducted-fan aircraft flew to the castle and landed on a rampart pad. A hangar door opened in the wall of the castle. The aircraft taxied in, and the door closed behind it.

The Freep drones that followed Funt's aircraft were detected. Explosions erupted in an umbrella over the castle. Funt's ground-to-air missiles carried aloft various kinds of explosives and detonated them in a pattern at two hundred meters. Another salvo went off six hundred meters higher, to be follow by another five salvos to kill anything in a death cube two thousand meters high. Two Freep drones were destroyed. Two limped home.

Joe, orbiting high above the border could see Funt's exploding salvoes. "Yahzorn, have you found me another way into that castle? Jasper is going to gang-lase through its walls. Funt might anticipate that and be ready for it. We need a backup plan."

Yahzorn said, "We're working the problem. Chertikoff's team is examining every bit of intelligence on the castle."

One hour later, Joe met Chertikoff and Yahzorn at his command center at the Airplane Works. Other top leaders were linked in through beetle packs and distant screens at locations where the dynamics of battle had put them. Joe said, "Teammates, we have driven out half of Funt's army. That is a great accomplishment; my congratulations to all of you. Funt has reneged on our deal to deliver Mary and get back the rest of his army. He is going to die for that. No matter how long it takes."

Joe turned to Chertikoff. "What have you learned?"

"Joe, our interrogations of captured castle workers hit pay dirt. There is a secret tunnel from the castle dungeon level that emerges three kilometers away in a building. We could attack through it."

"Or," Joe said, "we could capture someone escaping through it."

"You got it, Joe. If we know when they plan to leave, we can nail them on the way out."

Joe turned to Jasper. "Are you ready to attack the castle?" he asked.

Jasper said, "Ready to go on your command."

Joe said, "OK, Jasper let's go for it."

Joe, Jasper and their crews double-timed it out to their air vehicles.

Joe yelled to Jasper as he was boarding his owl-copter, "I'll be flying above the castle during your attack. Link in attack video to my plane."

"Roger that."

From his owl-copter, Jasper watched as a squadron of decoy drones led his assault. When they were over the castle, the Bikers set off a layer cake of explosions above the castle and destroyed them. Prisoner intelligence revealed it took thirty minutes for the Bikers to reload rockets for another salvo. Taking advantage of the reloading time, Jasper sent in his A and B team's owl-drones to blast breaches in the castle walls. His attacking owl-drones hovered in two groups fifty meters away from the castle walls and concentrated their fire at two aim points.

Jasper radioed Joe. "We've initiated attack. We'll have holes big enough to attack through in two minutes."

When the breach holes were wide enough for mini drones to fly through, Jasper ordered them in. Swarm attack, just like bees entering their hive. He linked videos to Joe of his swarm as it flitted around and then through the still-smoking breaches. Once inside, the mini drones detected human targets and lased them under direction of Algo-Net. One shot, one kill.

Jasper's team A and B troops followed through castle breaches when the surrounding wall temperature cooled. They flushed out hidden defenders, forcing those who weren't lased or captured to flee down into the lower levels of the castle. Jasper's C team was positioned at the tunnel outlet, half in a line facing the building, in case Funt made it out the door. The other half were in owl-copters, circling in readiness to fly in. Their orders: save Mary at all costs and kill Funt.

————

Mary lay on her stomach on a tattoo table. Her arms hung over the sides with her wrists cuffed to rings attached to the floor. Her ankles were shackled to the table's end. Her pants and underpants were pulled down to her knees. Funt's favorite tattoo artist, Big Tigren, was working on Mary's left buttock.

Funt, who was lounging in a couch with a couple of interns, had told Big Tigren to strip so Mary could see what was in store for her. Mary gasped at the erotic and brutal images that completely covered Big Tigren's well-conditioned body.

Mary was getting a castle intern's tattoo, a large inverted triangle with a bar of red along its inside left edge, placed on her left buttock. Big Tigren's needle and its grating buzz drove her mind to black sadness. But Mary didn't utter a sound that might bring perverse pleasure to Funt, who was looking on while fondling a couple of interns.

Mary was miserable but not despairing. She forced herself to think of rescue. To think of guys like Joe and Jasper—who could save her. She clamped her eyes shut. Not easy to keep her mind on them with the pain of the tattoo and her leering tormentor taunting her.

An alarm bell started ringing in harsh pulses. Funt pushed the intern snuggled against him away. He jumped up as the door burst open.

Kadjuk, in mottled gray camouflage, shouted in an urgent voice, "Freeps have bored holes through our walls in a couple of places."

Funt yelled, "How'd they do that?"

"They ganged lasers together, firing pulses at one spot until they had a hole."

"Shoot them as they come through."

Kadjuk said, "They are not coming through. They fly small drones through the holes. The drones fly evasive maneuvers that we can't draw bead on. They're killing our troops with lasers and bullets—right here inside the castle."

Funt said, "We'll escape through the tunnel. He turned to Big Tigren. "Free her, but keep her hands cuffed in front." Funt tapped a code into a cipher pad, and a door swung open in a seemingly smooth wall. "Kadjuk and Big Tigren, you're coming too."

The four of them ran through the door. It closed behind them. Funt led them through a maze of corridors, stopping at a dead end and keying another code into a wall cipher pad. Big Tigren and Kadjuk dragged Mary along roughly. Sliding doors opened to the tunnel entrance, where two sleek black three-wheelers stood ready to race through the tunnel and fly away at the other end.

———

Joe had been aloft with Yahzorn, Rod, and Alf at the beginning of the castle assault. Orbiting at two thousand meters, they were unseen by the Bikers. Joe wanted to see how weapons he had developed worked, but most of all he wanted to see Funt's downfall for himself.

Joe watched as videos relayed back Freep progress under the earth. The steady progress of Jasper's troops following their deadly mini drones deeper through the subterranean levels alerted Freeps to be ready for Funt breaking out through the escape tunnel.

With adrenaline kicked in and pulse pounding, Joe couldn't just observe the battle from afar; he had to be close enough to it to watch the action and be there to help his Freep troops facing desperate and unpredictable savages. Intense hatred of Funt welled up in his psyche along with an overpowering feeling of love for Mary who was facing death at Funt's hands. This pulsing mixture of hate and longing had to be answered. He ordered Alf to descend and told the other owl-copters to stay on station.

They peeled off and fell in a steep dive and then leveled off in a stomach-wrenching pull up one hundred meters above the tunnel outlet building.

Joe saw Jasper's C team troops in a line facing the building and then brilliant flashes and *KaBlam!*—explosions from buried mines around the building jolted Joe's plane. The C team troops were down—dead or dazed from the powerful blasts. The building door snapped open, and a black three-wheeler barreled out through the blast smoke. It sprouted wings and lifted off. Joe's owl-copter followed. Joe radioed Jasper to keep his owl-copters on station to protect his ground troops capturing the castle

Joe shouted, "Give me laser control. Got to force it down." From his position, he precision sighted the wings of the three-wheeler and burned off six inches on each side. Couldn't burn off too much wing at one time or it would flip over and crash. He had to force it down so those aboard survived. He shot off another six inches from each wing. And then another six inches. With the third wing-trim job, the three-wheeler lost altitude but still stayed aloft, flying meters above the ground along streambeds and around mesas and buildings to get out of the line of sight of Joe's owl-copter. Joe shot a laser bolt into one ducted fan, and it shed blades and flew apart. Now there was not enough thrust to stay airborne, even in the ground effect that had been cushioning it up. The three-wheeler slammed onto rough terrain, coming to a jolting stop against a pile of boulders. "Hang in there, Mary," Joe exhaled, barely audible.

"Land this thing," Joe shouted.

Alf banked at ninety degrees, snapped the wings level, and landed. Joe jumped out and ran twenty meters toward the three-wheeler. He looked into the left bug-eyed canopy, squinting to see inside when it snapped open, hitting his faceplate. He flew backward, stunned by the blow and the impact of hitting hard ground.

The pilot was out of the cockpit in a flash. It wasn't Funt! It was Kadjuk! "Who the hell..." Joe exclaimed, as Kadjuk ran to him, jumping on his chest with both feet. Joe grunted loudly, and fighting to suppress the sledgehammer pain, he grabbed one foot and twisted it as hard as he could. Kadjuk fell backward. Joe and Kadjuk both scrambled to stand up. Kadjuk yanked a pistol from his holster. Joe got to his feet at the same time and brought his laser to bear on Kadjuk's chest. He had the drop on him—lasing a killing bolt of lightning to Kadjuk's heart.

A death reflex in Kadjuk's trigger finger got off a shot through Joe's faceplate. A searing pain followed the bullet as it dug a furrow on the top of his scalp and exited the back of his helmet. He was stunned and stumbled into the arms of Rod, who came running up from the owl-copter. Rod said "I've got to check out your head to see how bad it is."

Joe, in a daze, heard screaming. It seemed far away. Then he saw smoke coming out of the three-wheeler; a blast of clarity shocked his brain into focus. He shouted, "Get Mary out! It's on fire."

Yahzorn and Alf sprang to the right copilot canopy and pried it open. It wasn't Mary screaming! It was Big Tigren looking like a demon from the underworld with smoke curling up around her illustrated body.

Joe stumbled up with Rod's help and yelled, "Let her burn unless she tells where Funt and Mary are."

Big Tigren cried, "No! I'll tell you where they went! They are going to the old headquarters in Banning." They pulled her out of the smoldering wreck, and the four Freeps took off for Banning.

As they were climbing out to cruise altitude Yahzorn took Joe's helmet off and put a bandage pad on his head on to staunch the bleeding. They secured it with gauze wrapped around his head and under his chin and put his helmet back on. The hole in the faceplate was above his eyes and didn't interfere with his vision.

Rod found pain and energy powders in the first-aid kit for Joe. Joe washed them down with high-alert fizz tea. Joe messaged Jasper, "Jasp, it was a wild-goose chase. The three-wheeler we chased wasn't carrying Funt or Mary. I'm heading for Banning to get him there."

Jasper said, "I read you, Joe. I'll follow you in minutes."

Joe said, "Bring mini drones."

"Roger, we're recharging them. They'll be underway in five minutes."

———

Twenty minutes later, Joe flew over the Bikers' old headquarters. It had been abandoned when the castle was finished. Joe studied the old buildings from above; no sign of Funt's three-wheeler. He asked Algo-Net which one Funt was in. Algo-Net said, "Probably the hangar—that's the large middle one. That was where their inner sanctum was in the past."

Joe commanded, "Alf, take us down and land near the front of the big building."

Alf rolled the owl-copter and descended fast, leveling out for a smooth landing by the building's door to the right of the large hangar door. Joe told the other three to stay on board. He jumped out and tried the door next to the main hangar door. Locked! He lased it open with a blinding flash. He ran inside to see Funt's three-wheeler facing toward the main hangar door. As his eyes grew accustomed to the light, he saw an upper level of scaffolding around the hangar walls.

The main hangar door opened enough for the three-wheeler to fire its nose Gatling gun into Joe's owl-copter. The owl-copter shuddered under the bullet impacts, but its deadly laser got off one last blast of energy, silencing the three-wheeler and setting it on fire. Joe put a laser shot into the opaque cockpit to make sure Funt was dead.

Joe thought, *That's the end of Funt.*

But it was not to be.

Funt's voice sounded in the smoke and haze. "Not in the three-wheeler, Joe. I shot up your owl-copter remotely. And now I am going to shoot you."

Joe ducked instinctually behind a row of crates. Then he heard Mary call, "Joe, help! Up here." He looked and saw her on the upper level with her arms above her head. She was held on her tiptoes by a rope from the rafters to the handcuffs on her wrists. Smoke from the burning three-wheeler was starting to block his view of her.

Funt said, "Hey Joe, I'm going to finish off the tattoo Big Tigren started."

Joe peeked out over the crates, and Funt sprayed bullets inches from his head. He ducked down and ran a couple meters along the crates, popped up again, and loosed a laser shot to where Funt had fired from. Missed. Funt wasn't there anymore. Then Joe saw a hulking figure lumbering on the upper level toward Mary and immediately fired a laser shot. It hit, but it didn't stop the black apparition. Funt said, "Joe, this is my new ceramic suit. Your sissy laser can't take it out."

Joe had one laser shot left. He thought, *Got to give her a chance to live.* He shot the rope holding Mary's hands. She dropped to the floor in a crouch and ran to the railing. Joe ran under it and yelled, "Jump." Seeing Joe below, she climbed over the rail and flopped into his waiting arms—flattening him. He couldn't move! She jumped up and dragged Joe under the upper level where Funt couldn't see them.

Joe couldn't get up. His back was pierced by pains that caused him to faint when he tried to move.

Funt yelled, "Coming down to get you love birds."

Buzzing noise filled the hangar. Joe saw Freep mini drones coming out of the smoke. They swarmed like bees around Funt. They fired—but without effect.

"Ha," Funt taunted. "Those pissant drones ain't worth shit." Funt was down the stairs and heading through the smoke toward where Joe lay. Mary jumped up and hit him with a crowbar she found in the smoky gloom. Funt backhanded her to the floor and she lay still.

Mini drones were swarming around Funt, still lasing him. No effect, even from one meter away. He approached Joe, who was trying to pull himself away on his elbows. Out of the smoke in front of him Joe saw Algo's eyes, and got the thought-message, *You really fucked up, Joe.*

Joe thought-messaged back, *Algo, tell those mini drones to gang-lase Funt between the eyes.*

Algo thought-messaged, *OK, I'll do it this time.*

The mini drones crowded in front of Funt, and their lasers blasted Funt's face mask, boring a two-centimeter hole and blasting the bridge of his nose out the back of his head. Funt's ceramic suit made a crackling sound as he crashed to the floor—dead.

Joe thought-messaged, *Algo, tell those drones lase a hole in the hangar wall so we can get out.*

Algo thought-messaged, *Can't, Joe. I used up all their power for that kill shot.*

Joe called Jasper. "Get us out of here. Bad smoke. Can't walk."

Jasper responded, "Owl-copters will blow their prop wash inside to clear the smoke. I'm coming in for you."

The owl-copters flew in front of the door two meters off the ground and rolled left one after another because the roll maneuver that blew air into the hangar pushed the owl-copters away from the door. Joe saw the owl-copters' gusts of prop wash pushing the fire and smoke away for a few seconds. Jasper and Rod, fully beetled up, ran in. They reached Joe, pulled him by the arms out the door.

"Where's Mary?" Joe shouted.

Jasper and Rod ran inside again, and with the next blast of prop wash, they saw Mary crawling toward them. They carried her out, coughing from the smoke, and put her in an owl-copter next to Joe. She screamed, "Joe!" when she saw him with a bloody bandage on his head. "Is it bad?"

Rod had rotated his seat to put a fresh bandage on Joe's head while a medic from Jasper's commando team was injecting him with medication to suppress his back pain. Jasper's engineering officer was cutting off Mary's hand cuffs off with a bolt cutter.

Joe said, "I'd kiss you, but we're all so busy."

Joe noticed there was a different pilot on board. He asked Rod, "Hey, where's Alf? And Yahzorn?"

Rod said, "Alf was hit, Joe, when Funt's three-wheeler opened up. He's gonna make it. Yahzorn too. Already been evacuated."

The new pilot said, "I'm Thad, where to?"

Joe said, "Head east."

The owl-copter lifted off. As it climbed out, Joe said, "Get Mary to an aid station."

"Oh no," Mary piped up. "Joe, I'm going back to my hospital."

Joe, surprised, frowned and said, "You're banged up. You need rest."

"You should talk—sitting there with a grooved head."

He laughed and humbly asked, "Can I come and see you sometime?"

"Call first."

With the bandaging done Joe leaned close and whispered in her ear, "God, how I love you."

She closed her eyes and felt aches and pains disappear in a reverie of pure happiness. She basked in its glow. The war was winding down. Peace was in the foreseeable future and fulfillment of her love for Joe was at hand.

Rod announced, "There is a medical plane two minutes ahead. We can land and transfer Mary."

"Do it," Joe said. And then softly to her, "I'll be there to see you when I can get away from this war for an hour."

"I'll be there to greet you unless..." She winked. "Something gets in the way."

An hour later, a medical copter dropped her at the hospital along with three casualties she helped care for along the way.

———

The hospital team was amazed to see her. Work pace there was at maximum tempo—handling war casualties from both sides. No time to answer questions about herself. She saw a new intern looking at her in awe. She said, "Sonny Jim, you come with me." They walked off to tour the hospital to evaluate its condition and needs.

The tour finished to her satisfaction, Mary went to wash off the battlefield grime and her hated new tattoo. She showered and noticed the intern's erection as he was soaping her down. She flicked it on the head with her finger to calm his ardor. "Get it under control, man, before you start working on me."

When Mary had dried off and was lying on a massage table, the intern put disinfectant on her cuts and bruises and then carefully did the same to the unfinished tattoo, to which he also added a healing salve and a large bandage. All the while, dripping wet folks from the showers dropped in to welcome Mary back and then disappeared back into the steam.

Mary was all business as she put on her hospital regulation underwear and scrubs. Back on her feet, there was no time for anything but keeping her hospital and all the others under her command humming along at top efficiency. The adrenaline from being home and seeing Joe masked her aches and pains. She took pep powders to keep the euphoria going.

From her office, she linked to other places in her medical network. It was nonstop, getting reports from her many medical facilities and working with them to solve problems. She was at the top of her game, doing what she loved. And she couldn't get enough! Members of her team hovered around, begging for a minute to discuss their problems. She worked them in, too.

Yet, in spite of the pace of work, fleeting memories intruded—memories of past days with Joe. Couldn't dwell on those flickers of happiness. Work to do. But the memories were persistent. She remembered their first Normalizer and the inkling of attraction for Joe that continued to evolve to the all-consuming love she'd felt when Joe rescued her. Just hours ago, she had gone from hell to heaven. Then she snapped back to the present. Back to triaging the wounded. Back to moving the barely healed out to make room for the barely alive. Back to supplies, doctors, nurses, food. Back to being a leader in the toughest challenge she would ever confront.

After ten hours at the hospital, she put her top assistant in charge and stumbled off to bed. She thought of Joe as she lay there in the dark. It hadn't all been rosy. There had been many disappointments as their attempted meetings fell through and calls seldom answered. In time, they learned it was Algo. Hadn't wrecked their love, though. She and Joe had found ways to have those ecstatic interludes, locked together surfing turbulence in Joe's owl-copter above the ambitious seashore construction sites of the south Freep Nation. She shared his dream as it grew from a catastrophic flood to a region of promise and hope.

For Freeps, it meant greater strength and stature as a nation that would, in time, strengthen their chances of survival. For individual Freeps, a chance to enrich their existence in many ways and to even enjoy some cooler weather. Mary luxuriated in those dreams as she lay there in the dark and saw them unfolding. Joe was making it happen, and she loved him for it. She sensed sleep coming on.

And then it was morning—and she was back at it.

Chapter 38
VICTORY NORMALIZER

After transferring Mary to the medical plane, Joe reboarded his command owl-copter. At cruise altitude, yellow rays of sunset retreated across the blackening sky. Joe said, "Rod, brief me on Biker-army status."

Rod replied in a rapid, clipped voice. "Second half of their army is inching its way west to the Out-Lands. We're distributing fuel for their personal air conditioning. We are selecting Bikers for reconstruction. Taking their best, men with skills who don't appear to be spring-loaded for revenge against us. Not perfect vetting, but enough to screen out the crazies who might cause trouble. Should have them equipped with prisoner beetle packs in a month."

Joe asked, "What are you doing for Juanacho?"

"We have invited Juanacho's people to come to our prisoner way stations to recruit. They'll be there tomorrow."

"Good planning," Joe said. "He'll be taking over a big hunk of Funt's Mid-Level protection service. Juanacho is a strong ally, and we want to keep it that way."

After a couple of hours of orbiting in darkness, Joe realized his presence above the battlefield was no longer needed. He was nearing exhaustion, and his scalp was hurting. He headed back to the Citadel.

The Citadel command center was staffed with specialists who were monitoring the battle winding down and directing reconstruction activities that were spinning up. Joe hadn't spent time there during the invasion. He had controlled the Freep defense from his owl-copter, from Jasper's command center, or from his own command center in the Airplane Works. The real command center was wherever Joe was at any given time. He knew that if it got right down to it, he could have run the whole war from his beetle pack.

Even though he had directed that the Citadel be built. He'd asked himself at times: Is the Citadel necessary? He came to believe it was—because without a government building, foreign officials would have to meet Freep officials in his Airplane Works command center or similar modest accommodation. He believed that those plein gray spaces wouldn't convey the image of a wily and brave nation that was not to be taken lightly. The Citadel was a place that represented strength. Joe believed that in time it would become a symbol of Freep military prowess in the Salton Sea War.

Grateful Freeps had constructed luxurious living quarters there for Joe and Mary. They acknowledged the goodness of those Freep hearts by moving into the Citadel quarters and playing host to a steady stream of visitors from just about everywhere.

The opulence of his Citadel office felt strange to Joe and took getting used to. That closeness to Freep comrades at work or at war was missing. It wasn't all that bad, though. He had more time alone, time for thinking—that was welcome with so much in a state of flux. Maybe colleagues were reluctant to burst into his impressive office with problems and questions because of the chain-of-command mentality at the Citadel. Whatever the reason, in his quiet moments he found himself thinking more and more about what was next.

What could Freep history tell him? He drilled into Algo-Net's vast memory to find out what he could about others like him. Other crisis jocks, pulled in to take over for Algo and lead the Freeps in times of deadly threat. Pulled in for their imaginations—and their ability to wield power. How many were there in the last two hundred years? Who were they? How long did they rule? What happened to them?

Algo-Net was slow to respond to his queries. Seemed to be stalling. Then, on a quiet afternoon, Algo itself responded to a thought-message from Joe, *Crisis leaders like you have always asked these questions. They usually ask after a climactic event that calls for brilliant exercise of their capability.*

They seek out the next challenge, the next threat. I am not hiding this information from you. I want to be the first to explain what we offer leaders like you, strong people who have experienced the deep satisfaction of wielding great power.

Joe frowned and then thought-messaged, *Sounds like I am going to get fired.*

Algo thought-messaged, *I've learned that our best leaders use up their civic creativity in an average of six years. Beyond that, they have little new to offer, and Freep Nation is just as well off with bland but competent leadership—like mine.*

Joe, not knowing whether to laugh or cry, went for the wisecrack. He thought-messaged, *Will my personal messages to Mary get through any better in retirement?*

Algo thought-messaged, *Yes, every call to and from your loved one will connect.*

———

Twenty days after Funt's defeat, Joe kicked off a national Normalizer to celebrate. The Citadel was alive with un-bridled joy for surviving the invasion and triumphing over powerful, malignant forces. A huge crowd had gathered there and waited for Joe to address them. The air was electric with anticipation.

After visiting Mary at the hospital on her coffee break, Joe flew to the Citadel in his owl-copter. Freeps had lined up respectfully and applauded as he strode by them from the landing pad into the Citadel's great hall.

He stood in the floating pulpit that levitated high enough for all to see him. Kaleidoscopic rays of light and color shone from the pulpit. He was beetled up to cover his head bandages but had his helmet faceplate rolled back so all could see his face—whether they were in the Citadel's great hall, or watching on Freep community screens, or on individual beetle pack displays. Wild cheering ensued. It abated after five minutes in response to Joe's raised hand.

Joe yelled, "Free power, free people!" The chant was returned with a roar in the hall and all over Freep Nation—wherever a Freep heart beat with pride. He raised his hand again for silence, and then he spoke. "Freep teammates, we prevailed over larger and stronger adversaries." More cheering. "Meet some of our team who made it happen and are too busy to join us."

In turn, images appeared of Jasper, Waxer, and Shirlene linked in from the recent battlefields. They waved and said a few words to great applause. Images of Shan, Lon, Yahzorn, Chertikoff, Chet, Rod, and other Freeps appeared from where they were hard at work on recovery from the war. They too were cheered by a grateful nation.

"There is another person I'd like you to meet. She runs our hospitals, takes care of our sick and wounded." Mary's image appeared, caught in the act of helping a wounded Freep limp to an examination table. After she had settled him in with help of a couple of nurses, Joe said, "Meet my partner."

Mary suddenly turned back to look at the screen and exclaimed loudly and happily, "Did you say 'my partner'?"

EPILOGUE

Algo learned over the last two hundred years that the "transition" of a Freep leader could be complicated. A lot was at stake. Early on, mistakes were made and damage done. Algo, lacking emotions and empathy, had learned the hard way that an otherwise brilliant Freep leader could turn angry and destructive if his or her transition was too abrupt or unrewarding.

Algo had learned how to reward leaders who believed they had more to contribute. Leaders who still loved power and desired to use it. Algo had worked the transition problem many times. Each time it was different—because people are different, times are different. Evolution ensures that many things are different as time passes. But Algo had learned that some things were always the same.

Love, for example, was often a big contributor to a successful transition. Algo frustrated a leader's love life enough to build a high level of longing so that when Algo got out of the way, and the lovers had full access to each other, their attachment was powerful, and their pleasure in being together immense.

In Joe's transition, Algo gradually took over more of routine management, leaving the new initiatives to Joe. The infiltration of Mainstream's infrastructure, for example, was complete, and Algo took over and managed the residual details competently.

The Out-Lands was a different matter. Joe had crafted a strategy for the Out-Lands to be controlled by six main gangs, with Juanacho's gang as the strongest and the Bikers left as an impoverished entity that had lost half its territory. Spies and infiltrators were established, to the extent that a gang's flimsy infrastructure could be infiltrated. Food and power exports to the Out-Lands set up dependencies whose chains could be yanked as an added incentive to stay friendly with the Freeps.

Two years after the war, Joe turned over the Out-Lands management to Algo. Algo was back in full charge again. Along the way, Algo interested Joe in other things that would use his drive and imagination in satisfying ways—in ways that gave Joe a stage to play on beyond the borders of Freep Nation.

Eventually Joe concentrated on an enterprise to mine plastic from the oceans for building jumbo drones with two-hundred-meter wingspans. These enormous drones built from reclaimed plastic were stationed above Salton Sea communities. Solar powered, clouds of them stayed aloft indefinitely to shade and cool the earth below. Joe marketed them in countries around the world, and Mary accompanied him on trips to exotic places to sell them.

Joe was grateful to Algo for the chance to get in the fight against an ever-hotter world—without any restriction on his love life. Algo thought-messaged, *You're welcome*, when Joe thanked him, but it seemed a bit mechanical. He felt disappointed that Algo didn't really seem to connect with being thanked, but he knew deep down that Algo didn't have the emotional chops to do anything else.

From their quarters in the Citadel Joe and Mary could see ships moored off the port, waiting for their chance to exchange cargoes and be on their way. They could see seashore communities, greenhouses, and solar-powered planes ghosting by. The fruits of Joe's dream were there before them in any direction they looked. Even Joe's parents' boat, could be seen placidly at anchor.

Life in the Citadel was good but not extravagant. Joe worked hard to prevent that. Nonetheless, Mary found the amount of entertaining that came along with Joe's fame hard to take. At first Joe enjoyed banquets and the company of foreign dignitaries. But with time Joe discovered that a life of fame and wealth was like life back at the Marina, with its rules and customs against which he had once rebelled.

Mary loved her job managing the hospitals and, eventually, the whole Health Works, where she upgraded the technology and talent of services offered to the community. She frequently used her professional commitments as excuses to avoid the celebrity dinners Joe was often corralled into.

In time living in the Citadel, close to an adoring public, had lost its luster for both of them. With their two kids, they decided to change to a lifestyle closer to what they had when they joined the Freeps. They acquired a homestead and moved to it, bringing along Joe's owl-copter for trysts above their beloved desert vistas.

Negla helped them launch their aeroponic vegetable farm. She lived half a day away and would trek in now and then to visit and spend time with Mary, with whom she had become close. She had no interest in other men since Freddo died. Her attraction to Joe and his attraction to her had matured into a deep and loyal friendship.

At first Joe was concerned about losing contact with the outside world. He surfed Algo-Net to keep him in touch with Freeps itching for a battle of wits. He was welcome in Strat Team and Cyber Station's rowdy meetings and was occasionally the butt of somebody's joke about tending his bean garden.

Joe and Mary were active in the preservation of Freep culture. She promoted the health benefits of the beetle pack to the outside world. The conditioned air of the beetle pack kept the wearer's skin moist and young looking, with atmospheric allergens and toxins filtered out.

Tourists came to trek beetled up through the Freep Nation to live the uniqueness of the experience and the rejuvenation of their physical and mental well-being. The fear that the beetle pack would disappear in the cooler areas of the Free Nation near the Salton Sea was dispelled as a result of beetle-pack technology evolving into everyday clothing configurations.

Joe was an enthusiastic spokesman for beetle pack developments and Freep technology in general.

Business colleagues, diplomats, and tourists visited Joe and Mary's homestead. They, and the newbie Freeps who were often trekking through, added to a heady mix of people who livened conversation at his rough-hewn dinner table in the evenings.

Lon and Shan visited, too. Their tales of high-level intrigue were a check on Joe's natural optimism. After all, they were the ones who had clued Joe in that Algo wasn't perfect. They thrived in a world that required them to know the way things should be and the way they actually were, so the Freeps could profit from the difference.

They were there the day Yasminah, the fortuneteller, hitched a ride on a crop-collecting drone that dropped her off at dinnertime.

After eating they sat around the dinner table and talked into the evening.

Yasminah said, "So many foreigners come to me now. Say they are tourists, but they don't have a tourist look in their eyes. They are here trying to understand."

Shan asked, "Understand what?"

"Whether to love Freeps or fear Freeps."

Joe, with an incredulous expression and a palms-up shrug, said, "We have bug suits, poor land, and slow planes. What's to fear?"

The others laughed.

Yasminah said, "They believed Mainstream and the Bikers were going to conquer the Freeps. But they couldn't.

"You won, Joe—and they want to know how you did it."

ABOUT THE AUTHOR

 Dick Heimbold spent his career as an aerospace engineer. His work, including serving as director of process engineering for the space shuttle, and his love of the deserts of the American Southwest gave him the experience and knowledge needed to write the science fiction thriller *East of the Out-Lands*.

Heimbold is also a professional artist and the author of *Dream Wrecks*, a suspense novel set in Malibu, California. He has recently adapted it into a screenplay.

Heimbold lives in Glendale, California, with his wife, Ursula.

www.ingramcontent.com/pod-product-compliance
Lightning Source LLC
Chambersburg PA
CBHW071205250626
47159CB00001B/210